To Crystal

Along Comes
A Wolfe

David Greer

E Cournos

Cover Design by Dimitrios Kounios.
Proofreading by Nathan Mader.

First Electronic Edition, October 2015
First Print Edition, November 2015

Visit us at www.swiftflowing.com.

PROLOGUE

ONE

Erika told Sarah she thinks u'll be mad if she goes 4 Derek

Jayce Morgan stands in the hallway of Gardiner High, staring at the text on her phone. Erika has the whole school to pick from and she goes after Jayce's ex? Of course she's mad. She taps out *hell yeah* and sends it off.

She heads towards the girl's bathroom on the second floor, in absolutely no rush to head back to class. She's looking for any excuse to wander the halls instead of sitting in her English class and this message gives her one more reason to stay away and cool off. No one ever really needs to go to the bathroom anyway.

The corridors are clean, empty, and quiet. *Bzzz*— her phone vibrates and she pauses at the bathroom door. It's her bestie, Molly, in Level Three Science on the main floor, making a dumbass face. Molly always makes her smile, and Jayce makes her own silly look and sends a pic back. She leans against the bathroom door and heads inside.

She stops at the mirror for a moment, looking over her teen body. She's indifferent to it, neither pleased nor displeased with her complexion, the fall of her hair, or the way her clothes shape her curves, so she moves on.

She steps into the stall in the corner, the one she always goes to. She takes her phone out and sets it on the small ledge. Last time she forgot her phone was there and nearly knocked it into the toilet, reeling as it clipped the edge of the seat and hit the floor. She settles in.

The door to the bathroom swings open. Footsteps. The stall closest to the door bangs open and then locks.

Bzzz—she receives another image from Molly. Jayce sees Mr. Fleet in the background pointing to a chart of a frog's reproductive system. She stifles a silent giggle.

The toilet flushes and the other person leaves the stall. The door squeaks open and the sound of Ms. Maple's history class across the hall spills into the silence. The door hisses closed.

Gross—that person didn't wash their hands. Who doesn't wash their hands? Jayce shakes her head as her face scrunches in disgust. She looks at her phone and realizes it's time to get back before Mrs. Drake busts her.

Standing, she tugs her jeans over her hips and zips them up. She pushes her phone into her back pocket and flushes. She steps out of the stall and heads for the sink. She hates washing her hands with the pink soap that stinks like a hospital and leaves her skin dry and ready to crack, but the germs around this school disgust her. She pumps the dispenser several times and rinses her hands thoroughly. She dries her hands off with the paper towel, wishing this school would buy some decent hand dryers, and reminds herself to stop at her locker and moisturize before she heads back to class.

Leaning into the mirror, she runs her fingers through her long, blonde hair and watches it fall smoothly around her face. She inspects the dark eyeliner under her eyes and carefully drags her middle finger to clean up the edges. She leans back, admiring herself in the mirror, satisfied with her refined appearance. She's wasted enough of this class period with her fake break. It's time to head back to English.

Two

The boy presses a closed fist against the bathroom door's metal plate. He makes sure to swing it hard and let it bang against the wall to signal his entrance. He steps inside and finds the area neat, without any scraps of paper towel on the floor. It's early and he knows it doesn't look like this at the end of the day. He also knows that a clean space is a more efficient space.

He kneels. Only one set of feet point from beneath the stalls, someone who wears a pair of trendy red Toms. He rises, moving to the stall closest to the exit and steps inside. It's cleaner than a guy's washroom, without graffiti on the walls. It even smells better.

He gets to business. He pulls off his backpack and puts it down by his feet. He lifts one foot, working to avoid touching the walls, and slips off his shoe. He shifts his weight and pulls off the other one, dropping them both into his backpack. He stands still, waiting, preparing himself for the next moment.

Bzzz—he listens. A slight hiccough of breath. Is she laughing? Is she texting while sitting on the toilet? His face twists in disgust.

He turns and flushes the toilet, moving out of

the stall and across the bathroom before the noise disappears. He walks to the door and yanks it open. It swings easily and he releases it, letting it close in a slow, hissing whisper. He turns back inside the room, moving quickly, one step at a time, towards a middle stall and pushes the door open with his fist again, careful not to bang it against the wall or leave any fingerprints. He steps inside and rotates on the ball of his foot, catching a glimpse of himself in the mirror as he pulls the door shut. A smile crosses his face.

He doesn't lock the door, leaving it slightly ajar. He lifts the toilet seat and places his right foot on the porcelain edge. Germs disgust him but he ignores the thought, pushing it away so that he can focus on his goal. He lifts his left foot and perches on the toilet. He presses his forearms gently against the walls to stabilize himself and takes a silent breath. He waits.

Swoosh—the toilet flushes, and he hears her zip up her pants. The lock clicks and the door thumps open. He looks through the space between the door and the wall and sees her move over to the sink.

She runs the tap and pumps the soap—a lot of soap—and washes her hands. While the water splashes in the sink, he eases himself down from the toilet seat. He leans close to the crack in the door and watches her cross over to the far wall and pull paper towel out of the dispenser before crumpling it up and throwing it away.

He readies himself, reaches around, and grasps at the plastic bag poking out from his back pocket. He slides it out silently, the black letters from the local grocery store legible in its creased folds. He tightens his fingers in its handle straps, careful not to make a noise.

She pauses at the mirror again, and he watches as she checks herself one last time. Her hair spills down her back as she plays with it. He can't fault her for her vanity. She is long and blonde, just like that girl he hurt in grade eight. She wears faded blue jeans that are tight against her ass, like all the girls buy now, and they look good on her. She never quits watching herself, absorbed in her own reflection, and he must clear his mind. He can't let those thoughts in—not when his moment is so close.

He takes a slow, calming breath and knows it's time.

He opens the door and steps out of the stall in one quick, sudden motion. She doesn't even see him coming. He makes no sound and raises the plastic bag over her head and pulls it down quickly. Her blonde hair hangs out of the bottom. He pulls back, the bag sinking deep against the folds of her neck. He can see her in the mirror, her face pressing against the inside of the bag, her mouth sucking the plastic in with each breath.

Her hands reach up to her face, flailing in panic, struggling to get the bag away. He realizes that she's stronger than she looks and he pushes his knee into her back for leverage. She bucks against him, and he stumbles, banging his thigh into the porcelain sink. He grunts in pain.

He pulls the bag taut and her fingers tear at the stretched plastic on her face, but then her knees give way and she crumples to the floor. He struggles to stay standing.

He doesn't know it yet but girls are taught to fall in self-defense and she's got the upper hand now. She kicks blindly and strikes him on the side of his shin. He stumbles and she kicks again, catching his sore leg.

He realizes he's losing the fight and steps away. She keeps kicking and before she pulls the bag away, he turns and rushes for the door.

THREE

"Can anyone please answer the question of why Scout thought the world was ending?"

The class sits in silence.

Mrs. Drake smiles as she waits patiently. "I know you guys read this."

A girl in the second row begins, "I think Scout—" but a bang interrupts her.

Mrs. Drake sees Jayce standing in the doorway, holding a white plastic bag loosely in her fingers. The color is gone from her face, her hair is a mess, her eyeliner is running, and she can't seem to speak.

Mrs. Drake immediately realizes something is wrong. "Jayce?"

Jayce says nothing.

Mrs. Drake sees all the other students watching and she moves to the girl and repeats herself more adamantly. "Jayce, what's wrong?"

Jayce makes eye contact with her and begins to hyperventilate.

"You're okay. Tell me what's wrong."

Jayce looks down at the plastic bag in her hand. Her breathing chokes and becomes heavier, and she gasps in panicked moans that burst into a deep, wailing cry. It sends a shiver down Mrs. Drake's spine, and suddenly she must catch Jayce as she collapses to the floor.

Deb, a friend of Jayce, sitting on the far side of the room, has her phone out and sends a text: *shits going down with J. Come quick.*

FOUR

Bzzz—Molly's phone vibrates beneath her science notebook.

She peeks underneath, expecting something about Erika going after Jayce's ex, but sees a photo of her best friend on the floor beside Mrs. Drake. Then she sees *shits going down* and believes it.

She doesn't hesitate and jumps out of her desk. Mr. Fleet calls out as she rushes for the door, "Molly, where are you going? Molly!"

She doesn't stop.

She bolts down the hall and through the indoor courtyard, rushing past a senior sitting on a bench who's putting on his shoes.

Molly sees Mr. Coogan, the vice principal, stepping out of his office and she knows she's going to catch hell.

"Slow down!"

"Sorry." She keeps running, all the way to Jayce's period 2 English class.

She rushes in and sees the crowd of kids circling. From somewhere in the middle, Mrs. Drake yells, "Owen, grab my water."

As Owen moves to the desk, Molly slips inside. She sees Jayce and she isn't prepared for how bad her friend really looks.

Owen comes back with the water bottle and Mrs. Drake gives it to Jayce to drink.

"Calm down. Breathe. You're okay."

Molly kneels down beside her and takes Jayce's trembling hand. Her friend's breath hitches as she fights back the tears.

"Tell me what happened."

FIVE

The boy exits through the nearest stairwell. He needs distance from the upstairs bathroom. It didn't go the way he planned. The girl fought too much, and now his leg hurts, and he never finished what he came to do.

He steps into the empty indoor courtyard, struggling to keep calm and relaxed. He's only thirty feet from the exit but he can't go anywhere until he gets his shoes back on. He didn't think things through to the very end, and he didn't imagine how the girl would react.

He moves diagonally towards the vending machines. Halfway across the large room, he sees the big window into the Principal's Office where a man stands, wearing a suit, staring out. He digs in his pocket and finds some change, hoping it's enough. He keeps his back to the man, pops in a few coins, not even looking, and chooses "E5." A Ziggernut candy bar drops down. As he reaches for it, he looks over his shoulder and sees the man in the suit still watching him. He's sure this isn't about the girl in the bathroom and that the man is more concerned about a student wandering the halls during class, but he needs to keep it together and get out of here as soon as possible.

He takes the chocolate and sits down at the closest bench. He pulls his backpack off, yanks out his shoes. He's tying the first set of laces when a girl around his age rushes past him. Now, this likely has something to do with him.

"Slow down," the man in the suit yells, and the boy watches as he rushes out of his office and chases after her.

He ties the other shoelace and sits up. He unwraps the candy bar and takes a bite, enjoying the chocolate and caramel in his mouth. He closes his eyes, listening to the quiet buzz of the school around him.

His brain turns, and he knows that next time he needs to be prepared and to think his actions through more clearly. He has to foresee the fight from the girl. He has to figure out when to get his shoes back on.

He stands, slings the backpack over his shoulder, and moves towards the exit.

With time, it'll get easier. The more he does it, the more it'll become routine. His mind will be ready and he'll work on instinct.

The bell sounds, signaling the next class. He savours the last bit of nougaty goodness and tosses the candy wrapper in the garbage. He slips out the door.

He starts to relax as he heads for the street. He thinks of that old aphorism that people say in times like this: Practice makes perfect. Today was his first try and with time he'll get better. All he needs is practice.

The sun is out and warm and he knows it'll be a good summer. He takes a deep breath and smiles.

PART ONE

1

"Anthony, you're up next."

Coach Davies has had us busting our asses running lay-ups for the last half hour. Even though we won our last game, he says we missed too many opportunities, and Coach's philosophy is that practice makes perfect.

I'm facing off against my buddy, Mike, who's defending. This is easy stuff, and I'm pretty good using either of my arms, so I've already got a plan. I drive the ball down the court, pushing strong to the hoop. I'm not even thinking about it, my mind zeroed in on the backboard. I easily dodge around Mike and move past the basket. I plant my foot and push off. I feel the spin I have on the ball and I know it's going in without even looking.

I'm feeling pretty good about it, but it doesn't last long. Coach is on me right away.

"What the hell was that?"

"Reverse lay-up."

"And why'd you do it?"

I'm not exactly sure how to answer this. "To guard myself with the net?"

"No! Why the hell did you do a reverse while the rest of us are doing standards?"

"Come on, Coach, this is easy stuff." I know I've

screwed up as soon as it comes out of my mouth.

"Well, I'm happy for you. And when you get your ass handed to you by Cornwall next Friday, I'll be the first to remind you about this little chat of ours."

Cornwall High is currently in first place in points and rebounds and has destroyed us in the last two games.

"Quit thinking about what's just in front of you. You've got to start thinking about what's coming up from behind that might blindside you."

Coach moves on and looks at the whole team now. I'm grateful.

"You guys need to respect the fundamentals. It's what'll get you out of a jam when things start falling apart. Now, hit the showers because I'm done with you."

2

I step out of the shower, wrapping a towel around my waist.

"Geez, Shepherd! You just had to show off."

Mike's at the mirror shaving his three chin hairs while I sit on the bench drying off.

"Well, I knew you'd be too slow to catch me—"

"I don't need the speed when I got the shots." He air-swishes an imaginary ball.

"Not if you can't get to the basket." I'm beside him at the mirror now and watch him finish. "I don't know what you're even trying to scrape off there."

He grabs his towel and wipes his face clean. "You're just jealous that I've got something to shave." He admires his jawline then heads to his locker.

I stand in front of the full-length mirror, pleased with my well-formed six-pack. Every sit up, every crunch, every chin up that my drill sergeant of a coach has us doing is worth it. I barely have to flex. My abs are solid.

I look back at Mike. "This is a form to be admired."

Mike shakes his head as he pulls on a shirt. He's a big guy for being white, but he's still got a bit of baby fat on him that he can't seem to shake. I imagine that in twenty years he'll be that chunky guy in an office selling life insurance. For me, this stomach is a little preventative medicine for my own mid-life crisis in thirty years.

"Save it for your girlfriend, buddy."

I head over to my own locker and start getting dressed. I let my boxers hang out just enough to give a tease over the belt of my Hollister jeans. I grab my top, even though it seems a shame to cover this magnificent stomach up.

Mike catches me rubbing my abs in admiration.

"Do you need to get yourself a room?"

Maybe.

3

On my way home, my phone rings out "Pumped Up Kicks" by Foster The People. It's my girlfriend, Sheri. She's on the track team and she's fun and easy going, so the ringtone suits her. She's sent me a picture on Picta-bomb, one of those image apps that self-destructs, of her holding a photo of me. Her eyes are shut tight and she's got the biggest pucker. She's adorable and goofy and I can never figure out why this combination makes her the hottest damn girl.

I let out a quiet laugh and feel a little shudder run up my back. The image disappears and I realize I should have taken a screenshot.

I text: *Send another.*

It takes a mere moment, then I get another image notification: *run baby run faster than my bullet.* I open it and she's holding her hands in the shape of a heart and I feel lucky and happy. This time I'm ready and I save it to my collection.

My phone chimes: *You screenshot that didn't you? Maybe? :-P*

I move across Albert Street, my ankles nearly skimmed by an impatient asshole in a car-turning north. I step onto the curb, look over my shoulder, and see he's already half a block away. I adjust my gym bag on my shoulder and text back to her:

How'd the test go?

Good enough.

And the track meet?

The typing indicator bubbles away. This reply is longer, because she loves being competitive: *It went well. Made great time. Need to pace myself better but I don't think Broadhill will be real competition. Track isn't their thing. Coach said there may be some university scouts at the next race.*

I'm so proud of her: *That's great babe.*

She adds: *You?*

I want to reply in my cheeky way, but I hesitate. She deserves a real answer once in a while: *Practice was hard, but good. No pain. No gain.*

I don't realize in the texting how far I've walked. I'm already in my neighbourhood, but I want to chat more. Yet, Sheri is like me—busy—and I know she's likely itching to get to her run. She's not one of those needy girls always looking for her boyfriend's attention and I love her for it.

Bzzz—another text: *hanging out with Brody tonight, maybe help him with science. You?* Sheri's the oldest in her family and Brody is her younger brother. Since I'm the youngest in mine, they (who ever they are) say that this is a good match for a couple. In my opinion, that is one in a long list of reasons why we're a good match.

Almost home. Supposed to be reading a couple chapters of Catcher in the Rye for English, but I have my science test coming up.

Send me a pic?

I smile. I suppose I owe her one. I turn my hat

around and duck face the shit out of the camera.

Bzzz—BAHAHAHAHA! Get yourself home babe. We'll talk later.

I text her back quickly: *Make plans for the weekend?* It's only Wednesday, but it's good to plan ahead. I send it and slide the phone into my pocket.

4

I cross the street towards my house. We're west of the school and the neighbourhood always gets nicer. Although the area started at the turn of the last century, our house is one of the newer ones on the block. It's a white two-story, constructed to blend in with the older homes around it. It has the big pillars and the porch, but not the dark, leaking basements that all our neighbours have.

I run up the steps and go inside to find Dad on the couch. He smiles as he puts the book he's reading on his lap.

"You're late for supper."

I pull out my phone and look. "Almost late."

"Tell that to your mother."

Mom hollers from the kitchen, "Is that Anthony? Tell him he's late for supper."

Dad yells back at her, "Geesh, woman, you in my kitchen? Leave my food alone. You're the breadwinner and I'm the cook."

We are traditional in a lot of ways, but Mom and Dad carved their own path a long time ago when they started dating in college. Grampa freaked out when he found out Mom's new boyfriend was white. Dad tried to cook every holiday meal for three years until he felt he proved to her father that family and tradition were something special to him. The two of them still laugh about it, Grampa admitting he liked Dad after the first year but didn't want to lose out on all the good food. Back then, interracial relationships were a big deal but now that label is mostly gone—Mom and Dad are just a couple and my mocha skin is a blessing.

Dad looks at me and wrinkles his nose. "You stink."

Mom calls again, "Tell him to change his shirt. He probably stinks."

"How do you two do that?"

Dad holds up his ring finger with a knowing nod. "Gives you magic powers, Son."

I know a little interest in my parent's stuff goes a long way, so I nod to the book on Dad's chest. "What are you reading today?"

"Le Carré."

"Ah." I nod but don't really know who it is.

"How was practice?" Seems Dad uses my tricks too.

"Good."

"What'd you do?"

"Lay-ups."

"Coach worked you hard?"

I nod.

He picks up his book again. "Go get changed before your Mom gets a real whiff of you."

"You just want to finish your chapter."

"Maybe, but I wouldn't debate that with your mom."

My sister Heather comes out of her room as I head up the stairs. "Did you listen to that download

I shared?"

I nod. "Yeah. It's good. Your taste in music is improving, College Girl."

I think all those pre-law classes have got her thinking in a different way. She'll end up working for some high-priced firm far away one day and I'll miss her when she does.

"Shouldn't you be at some sorority thing?"

She's two years older than me and we're finally starting to click as siblings. The banter is fun—way better than the cat and dog fights we used to have, and I'm sure Mom and Dad are grateful too.

"That's just in the movies, smart ass."

"Easy or I'll give your number to Mike." I know all my friends think she's hot. I'm grateful that it happened after graduation though, because no guy wants to deal with that growing up. Just way too much hard work.

Mom yells up the stairs, "Are you two ever going to make it down here?"

Heather turns back to me. "I think supper's ready."

"A magnificent feat of deduction. You'll make a great lawyer someday."

Heather winks and heads down.

I head into my room and see a laundry basket full of fresh, clean shirts on the chair next to my desk. Nice—Dad makes a good housewife.

I pull both a red tee-shirt and a yellow tee-shirt out, trying to decide.

Mom yells from downstairs, "White."

How the hell does she do it?

"You heard your dad. Magic powers."

Damn.

I dig a little deeper and sure enough there's a white tee. I pull it over my head and check my messages. One from Mike and a couple from Sheri.

"Anthony!" Ah, the call of a mom telling you to get your ass in gear, which is very different than the call of an angry mom.

The texts can wait. I toss my phone on the desk and head downstairs for supper.

5

Standing on the path, Sheri folds into a forward bend. Her face almost presses against her legs with very little effort, her arms reaching to the laces of her Asics runners. It's the end of a beautiful fall day. The leaves haven't started to turn yet and she wants to take advantage of the warm weather and practice her race strategy before the next cross-country meet.

She comes up, feeling the stretch along her straightening back. She wears short, black spandex running shorts that hug her strong, long legs, and a white sports bra that peeks out from beneath the shoulders of her loose, grey tank top. Her body is fit, firm, and naturally athletic.

She pulls her long hair back into a ponytail at the top of her head and ties it with a white bandana. She snuck it from Tony's drawer because he's a boy and a slob and probably won't notice it missing, and she likes to keep a part of him near. It helps hold back the little hairs from her face that tickle and annoy her and keeps the sweat out of her eyes when the run is long and focus becomes important. Today is all about focus and she doesn't want anything to distract her.

Two older men jog by, giving her a gratuitous wave, and she smiles. It's a lovely courtesy to acknowledge each other when running and keeps one going when the distance is long. Today her goal is six miles. It's a little further than a regular practice run, but she wants to push herself all the way to the tracks outside the city. Her goal is to finish in 51 minutes. After all, it is still training.

She hopes that when she gets back to the car, there'll be a text message from Tony. That'd be perfect. What she doesn't want is a text from her ex, Dillon, who keeps trying to rekindle things. She finds it annoying but hasn't figured how to cut him out completely.

She clears both of the boys out of her mind and presses into deep, long lunges, until her hams stretch and she feels the surge of blood in her veins. She comes up, slips her earbuds into her ears, and hits play. "Jesus of Suburbia" by Green Day starts up and she takes her first few strides. It's easy and smooth and she quickly puts distance between herself and her starting point.

She jogs past a woman in her 40s, who keeps a good pace. Sheri imagines she'll be like her later in life, still running, still happily taking care of herself, and maybe with a special someone like Tony. As she travels along the golf course, she passes by the Ferguson memorial bench, her personal reminder that the warm-up is done and the serious workout begins. The creek twists away from the city and she picks up her pace.

A Tiesto mix of the love song "All Of Me" by John Legend plays and she giggles as thoughts of Tony slip between the *thup-thup* rhythm of her run. He hates her choice of music, dismissing anything even slightly mainstream as crap. He likes hip-hop and anything that's never graced the top twenty. He's a music snob, and his strong opinions put people off, but it was his manners that drew her in.

They met at a party in the gravel pits. He didn't use any cheesy pick-up lines and didn't try to get her drunk. He swept in while Ross from her English class was attempting to ply her with drinks with absolutely no good intentions. Tony appeared out of the crowd and grabbed the bottle out of Ross's hand before he even had a chance to know what was going on.

"Hey, it's Mr. Unsportsmanlike Behaviour!"

"Back off, Shepherd."

Ross went for the bottle but Tony towered over him—he was tall for a sophomore.

"Oops! Sorry! Was this for her? Did I break up your *thang*?"

That's when Tony looked back at Sheri, and she realized he had the sexiest eyes.

"Was this yours?"

She was about to answer but Ross reached for the bottle again and Tony didn't even look at him, raising it higher out of his reach. He kept looking at her. She felt her drunken head as it smiled and shook out a wobbly "no," but she was spinning into those hazel centers.

"Are you sure?"

This time, she nodded. Tony turned back to Ross.

"Doesn't seem she wants your drink."

That's when Tony, always the cocky one, let the bottle slip out of his hand and it shattered on the gravel. "Oh no."

Ross looked Tony in the eyes. "Screw you!" But he knew he was outmatched and walked away.

He turned back to her. "Well, that was close. I would seriously have hated to break a nail."

The two of them clicked and they spent the rest of the night side-by-side near the fire, watching the drunken antics of their friends. Near dawn, he drove her home and said good night but didn't try anything. She was a little stunned.

After that, they texted back and forth. Their conversations were fun but brief, and she never thought he was going anywhere with his flirting. That is, until things unexpectedly heated up. She had gone to a post-game backyard party and saw Tony playing the guitar and commanding an audience, as Tony often did. He was singing a parody of Taylor Swift's "22," changing it to a song about teachers and what only could be described as their love for shaved genitals. When he was done, he moved out of the crowd towards her and took her hand.

They were sitting on some lawn chairs by the pool when a shooting star fell across the sky.

"Should we make a wish?" It was cliché but she said it.

"Why? It's only space garbage burning up in the atmosphere." That was Tony's response and now she regretted her wish comment.

"Well, aren't you romantic?" It was her only comeback.

"I have my ways."

He leaned close and raised his hand to her

cheek. She could feel his warmth against her skin and thought he was going to kiss her, but nothing happened.

When she opened her eyes, he held her eyelash in his hand.

"Wish on this." She liked the effort but the gesture was cheesy. He leaned closer, whispering in her ear, "Wish for something special."

She shook her head at the mushiness of it all but closed her eyes anyway and blew. She figured he was going to kiss her, so she waited for a long time, but when she opened her eyes, he was gone. She looked around—he was nowhere. Vanished. All she could think was WTF?

She asked around the party, but her friends, Katie and Jessica, never saw where he went. She was feeling pissed off when she turned around and suddenly saw him.

"Where the hell did you go?"

He wrapped his arm around her waist, pulled her close, and then kissed her in the middle of all those people. It was bold and confident, and he seemed so sure that he could kiss her. And he was right.

"What? Wasn't that what you wished for?"

She grinned, completely pleased with his game, but wouldn't let him have it. "You are such a weird asshole."

He smiled. She smiled. It was then that she knew he was the boy for her. That was eight months ago.

He kept her guessing and always on her toes. He challenged her to be her best. He came to every one of her meets but gave her the space to be her own person. Now, the only real issue they face is that they plan to attend separate colleges after graduation. She knows couples do it all the time, no matter the space between them, but long distance is never easy—unless it's a run.

She realizes that she's let her focus shift and begrudgingly shakes off thoughts of Tony as she slips back into her running brain. There's time to think of the drama in her world, but at this moment she needs to make her goal.

She starts to sweat just as a slight breeze picks up. Perfect. Maybe a good run has to do with luck as well as training. She heads over the road that takes her on the path toward the old tracks.

She pushes herself up the small incline, knowing that the next mile is the part she likes the most. It's a series of gentle rolling slopes that pushes her hard, and on the last rise she gets to really dig in.

She moves through each dip towards the picnic area by the pines. In the summer, people come here to get out of the city and relax in the grass while their kids climb on the play structure. Yet, at this time of year, even in the warm afternoon, it's abandoned and quiet.

She looks down at her watch. She's making excellent time—better than expected. If she continues on without stopping, she'll crush her personal time, but she only needs to prepare herself for the upcoming meet. She's done well and there's only a mile left before she turns back. She re-calculates in her head and knows that if she stops for a quick bathroom break she'll still end strong.

She heads across the grass towards the playground by the trees. She winds herself down, takes in a deep breath, rolls her neck, and stretches her legs. "The Kids Aren't Alright" by The Offspring starts up and she can already hear Tony getting riled up by the song. It makes her laugh. After her run, she'll take a long shower and drop by his house for a short visit.

She pushes the washroom door open and enters.

6

He first spotted her three weeks ago.

After his first attempt failed, he decided to scale back his efforts. He started with cats and small dogs. Then, his training was interrupted by the move brought on by his idiot brother. Once the family settled in this new city, he rededicated himself to his practice. He learned to suffocate larger dogs with plastic bags, and while he was burying a neighbourhood dog by some pines outside the city, he saw her. She was strong and lithe, and she looked like a solid challenge. If he was to be successful, he needed to take his time and prepare.

He believed this wasn't a one-time occurrence and that she'd return again. She had the pertinacity and agile glide of someone confident in the steady movement of her body. He returned the next day at the same time, sitting by the edge of the play structure, but she didn't appear.

Although disheartened, he vowed to return. When he arrived, he saw someone moving far away, back towards the city, and he decided to repeat his watch again the next day. He arrived at an earlier time and his diligence paid off when he saw her round the curve towards him. She moved past without seeming to notice him hidden in the shadows of the pines.

Again, he arrived early the next day, eager to see her. He brought a thermos of tea and F. Scott Fitzgerald's *Tender is the Night,* and waited. He enjoyed the process of the hunt, the focus he felt in unwrapping the mystery of his act. He worked it through his mind, careful to not put anything on paper, to leave any trace of the plot. He knew that crafting his performance in his imagination made him sharper and more in control of his faculties.

Except, he couldn't envision the circumstance of their meeting, the moment in which he'd happen to her. The picnic area sat on a plain beyond the undulating hills and unless he wore camouflage, he'd be conspicuous in the knee-high grass along her route. There were the pines but they were too far from the path, and any attempt to cross the distance between them would likely alert her, leading to her escape. His choice was to find a more opportune location either by arriving earlier, closer to the start of the path, or to follow her at a distance through the inclines. These musings were interrupted the steady *tick-tock* rhythm of her soles against the bituminous surface of the nearby path.

He looked up and she was moving towards him. He didn't move and he barely felt the tea spill out of his cup onto his hand. She looked at him and he forced a smile, but she didn't return it. She looked right through him and crossed to the bathroom. He stayed still, unsure of his next move. He set the tea down, wiped off his hand, and picked up the book he didn't plan to read. He kept an eye on his watch. It was 5:37 and the second hand ticked slowly. One minute. Two. At four minutes, she exited the building. He didn't look up when he heard the door bang against the stop and her feet pick up their steady rhythm, the sound fading into the distance. He had his answer.

Now, three weeks later, he's waiting and practice has made perfect. He arrives early, slips inside the farthest stall, and locks the door. He takes off his shoes, placing them in his bag, and sits with his legs crossed on the toilet seat. He's rehearsed his moves repeatedly, hitting all the right marks and making sure to remove any hint of noise. He knows all of his polishing, all of his perfectionism, will pay off.

He leans back against the wall. There is no electric light and the skylight casts a soft shadow on the floor. The mirrors are metal and create distorted shapes like figures in a fog. It helps hide his approach, but he dislikes not being able to see the show.

He wraps the bag around his hands. He uses a white garbage bag this time because it makes less noise and, after a particularly vicious canine bite to the hand, he found the cheap plastic shopping bags tore too easily. He doesn't check his watch because she never runs on a tight schedule. She fluctuates so much that he knows he needs to wait for nearly an hour before he can leave. At the start, there was more than one time that he almost got caught, but he's grown to be patient. He closes his eyes, calming his mind, listening to the silence around him.

When the door bangs open, the noise surprises him. He isn't sure if he had fallen asleep or not. He hears the person cross to the bathroom and shut the door. In the silence, he can hear quickened breaths and he believes it's her. He lowers his feet to the ground and rises off the seat. Even this action, the fundamental act of standing, he's trained for. He reaches over and turns the lock but keeps the door slightly ajar.

He listens to the toilet flush and knows he only has seconds to act, but only if she washes her hands. He pivots the door open, not hitting it against the wall. He sees her cross to the sink and push the self-closing tap. He rushes towards her and she doesn't even see his distorted image in the mirror. He wraps the bag around her face and she immediately drops.

All of his rehearsal, all of his considerations, have prepared him. He throws all of his weight on top of her, keeping his body low and his legs protected. Her fingernails scratch at his arms, but his jacket protects him. She tries to leverage her body into a different position, but he predicts her every move. He's ready this time. Ready for it all.

He leans against her and the tight lip of plastic presses against her neck. Her defenses aren't working and she realizes it. She needs air. She claws at the bag and he knows that the struggle is tipping in his favor. He twists the bag in his fist, the white plastic wrapping around his hand, and he yanks hard and shoves his arm deep into the flesh of her neck, pressing against her windpipe. She coughs as he cuts off her air.

He leans in, pushing his whole forearm against her and pulls her hands away from the bag, but she doesn't fight because she can't see and she's scared and crying and screaming and he can feel her slipping away. He can feel the fight in her arms getting weaker, the strained breaths between each gasp growing longer, the heaves of her whole body as it chokes on all that's left, all of her world contained in the white plastic bag.

Her legs stop first, and he can feel death move up through her body. Her hands slide from the bag, and he waits a moment until he can't feel her chest move. He lifts his arm off her throat and then lifts the bag. He sees her, eyes open, tongue out, vomit and spit on her cheeks and in her hair. Her skin is mottled blue—no, gun metal grey—and he looks at her bloodshot eyes. All the little spasms and twitches are gone, and he wants to keep staring—but he can't because there is still work to do.

7

Dad has this great way of feeding us healthy food without it looking like a hospital tray. I'm not sure if it's a 'stay at home dad' thing or a 'being married to a doctor' thing, but either way he does some pretty badass tricks with greens and quinoa. He knows he has to make us healthy food or listen to Mom lecture him on what happens to your insides when you don't take care of your body. I guess looking at sick people all day long does that that to a person.

I'm at the bottom of the stairs when Dad yells, "Last one here can grab the milk and the glasses." Heather appears out of nowhere, pushing me against the wall, racing to get to the table first.

"You stepped on my foot."

"Sorry, little brother, but a rule is a rule."

I head towards the kitchen and open the fridge. Seeing nothing, I yell out, "Where's—?"

"Don't yell," Mom says over my shoulder, "It's the soy milk."

I wrinkle my face. "Making changes without asking? Not cool, Mom."

She reaches in and hands it to me. "Deal with it."

I take it to the table and plop the carton down in

front of Heather.

"Soy? That stuff tastes like chalk."

Now, I have to try it. I grab another glass from the cupboard and pour a glass of water. I feel my family's eyes on me. "Just in case."

Heather raises her empty glass in a mock toast. "To your health."

"It's better for both of you." Mom looks over at Dad. "For all of us."

"Sorry, hon. Tonight, I partake in the wine."

I shake my head. "Cheater."

"No, Son. Studies show—"

I grunt my disapproval but he cuts me off.

"—a glass of red wine is very good—"

Mom tries to interrupt him too, but he doesn't stop.

"—when that person is an adult—"

Heather reaches for the bottle but he pulls it away.

"—and living on their own."

"Fine, old man, you win this one, but only because you made the meal." I dig into the salad, put a billy goat's worth on my plate, and pass it to him. "But make sure to eat your veggies."

Mom nudges her glass Dad's way and he pours her a glass of the vino too. She savours it, then says, "Jodi called. She and Bryan are thinking about selling their place." Jodi is my oldest sister and Bryan is her husband.

I take a slug of the soy milk, hoping for the best, expecting the worst. Yup, chalk. I put the glass down and take a long gulp of water to wash the taste away.

Conversation moves around the table. Ollie, our golden retriever, lies under the table with his butt on my toes. Dad talks about a contract he's working on. I have no idea what he actually does, but I know he does it at home in between the cooking and the cleaning. Mom wants to fire the receptionist at her clinic, saying that this one isn't very good with paperwork. Heather loves college. Everyone shares their day.

I try to appreciate this moment, to savour it all. It won't last forever, because like Coach said, you never know what's coming up from behind.

8

After supper, Heather and I share the duties of cleanup and give Mom and Dad some quiet time. The everyday business of the family is a lot like a good basketball game. It's not the whole game that matters but all the small plays that lead up to the win. I always say sports makes a good analogy for the family because you always have to be on the same team.

As I put the dishes on the counter, Heather gets containers out of the drawer for the leftovers. Ollie sits in a corner, close but not underfoot, ready to catch any scraps we send his way.

"Some of us are going out tonight. Do you want to join us?"

She snaps the lid on the salad and chicken, and I'm already thinking they'll make a good lunch for tomorrow.

"No. I'm beat and I still need to get homework done." She grabs the food and heads to the fridge. I help her with the door.

"You just want to hang out with Sheri."

"I wish."

The fact is, I'm exhausted. It's been a long week and I've learned that knowing when to hit the pause button to regain focus is important. I open the dishwasher and Heather stacks dishes on the racks.

"What about you? Is what's his name going to be there?" Some boy has been calling her lately but she's being secretive about him. She's still getting over her old boyfriend, so she may be thinking this new guy isn't worth her time.

"Isaac."

"Right. Isaac…" I swig down the last of my soy milk and cringe. I gladly put the glass on the rack and close the dishwasher.

Heather hands me a wet cloth, and I go to the dining room to wipe the table.

"No. He's busy—which is fine. He's just not—"

I step back into the room. "Outstanding?"

She leans on the counter, shakes her head, and laughs. "I'm only here for another year and then it's law school. I don't know where he's going or where I'll be, so what's the point? Besides, he's a bit wishy-washy."

I toss the cloth in the sink and lean on the counter beside her.

"Hey, no judgments here. This is all between you, me, and Ollie."

My sister looks around at the kitchen and nods just like Mom. "Baby brother, you're getting really good at this cleaning up thing. Who'd have thought?" She heads for the living room. "I'm leaving in ten to meet Hayley, Lindsay, and Chad at McLarens—if you change your mind."

"Thanks." I won't be going and Heather knows it, but I'm grateful that she asks.

I head upstairs to my room and shut the door. I'm not in the mood for schoolwork, but I grab a seat at the desk and drag out my biology text. Mr. Harriet's class has a test coming up next week, so I need to memorize the biological classifications of fifty plants and animals from kingdom to species. I stare at the page and all the words meld into an ugly mass of -phyla and -zoa. My eyes glaze over, and I move over to my bed and grab my phone.

Mike pops up first with a text about him killing 200 lbs on the weights. I shake my head. He always thinks about size and never about speed. I move on to Sheri's text. It's her response to my question about the weekend.

yes.

Her next text reads: *visit tonight?*

It kills me, but I text back: *can't.* I don't want to leave it at that, so I continue: *text me when you're done.*

I don't expect to hear from her until after her run, so I go back to my studies. Somewhere between the family and genus of a mountain lion, my head hits the pillow, and I don't lift it until morning.

9

I wake up Thursday morning and wipe the little bit of drool off the book I fell asleep reading. Out of habit, I reach for my phone. The screen is too bright and I squint to see who's texted: two from Jessica, Sheri's best friend. It's likely girl drama so I disregard it. Two from Mike. One from a number I don't recognize. And one from Katie.

I don't see any message from Sheri. I know she's been working hard for competition lately, but it's strange. She must have been as knock-out tired as I was.

I tap on her name and text: *Morning, babe* and send it off. It's painfully early and I fall headfirst back into the pillow.

"You're going to be late for practice!" Mom hollers from the kitchen.

I look at my phone again and realize half an hour has passed. I groan quietly and drag myself out of bed. I know that as soon as my feet hit the ground the rush will begin.

I shower and quickly pull on my Adidas sweats. I toss socks, a tee-shirt, a pair of shorts, and a towel into my bag. I double-check for deodorant. Got it. Don't want to be late, because Coach will make us do extra laps. Damn—I still need a shirt.

Bzzz.

Sheri? I grab my phone off the dresser and check. It's Mike. *Hey man. On my way. Picking up breakfast. Order?*

I text back a delicious and thoroughly unhealthy choice from Mike's favorite fast food place. I'm hoping it'll get me through the grueling basketball practice that Coach has planned for us.

"Anthony!" I pull the tee-shirt over my head as I grab my gym bag off the bed. I text one last message to Sheri: *Heading to practice Babe. Talk later.* I stuff my cell phone into my front pocket and go downstairs.

Mom's on me. "Practice starts in twenty minutes." Along with being magic, Mom's also a precise time-keeper. Although I act annoyed, I'm secretly grateful.

Bzzz — I take my phone out of my pocket. It's Mike and he's on time.

"You better get going or you'll be late for practice. Don't need to hear you whining about Coach Davies being hard on you again." She puts my water bottle on the counter.

"Thanks." I toss it in my bag.

"You have enough gas?"

I smile, knowing there's an offering for money coming. This is the advantage of being the youngest, the only boy, and the last teenager left in the house.

"Mike's driving." I hesitate. "But if you want, you can give me a little extra cash...maybe a ten?"

She laughs and looks over at Dad, who's deep into his newspaper at the breakfast table. "Ben, the boy needs ten dollars."

Dad looks up from his paper, smirking. "I'm a

bank now?"

"You know what I like about you, Dad," I nod at the paper, "You always keep it old school."

He hands me a little pocket cash. "Spend it on Sheri. Women like that."

I take it, always grateful for whatever they give.

"What's practice today?"

"Passing and handling."

Mom moves in with a refill for Dad's coffee. "It's good that Davies makes you sweat."

Mike's truck honks outside.

"When's the next game?"

I love having my parents in the stands. "Friday. Seven. Against Cornwall High." Dad nods and I know he's listening. Sheri says I'm the same way. It's like they say—apples and trees, chips and blocks.

A longer honk from Mike. He's in no mood to run laps.

Mom breaks the moment when she kicks the dishwasher door shut with her heel. "Tony, get moving. Ben, quit wasting his time." Mike and Mom would get along great.

I move to the kitchen and grab my lunch. "Nice shirt. Teal looks good on you."

I stare at her. "Really? You can't just call it green?"

She shakes her head. "What time will you be home?"

"Supper."

Honk.

"Go."

"Kay. Love you." The door shuts as I hear her reminding me to walk the dog when I get home.

I move to Mike's truck and toss my bag into the back seat. I barely plop myself into the passenger seat before he's moving. He has the radio station on some Top 40 garbage.

"What the hell are you listening to?" I change the channel to an indie station that plays some pretty sick hip-hop.

Mike shakes his head and says nothing. He hands me my breakfast.

I unwrap my breakfast sandwich and see that the bacon is missing. "Did you mess up the order?"

He keeps his eyes on the road. "No. I ordered it right."

I bite into the sandwich. "Well, where's the bacon?"

"I ate it."

"You took out my sandwich, opened it, ate the bacon, and then rewrapped it and gave it to me?" I really need to hear the logic behind Mike's thinking.

"Yup. Fair trade. You get to listen to hip-hop. I eat your bacon."

I shake my head. The guy is a great power forward, but he really thinks in unusual ways.

Before I can say another thing, we pull up to the school and hustle to the gym to get changed for practice. If all goes well, we'll finish by eight, right before first class.

We get our uniforms on, stow our bags in our lockers, and rush out of the gym door. Yet, as we step out onto the court, we move like we're cool and composed, dropping our water bottles by the team bench.

Coach shakes his head. "Nice for you two to be a

part of the team."

I glance over at the clock—just in time. "Well, Coach, we do what we can."

10

The next hour is a blur. Coach works us hard with drills, plays, and strategy. There are a lot of do-overs, yelling, and whistle blowing on his part. His expectations are high. At the moment, it's hard and I'm exhausted, but I know it's worth it in the long run.

Finally, Coach blows the final whistle and we all nearly collapse.

"Alright team, huddle up."

I walk over to him along with the rest of the players. We're dripping sweat and barely able to breathe. I savour the fact that I don't have to use my legs, or I might collapse.

Coach goes over his notes. "Solid effort. James, you need to focus a little more on defense, and Leo, you've really got to stick on your man."

Leo nods. We all start to relax. It looks like Coach is letting us off easy today.

"Good work boys. Practice is over…after you do your lines."

We groan and drag our asses to the far end of the gym. Coach blows his whistle and I push myself to the first line.

Touch. Run back. Next line. Touch. Run back.

By the time I finish, I'm sure I've lost ten pounds

in sweat. I head for the shower and quickly rinse off before first class.

I dress, exit the change room, and head towards my locker. I grab my binder for my first period history class and my psychology textbook for second. I check my phone. Still no messages from Sheri. She really must be running late this morning.

I send off a quick text: *Have a good day babe. I'll text you at lunch,* and slam the locker door shut. I spin the combination lock and put the phone in my pocket. I still have a few minutes before class.

Mike approaches.

"Man, that was a tough one today." He sees Sarah, a girl from my English class, and he pulls himself up a few inches. "Tough but good, right?"

She ignores his obvious stare and passes by. He leans back against the locker and sighs deeply.

I try to change the subject. "Are we training after school?"

He mumbles, "Yeah," still staring in Sarah's direction.

"What about that girl from the movie theater?"

He looks at me. "Who? Chrissy?"

I nod.

"Oh, you know, I'm trying to keep my options open."

"Have you even spoke to her?"

Mike nods, but I can tell by his look he isn't even listening to me.

I yell, "Stay focused, Mike!" but it doesn't matter as his groin leads him down the hallway towards Sarah. I shake my head and wonder why he even bothers to carry a backpack. I head to class.

The rest of the morning passes by and I don't hear back from Sheri. Deep in my gut, a small, uncomfortable feeling settles, but I bury it away. I don't need to be insecure. Besides, it's something I'm going to need to get used to once we start college. She's way too driven and busy to have time for a clingy boyfriend.

The bell rings and now it's time for psychology. I slip in and drop down in my assigned seat by the door. The teacher, Ms. Statten, stares at her computer. Her glasses sit buried in her strawberry blond hair, and her long legs stretch out beside her desk showing off whichever pair of heels she's decided to wear today. She's not old enough to be a mom but not young either—she's just in the neighbourhood of cougar. It's her second year at our school, and the entire male student body knows about her ever since Black Panty Friday.

Some freshman claims to have caught a glimpse of something peeking out once, and since then, the rumor has grown and all my buddies have had perfect attendance. Not one guy seems to miss a day in her class, just in case.

All that aside, she's an interesting lady because she hardly talks about anything outside of school. She's down to business—not like any of the other teachers who tell us about their weekends, their kids, their spouses, dogs, whatever—but Statten? Nothing. Maybe she has boundaries or it's about respect, but for me, she's a secret—a riddle with really nice legs.

The bell goes and I'm pulled out of my quicklived little fantasy. The data projector is on, her notes are up, and she's ready to go. The first slide up—Disorders.

I write as Statten speaks: "Antisocial Personality Disorder, Avoidant Personality Disorder, Borderline Personality Disorder, Narcissistic Personality Disorder, Obsessive-Compulsive Personality Disorder, and finally, Schizotypal Personality Disorder."

I stare down at my notes and can't help but wonder if learning this stuff is the reason why I question whether or not my neighbour has it. Do I?

Ms. Statten finishes up and tells us to read the first ten pages of Chapter 11. The class settles into silence.

The intercom pings on. "Good morning, Ms. Statten. Is Tony Shepherd there?"

I look up from my textbook, surprised to hear my name.

"Yes, he is."

"If it's convenient, could you send him down to the office?"

"I will." Ms. Statten looks at me and nods.

The intercom pings back. "Also, he's not likely to be back before the end of class." That gets everyone's attention—including mine. A hushed, collective taunt rumbles through the room.

I grab my books and head for the door, not wanting to look back. I hear Ms. Statten call out, "Tony, questions one through eight—"

"For tomorrow. Got it, Ms. Statten."

11

I head straight to the office and enter. Mrs. Opal, the school secretary, sits at her desk on the phone. She looks up, sees me, and turns away, lowering her voice to a whisper. Constable James Blake, our Resource Officer, leans against the edge of the desk listening to the call. He's jotting notes down on a pad of paper that sits on his lap. He's the school cop, and I rarely see him at the front desk in the main office.

Mrs. Opal ends the call and turns back to me. She smiles but it feels forced. "Hello, Tony. The principal wants to see you, but it will be a few more minutes."

I nod and stand there, feeling awkward.

She doesn't seem that comfortable herself. She points to a plastic chair against the wall. "Please take a seat."

I sit and keep thinking this has to be a basketball question or something, but the door to the principal's office is closed. Through the frosted glass I see several people moving inside. Mrs. Opal and Constable James talk between themselves, but they keep looking over at me and I start to worry. I've never been in real serious trouble before, but I sure feel like somehow I've landed myself in the middle of it now.

"Do you know why I'm here?" I ask.

"Just a few more minutes," says Constable James. He tries to look relaxed, but he's got his arms crossed stiffly and awkwardly.

I suspect they don't have any more of an idea of why I'm here than I do, but I know something is going on. I haven't done anything that could justify a serious response and the worst I can come up with is a low grade on a test that might bench me from a game.

I decide to try and quit worrying and I grab my phone. There are two more messages from Jessica. She's the kind of girl who gets really worked up about nothing. I think she should text Sheri or even her boyfriend and leave me alone. I skip over her messages and I see Mom called—twice, which is weird. I go straight to her message and listen: "Anthony, please call as soon as you get this message." This doesn't help me relax at all, so I keep pushing through my texts. Still nothing from Sheri, so I decide to send her another message: *Hope you're having a good day babe? What's on for lunch?*

This is the usual routine for the two us, since her noon hour break starts twenty minutes before mine. As long as she's not in class, she'll text back quickly.

As I send it off, the door to the principal's office opens and Mrs. Johnson steps out. She's a great principal. She always makes it to our games and knows us all by name when she walks the halls. But she isn't smiling when she sees me. That's when I notice the other woman behind her. She's not a teacher but something tells me she isn't a parent either. She wears jeans and a black cord jacket and there is something about her posture that makes her look like someone off a show about hard-nosed New York cops.

Mrs. Johnson crosses the room to the secretary and lowers her voice—what's with everyone whispering around here? I hope she's only setting me up for a drive-along for my law class with that police officer, but I know it's doubtful.

Mrs. Johnson tells Mrs. Opal to hold her calls and my mind races. When was the last time I drove? Did I speed? Did I blow through a light? Maybe it had to do with the last party I was at. Maybe I've been too friendly with the school dope dealer? I try to calm my spinning mind, but part of me feels like I've slipped unknowingly into a mess of trouble.

"Tony, I think we're ready. Can you come into my office please?"

12

I follow Mrs. Johnson into her office. She takes a seat behind her desk and I notice that Constable James and the tough city cop have followed us into the room. Constable James shuts the door and takes a seat, but the woman remains standing just behind my left shoulder. I want to turn and look at her but stand there feeling really uncomfortable.

"Have a seat, Tony." Mrs. Johnson motions to the chair.

I sit down.

"You know Constable James. And this is Detective Gekas."

I twist in my chair to look at them and feel myself forcing a smile.

"Hello, Tony." She puts out her hand and I shake it. She's tall and slender with dark, wavy hair. Although her face seems kind, she looks like she hasn't slept in several days.

"Tony?" Mrs. Johnson addresses me and I have to turn back to face her. "We've called your parents to let them know we'll be talking to you, but for now we have a couple of questions."

Detective Gekas starts. "Do you know why you're here?"

I shake my head. I don't have a clue.

"We understand that you have a girlfriend?"

As soon as I hear the words, my stomach drops. I twist back around to look at her and nod.

"Good. Her name is Sheri?"

"Sheri Beckman."

"And how long have you been dating?"

"A little under a year."

"It's serious?"

"Yeah, I love her." Detective Gekas takes a deep breath in and her back straightens.

"Would Sheri say it's serious?"

"I hope so."

Detective Gekas moves around and sits on the edge of the desk across from me.

"When was the last time you spoke to her, Tony?"

I feel my phone in my front pocket with my hand. "Like ten minutes ago."

Detective Gekas, Constable James, and Mrs. Johnson look at each other.

"I sent her a text asking her what she's having for lunch. I do it every day. It's normal."

Officer James leans in. "When was the last time *you* heard from *her*?"

I realize I've stopped breathing and inhale into my already full lungs. I haven't heard from her all morning. I hear myself saying, "It's not weird. We're both busy—" I hear the words crystal clear in my head. I breathe out.

"Um. Yesterday after school. I had practice. She had a run." I look up from Mrs. Johnson to Constable James to Detective Gekas.

Then I hear myself say the words that I've been

holding back, "Why? Is everything okay?"

Mrs. Johnson's one eye twitches and her mouth curls. She's about to speak when my phone buzzes against my thigh. I look down and don't ask for permission. I reach in, take it out, and see the name.

"It's my mom."

Mrs. Johnson looks at Detective Gekas, who nods to me.

I answer it. Mom's voice sounds calm but distant. "Tony, are you okay?"

"I think so."

"Mrs. Johnson called me."

"I'm in with her now."

There's a long pause. "When you need me—just say the word."

"Okay, Mom."

"Everything will be alright. I love you, Anthony."

I don't say even goodbye when I shut the phone off.

"Tony, we just have a few more questions to ask you."

I look over at Detective Gekas. A thick, dark feeling in the pit of my stomach slowly makes its way to the surface.

"When did you last see her?"

"What's going on?"

"Tony—"

I realize I'm standing. Detective Gekas raises her hands trying to usher me back into my seat. "Please stay for a few more minutes."

I look at Gekas and I'm no longer sure I really like her, but I sit down again.

"When was the last time you saw your girl-friend, Sheri?"

"What happened to her?"

"Tony, I need you to focus—"

"The night before last. I went over to her house after supper."

"For how long?"

"A couple of hours."

"And what did you do?"

I close my eyes and I see Sheri before me. Her lips, her eyes. She's smiling. I look at Gekas and I know she isn't going to give me anything until I answer her questions.

"We hung out." Now it's my turn. "What happened to her?"

"Her parents filed a missing person's report last night when she didn't come home from her run."

My mind starts to spiral, "Have you talked to her friends? There's Katie and Paul and Jessica—"

"Yes, Tony—"

"And there's her ex, Dillon, who's a douchebag. And there's this guy who is always trying to get her drunk at parties—"

"Okay, Tony—"

"And, I could—"

Gekas raises her hands. "Tony!" She takes a breath and leans back. "Thank you. We're exploring all leads."

I glare at her, uncertain if I believe her.

"What I need from you is to help me answer a few more questions."

What I need is to get up and leave this office so that I can go start searching for her.

She leans forward again. "Tony? Okay?"

I agree.

"How was she the night you saw her? Did she seem distressed? Overly worried? Sad? Happy?"

"She was fine. Normal."

"Did she talk about going anywhere? Maybe she has a favorite place?"

"Running. She likes running— Have you checked the Trails?"

"We've got officers working out there now." She clasps her hands together, coming in close to my face.

"Tony— Is there—anything she might have been keeping from her parents?"

I know I'm supposed to fill in the gaps, that she is asking for something underneath the question, but I can't think. Her perfume is too strong and I shrink back, trying to ignore the smell. I keep thinking about how my last texts to Sheri before she disappeared were duck faces and questions about the weekend. All that she was worried about was how to handle the long-distance relationship when we both went to college. Now, she was missing, running into the distance without an end.

"Tony? Were there any secrets she—"

I feel the tears coming and I don't want to deal with any of this now. "No. Nothing. Can I go?"

Gekas sits up and looks away. I quickly wipe my eyes with my sleeve and try to get myself under control. She looks at Mrs. Johnson who rises up from behind her desk.

"It's alright Tony. Thank you. You can head back to class now."

I get up and move towards the door.

Gekas opens it for me. "If you think of anything else, you give me a call."

I take a card she hands me and I get out of the office fast. Yeah, I'm pretty sure I don't like her much at this moment.

13

I head to my locker, doing my best to avoid anyone in the hallways. I get my backpack and go out a side door by the stairs. I feel like I'm going to vomit, and as soon as I hit the fresh air, I take a deep breath. I push around the corner and at some point I realize I've slid down the wall, my legs going out from under me, my knees bunched up in my face. I keep breathing deeply, trying not to be sick.

I don't need someone finding me here, freaking out. I've got to get myself up and moving, but I feel a frustration I've never felt before and want to hit something. I don't have time for this and I stand and rush to the street and break for home.

I don't know where else to go, but I know can't stay behind the walls of this school any longer. I need to put distance between myself and this place. I could probably call Mom, but I need the walk, to surround myself with the noises of the city and drown out the buzzing thoughts in my head. I don't want to be asked questions about how I'm feeling, because frankly, I have no clue.

When they called me into that office, they had to suspect that I might have had something to do with her disappearance. And that detective—Gekas—she was trying to get me to confess. She was hoping I would say something.

I realize that it's been almost 20 hours since Sheri and I texted. Man, almost an entire day has passed and Gekas and her buddies haven't got any further than questioning me about what I know. Talk about a bunch of heads up the collective ass. It also means they have nothing. They have no clue what happened to her—whether she ran away or got taken or—

I push the thought out of my head and start running other scenarios.

Sheri isn't the type to take off. She was happy at home, happy at school. She had plans that required a sensible and stable family life. Also, she was strong. If there was a problem, she would face it head-on and deal with it.

Yet, Gekas kept asking me whether there was something going on or if she seemed in distress—

Still, we were good together. She would have talked to me if something was bothering her. She would have said something. I'm sure of it.

I want to clear the possibility of her running away off the table, but I don't have the energy to face the alternatives. She said she was hitting the Trails and then helping Brody with his homework, but before all that she was at school. If I want to figure out where she's gone, I have to start there.

I move up my street but go through the alley and open the back gate. I figure if Mom or Dad is home, they'll be waiting for me. I need to get in and out of the house with the least amount of confrontation, so I open the back door quietly and wait before I enter. I hear someone moving around on the second floor and sneak across the kitchen to the bowl of car keys. Whoever is in the house is coming down the stairs. I grab the set for Dad's car without asking and head for the exit. I'm pretty sure I hear my name before I shut the door, but I don't turn around. I head to the front of the house, jump in the car, and pull away.

I don't look back in the rearview mirror to see if anyone's there.

14

I head across the city, and the traffic is relatively quiet. I realize that I missed lunch entirely with my trip to the office and my walk home. I remember that I have ten bucks in my pocket from Dad, but really, anything I try to eat isn't going to sit well in my stomach. Besides, if I have to sit in a line-up for a craptastic burger and salty fries, I might want to punch a plastic clown, and I just can't have that. I focus on the problem, forcing myself forward to find a solution and let nothing else in. It's the best thing I can do right now—I'm sure of it.

Sheri's school is on the southeast end of town and as soon as I cross Ring Road, I hit the big box stores. I turn, making my way into the soulless suburbs. The cookie cutter mini-mansions for the wannabe wealthy appear. The streets wind and twist around corners and cul-de-sacs and along the high walls that separate the neighbourhoods from the rest of the world. Sometimes I wonder if these manmade boundaries are meant to keep the riff-raff out or to keep the inhabitants in where they belong—like an asylum.

The trees disappear and the road opens wide. It intersects the highway, and as I drive across, I see the paved asphalt stretch out of the city, slicing through the open prairie. If I needed to, I could turn right now and make a run for the border. I'd be there in only a couple of hours—if I needed to—if I were guilty—which I'm not. Sometimes it's hard to remember with all that's going on.

I keep driving until I pull up to Sheri's school, Guthrie High.

By now, it's fourth period, and I have almost half an hour before the bell rings. If I'm careful enough, I should be able to pass through the halls without anyone noticing. I grab the door handle and—dammit—it's locked. I pause for a moment and consider other options before moving along the building to find another entrance.

"They're all locked."

I look over and see a guy about my age with blond, shaggy hair, kneeling in the bushes, digging in the soil.

"What did you say?"

He doesn't really acknowledge me and keeps working the dirt with his hands. "All the doors are locked," he pauses, looking at the ground, "you'd think it's to keep out the troublemakers—" he looks over at me, "like you and me. But the wardens of this prison actually expect it to be protection for the students who give a shit."

I am pretty sure this kid must have just escaped from a psych ward. He rises, dusting off the knees of his jeans. He crosses over to the sidewalk that skirts around the school and stops, looking back at me.

"You following me or what?"

"Uh, no."

"Don't you want in?"

I size him up. He's shorter than me but he's built stocky and solid and likely enjoys getting into the occasional fight. I should be able to keep away from him if he decides to take a swing—but if I get too close, I'm sure I'd be down for the count.

"You know how?"

"You think I just hang out, digging in the bushes of any school?" He stares at me as if I'm the idiot. Since I'm considering following him, maybe I am.

"Yeah, what was that all about?"

He sighs, looking up at the sky, squinting from the sun.

"Are you coming or not?"

I walk towards him. He turns and heads to the corner of the school.

"Why were you digging?" He doesn't answer, so I jog to catch up to him. He glances over his shoulder at me and goes around the corner. I stay close to him.

This side of the school is shaded and it's cool and windy.

"There's a side door used by the mechanic class, so the grease monkeys can drive their cars into the workshop."

"Isn't it sort of dangerous to show strangers into the school?"

"You know why they lock the doors?"

"Listen, I've had a real long day—"

He studies me before he answers, "It's because our keepers expect students want to be here. They think that when we're late and we can't get in, we'll seek redemption to ease our suffering. The sad thing is that most of us buy into this belief."

He walks up to a big shop entrance and peers through the window. "Looks all clear."

He moves to the smaller entrance and tries the doorknob. It's locked, but he barely pauses before he reaches into his pocket and pulls out a ring of keys. He thumbs through them and picks one. He slides it into the lock and opens the door for me.

He looks at me. "I haven't seen you before and no one goes into a school unless they're looking for answers or got a personal score to settle."

I think about all the students that must go to this school—hell, that go to my school. "How would you know? How could you recognize them all?"

He just smiles, and I know this guy's definitely got a few screws loose.

"I hope you figure out what happened to Sheri." Before I can say anything, he shuts the door and is gone.

15

I move through the shop and find myself wondering who that kid was—and how the hell he knew who I was. This all disappears when I see students in a classroom. The day's events have knocked me out of sync with the rest of the world, and I keep forgetting that school is still on. I take another look and see a teacher at the front talking about the differences between a two-stroke and a four-stroke engine. I move past the window quickly so that no one notices me.

I've been in this school a couple of times to meet with Sheri or for a game but never in this area. The odors of oil, gas, and exhaust drift out into the hall, and although the walls are painted white, everything feels greasy. The smell of machines blend into wood shavings and dust, and the high-pitched sound of a table saw tearing through boards screams somewhere down the hall. The corridor tees off and I head towards a set of double doors that I hope leads me to the main area.

I come out a long passageway with lockers and classrooms on both sides. I see a set of stairs halfway down and head towards them. Sheri's locker is on the second floor, near the main staircase by the office. I'm hoping that Gekas hasn't found her way over here yet. I know that she will—but if I get enough time, and because I know Sheri, I think I might find something that Gekas won't. I am half-way down the hall when a teacher steps out of their classroom. I move into the recess around a water fountain between the lockers and hope he doesn't notice me. When I look up again, he's moved to the end of the hall, and I head for the stairs. As I duck through the door, he exits the hallway, and I see the open foyer by the front entrance where a huddle of adults stand in a circle.

I climb the stairs to the second floor and turn right.

The halls are empty. Sheri's locker sits between the bio and chemistry labs and I walk up to it, staring at the black number "223" stenciled onto the small brass plate. Two sticky notes, "Come back Sheri" and "We <3 u", hang on the outside of her locker. They're signed in colourful, glitter gel pens by a dozen or so names.

I feel a surge of frustration. These notes piss me off, because I'm sure some drama-seeking ninth grader who likely jumps on any opportunity to draw attention to themselves has placed them here. I think about crumpling the notes up and throwing them on the ground but I don't. I need to stay focused. I take the combination lock into my hand and realize I'm shaking.

Nineteen right, thirty-seven left, thirty-one right. I pull on the lock gently, not wanting to make a lot of noise, and it pops open. I look to the left and right—still no one. I've only been here a moment but it feels much longer. I open the locker and the faint smell of Sheri fills my head—*pang*—and my gut lurches. I close my eyes and breathe in. Enough. I have work to do. There's got to be an answer here about where Sheri went.

I look on the top shelf and only find two textbooks and a novel. I reach up and feel towards the back of the locker but there's nothing else. Three hooks are below the shelf, one empty from where she'd put her jacket, the other hook has one of my old hoodies on it—

pang

The third hook has a gym t-shirt of hers and a small canvas bag. I quickly dig into its centre pocket and pull out some lip gloss, a hair brush, deodorant, and a small cosmetics bag. Inside are tampons and a bunch of hair elastics, like the ones she leaves everywhere that I end up putting in the glove box or my pocket or wherever, just in case she needs one. I put everything back as it was. I take her tee-shirt down, rubbing it between my fingers, thinking.

What am I looking for? What's not right about her locker? Is anything out of place? If she was in trouble, she'd text me, wouldn't she?

I hang everything back on the empty hook and look down at the cross trainers snuggled in a nest of mismatched, colourful socks on the locker floor. I shift to the inside of her locker door. There's a magnetic note pad and pen. Attached to it is the small map of routes she takes with her when she runs, with kilometer distances written in marker on each loop. A calendar hangs under the map. Each day is marked with times and distances and the type of run she plans on doing:

THURS
RACE STRATEGY
EAST TRAILS, 6 MILES

A photo of us, held by a heart-shaped magnet in each corner, overlaps the bottom of the map. She's laughing directly into the camera. I have my arm around her and I'm looking down at her with the biggest smile. I remember this moment. We were at the lake and we had spent the day swimming and that evening, I asked her out officially.

pang—pang—pang

It's a wave I can't control. I close the locker and snap the combination lock shut. I rush to the nearest washroom and straight into the stall, locking it. I lean my head against the door and squeeze my eyes and fists tight. I'm breathing hard and I realize I'm still holding Sheri's tee-shirt. I try my hardest to keep quiet, inhaling and exhaling deeply, trying to find my composure. I want to believe she's okay, but I can't explain why I haven't heard from her.

I take out my phone—several missed messages from my parents and one from Mike. I don't have time for them. I scroll to Sheri's name and see the long column of texts from me—and none from her. I type one more: *Babe, text me back. I'm worried. Where R U?*

Send.

16

I want to punch something. The clock is ticking. The bell will sound soon and I need to get back to Sheri's locker. I suck up my courage and stuff her tee-shirt into the pouch of my hoodie. I take one deep breath and step out of the stall. I give myself one last check in the mirror and leave the bathroom—and immediately slam on the brakes.

Two uniformed officers stand behind a maintenance person with bolt cutters at the end of the hall beside Sheri's locker. They break the lock and start photographing, removing, and cataloguing each piece of her belongings before zip-locking all of it away into a box likely headed for the station.

Dammit, Gekas, you got here too soon.

Before they see me, I duck back downstairs and leg it to the closest backdoor. The last thing I need is to be found lurking around my missing girlfriend's school, especially when I seem to be their prime suspect.

I get to my car and toss my phone on the car seat. As I drive home, I look over at it frequently and pray that Sheri will message me.

When I pull into our driveway, I see Dad at the window. I haul my ass out of the car, ready for whatever he and Mom have to say. I don't expect it to be fun—I spent the morning talking with a cop about my missing girlfriend and they likely know by now that I ditched school. On top of it, I took his car without permission and didn't return a single text. This isn't going to be good.

I walk in the front door and kick off my shoes. Dad comes around the corner and waves me into the kitchen. I don't argue. Mom's there, but she's drinking tea at the counter. Dad takes a seat and fills a cup for me. I don't think I have a choice. I take a seat on a stool at the island. I don't look up right away and watch the hot steam rise out of the cup, weaving tiny swirls in the air. It distracts me for the moment until Mom's voice pulls me back.

"Anthony."

I look up at her.

"We love you."

I keep staring, waiting.

"Where did you go this afternoon? After the principal and the detective talked to you?" I hold a long silence, or at least it feels that way.

"I went for a drive."

"Son..." Dad's voice is so gentle, like he's trying not to shake loose the reality that hangs above us like broken glass. I close my eyes, taking a deep breath as he continues, "It's fine that you took the car, but we wanted to make sure you were okay."

Mom leans on the counter across from me—she's not a very big woman but right now her presence looms. "We're asking because we want to help you. To keep you safe. To know there are no surprises."

I open my eyes, exhaling, "I went...to Sheri's

school." I swallow. I really don't want either of them to get angry. "I wanted to see if there was anything in her locker that could help me understand why she hasn't texted since her run. It just doesn't make sense."

I feel my chin quiver and I look up at the ceiling in an attempt to keep the tears in. "I have this really bad feeling in my gut. I'm trying not to listen to it. I'm trying to believe that everything will be okay, that she'll turn up in some hospital with amnesia or something—"

Dad cuts me off.

"You went to her school?"

I nod.

"Did you find anything?"

I shake my head and add, "Not before the police showed up."

"Did they see you?"

I know I shouldn't be angry but I am. "No. No one saw me. But what does it matter? What if someone did see me? Don't I have the right to find out what happened to her?"

I can see the strained look on Mom as she fills another cup of tea for herself. It reminds me to drink my own, and I wish for a split second that there were something alcoholic in my cup instead of herbal tea. I take a big gulp.

Dad thumbs the edge of his cup as he speaks, "We ask because you are our priority, Anthony. We want Sheri found, but we also want you to be safe and okay. This is hard on us, but we also know that it's a thousand times harder on you."

I nod slowly.

"So if we ask something that doesn't sit well with you, please try to understand why we're asking." Dad has an innate ability to settle me down. "So, let's figure some things out together."

In this moment, I realize I'm safe but also still a kid in a lot of ways.

"You went to Sheri's school to look in her locker?" Dad asks.

"Yeah. To see if there was some clue to figure out where she went."

My mom pipes in, "You know her combination?"

"Of course, Mom." I roll my eyes a bit and as soon as I do I feel like an asshole. She says nothing else for the next few minutes.

"Did you find anything?"

"No. I wish I had but there's nothing. There's never anything unusual or different with Sheri, ever."

Dad leans back, looking up at the corners of the room as he thinks things through while Mom continues to listen intently.

"Then, I went to the bathroom for a minute."

Dad gives me a look, and I can only shake my head and keep explaining myself.

"On my way back, I saw the cops, so I left." I push my empty teacup to the center of the counter and Mom takes it.

"Good choice." She pours another cup to let me know we aren't done talking, which is fine by me. I need my parents right now.

Dad asks when I saw Sheri last and what she was planning to do the night she went missing. I get it. They want information, and I try to answer them unguarded.

"We're going to call our lawyer to be safe. We know you didn't do anything wrong."

I'm relieved that they're ready to fight for me.

"When her parents called last night while you were sleeping, we didn't think anything of it and suggested they try a couple of her friends."

"They called? Why didn't you wake me?" I'm stunned and feel like a stack of wooden blocks that threaten to topple over. Every minute counts and now those minutes last night are lost.

Mom answers, "It seemed normal. They've called here before looking for her. It was probably before they even called the cops."

Dad leans in and says, "People get mean, especially when they're scared and looking for reasons or explanations. You're going to be a target since you were Sheri's boyfriend—"

My emotions teeter and tip and crash down.

"Were?" I slam my hand on the counter and both my parents jump.

Dad rises. "Anthony, I'm sorry, that came out wrong—"

"I'm done." I push my teacup away and it spills. I go upstairs to my bedroom and shut the door. I toss myself on the bed and stare at the ceiling. I feel bad for yelling. I feel bad for spilling the tea. I know I should go back and clean all of it up, but right now, I don't care.

I stare at my phone. I want to pick it up, to look, to hope. It seems like it's been silent all day. A few minutes later, I hear my parents come up the stairs and stand outside my door. I roll over and face the wall.

Dad knocks. "Son?"

Mom follows his lead. "We love you."

I close my eyes and wait for morning to come.

17

I wake Friday morning and don't even want to get out of bed. Although it's a game day, I could really care less. Coach is tough, but I'm not sure if he'll even want me there. I don't move. I just stare at the soft light on the ceiling.

The landline downstairs rings a few times then goes silent. I close my eyes even though the idea of sleep seems something that was lost with Sheri.

"Anthony. Phone!"

I'm guessing Coach has realized I'm not there. He might have to get used to it. I drag myself out of bed.

Mom stands in the kitchen clutching the phone in her hand. I go to reach for it, and she pulls it back. I give her a look and realize she's upset. "It's Sheri's mom."

My hands fall to my side and I whisper, "I don't want to."

"You can. You will." She hands me the phone.

I run through the decision in my mind—if I walk out of the room right now, I'll only make it upstairs before Mom and Dad are on me, telling me how deeply disappointed they are. But, I know the moment I put the receiver to my ear I'll hear the pain in Sheri's mom's voice, and I don't know if I can handle it.

I take the phone from Mom's hand and take a deep breath, maybe a little too loud.

"Anthony?" She sounds likes she's calling from Mars—isolated, far away—just like Sheri.

"Hello, Mrs. Beckman."

She gulps a deep, rattly breath. "I hope the police weren't too hard on you?"

It feels like she's searching. "I'm okay," I don't want to say it, but I feel I must, "How are you?"

It takes her a moment to get it out, "We're just so worried…" I imagine Mr. Beckman standing beside her, holding her close.

"The police will find her." I can hear the disbelief in my own voice, and I'm hoping she doesn't pick up on it.

"That's why I wanted to call." I worry that she's going to ask me details about my meeting with Gekas, or worse, someone saw me around Sheri's school. I didn't plan to make people doubt my innocence or make this any more complicated than it already is.

"The police say they've finished searching the running path and are going to explore other leads." She pauses and continues, "They don't seem to think it's significant that her car was found at the head of the trail…" I can hear her voice breaking, "…we can't keep waiting… I can't wait for the phone to ring and—"

The phone drops with a clunk onto a distant counter and a low moan rises and cuts into my heart. There's a rustle and another clunk and the sound of a muffled receiver before Mr. Beckman comes on the line.

"Anthony? Sorry about that. Sheri's mother— It's hard, you know? We wanted to know—we've got some people together to walk the Trails. See if we can find anything the police might have missed." For such a big guy, such a doer of things, it's hard to listen to the hesitation in his voice. "Would you be able to come out with us? To help us search?"

"Absolutely." Anything is better than hanging around here, waiting for bad news to kick you in the ass while you're down.

18

An hour later, Mom, Dad, Heather, and I pull up to the crowd of people who have gathered to comb the path. The Beckmans stand beside a pickup handing out sunscreen, insect repellant, and water. Beside them on the tailgate are a couple boxes of coffee and doughnuts. How they organized all of this is beyond me. Sheri's parents see us and they give me huge hugs, thanking me for coming. The Beckmans, who sounded broken on the phone earlier, seem rejuvenated by this fight against fate.

They hand us some wire flags that we're supposed to use in case we find something that might be of interest to the police. They send us across to the far side of the creek that stretches out into the prairie surrounding the city. The plan is to move east, away from the golf course, walking towards the first grid road outside of the city. Mrs. Beckman hands me a walkie-talkie, hoping that we'll find something and need to report back.

We jump in the car and travel back to Fleet Street before pulling to the side of the road after we cross the bridge. There are more people at this position, all waiting to begin. Yet, there is no real order or plan, so Dad steps in to organize the group. He fans the crowd out into a straight line, asking us to separate ourselves by an arm's length. Once we are in place, Dad has me radio to the Beckmans to be sure that no one else is coming.

We all move at a slow and equal pace, sifting the deep grass. As the banks of the stream twist and turn, so do we. Sometimes we wrap around each other like a serpent's tail, stumbling into each other's lanes and, although it's frustrating, the mantra we start to spout is that twice the eyes on every patch of ground are better than none. By noon, the clouds have passed over and a wind pushes in from the fields, bringing bits of straw and dust that gets into our eyes. When someone needs a rest or twists their foot stepping into a prairie dog hole, word comes down the line to halt and I radio the main staging area for a replacement. Food is brought out to us in the early afternoon, and we walk and eat, our eyes and free hands ferreting the land. There isn't much chatter on the walkie-talkies, so we don't know how it's going on the other side of the creek, but we know they're further back because we hear the occasional indiscernible shout. It's late afternoon and everyone is exhausted. By the time we reach the grid divide, the foreboding notion that sticks like a nail in our guts is that this day has come up empty.

We move along the gravel road back towards the morning staging area. We see the other group as we walk and can see it on their faces—nothing. It's been an all day thrashing of uneasiness and frustration, and when we reach the Beckmans, I notice they no longer seem like they have power over their destiny and have resigned themselves to the worst.

"Anything?" Dad asks.

"We got a few flags that we'll report to Detective Gekas, but..." Sheri's dad pauses for a long time. "We hoped...Even for the most dreadful...Just so this..." He sighs, holding his hand to his chest, "...could start to heal."

That's when Mrs. Beckman looks at me. "Anthony, if you knew where she was, you'd tell us, right? Right? You wouldn't lie to us, would you?" She comes at me. "Tell me what happened to my baby girl. Tell me! Tell me where she is."

People from the search party stare, and Mr. Beckman shifts between us, pulling his wife back towards the truck before ushering her into the passenger seat and closing the door. I can hear her screaming and crying from inside the cab.

Mr. Beckman doesn't look at my family or me and moves around to the other side. "She hasn't slept much the last two nights. Neither of us have."

I feel Dad's arm around my shoulder and he's pushing me towards our car as I watch Mr. Beckman slam his driver's side door shut.

"They need some time. There's nothing else we can do. Let's go home."

19

At night, I don't feel like sleeping but close my eyes anyway. Every time I start to drift off, I stand among endless fields of grain. I sink into the long, yellow stalks and can't rise above them. I see the grid road in the distance and I try to wade toward it, but the wheat wraps around my feet and it's a struggle. I trip and fall into the thick, black soil where worms and spiders creep. They crawl up my arms and into my mouth and eyes. They choke me and blind me and I wake in a sweat.

I push the covers away and have to wait in the dark before my heart slows down and I can move. I go to the bathroom and wash my face and neck off with a washcloth. When I see myself in the mirror, I know it's going to be a long night.

20

On Saturday, I wake and feel exhausted. I must look like hell because when I head downstairs Dad sees me and says, "We're not going back today."

I wave it off but he doesn't break. "We won't help. We'll only...get in the way."

I realize what he's telling me. Either he and Mom talked last night and decided that the best thing for me was to stay away—or the Beckmans called and suggested I shouldn't come back. Either way, I don't like it.

"But I can help. The more eyes out there—"

"I know—the better. I get it. But we need to let things cool down."

"But, I didn't do anything."

Dad comes over to me, placing his hand on my shoulder. "The Beckmans are trying to comprehend that their daughter is missing. The world they know isn't solid anymore and they'll need to concentrate on what's ahead, especially these next few days. I appreciate you want to do what you can, but right now, that means giving Sheri's parents time to handle the situation in their own way."

I hear what he's saying. I don't like it, but I get it.

"So, what do I do then?"

"Well, first of all, you can do all the chores you've been skipping out on."

Chores are the last thing I want to do, but he gives me a look that tells me it's not an option. I head upstairs and get into sweatpants and grab an old tee-shirt of Dad's from the University of Toronto. For the next four hours, Dad has me taking out garbage, raking leaves, cleaning the downstairs bathroom, cleaning my room, and sweeping out the garage. During all of it, my mind rolls over thoughts of Sheri, of my texts, of my meeting with Gekas and the principal, and Mrs. Beckman yelling at me after I spent all day searching for the girl we both care about. When Mom calls me in for a bite of lunch, I am surprised how quickly half the day has gone.

I eat a chicken sandwich in the kitchen and check my phone. Mike texted me: *We missed you yesterday buddy*. Down below are the results from yesterday's game. We lost.

I stare at the scores and know I should care, but I don't. I am too numb to feel much of anything. The numbers are just strange squiggles and twists divided by a thin line. On one side is a winning team and on the other side is the loser. All that divides them are a few points. I push my phone aside.

"You okay?" Mom asks.

"Yeah…" She knows I'm not. "I was just thinking…What could be buried in the flower bed in front of a school?"

Mom scrutinizes me and I'm sure she wants me to talk to someone, one of her professional friends. I know it would probably do me some good. But I am thinking I might want to talk to another kind of professional—someone with a little more unorthodox methods.

Mom takes over for Dad in the afternoon, and I spend most of my time helping her organize the storage room in the basement. I take out three big bags of garbage and make one trip to the recycling depot. Mom tells me I can keep the $16.85 that I get for returning the bottles—and that's when I know she must really be worried about me.

By the end of the day, I'm exhausted. My head hits the pillow and I surrender to sleep. Nightmares of prairies and creatures and dark, rotting earth don't invade my deep slumber.

21

When I wake the next day, Sunday, it's raining and I don't even try getting out of bed. I pull the pillow over my head and turn to face the wall. Mom, Dad, even Heather, all come into the room to check on me and I lie still with my eyes closed until they leave. By lunchtime, I decide it's time to face the world, so I drag myself out of bed and head downstairs. Everyone has left and the house is quiet.

Ollie runs over. He's attentive and happy and I open the cupboard and find his dog treats. He sits, tail wagging.

"Shake a paw." Ollie puts his paw in my hand. I give him a treat.

"Good boy." I rub the top of his head as he swallows his treat whole.

"Geez, chew it, would you?" This time I get him up on his hind legs. I toss his next treat and he catches it in mid- air. I pat him again.

I grab a glass of orange juice and sit in the living room. I turn on the radio and some crap song is on, but it's good enough. I don't care—I just need some noise. I see my phone on the counter and text my parents: *Hey mom where r u?* I drink my juice and realize I've barely eaten since Thursday.

The phone chimes. Mom? No. It's a Facebook

notification. I click and it opens to a page: *Find Sheri Beckman*. I don't know who started it, but it already has 400 followers. I feel sick and don't know what to do. If I join, all the drama will piss me off, but if I don't, it looks bad. I decide to join.

My phone chimes again—Mom. *We're out. Be home soon. Hungry?*

I'm relieved and reply: *Burger and fries?* Slim chance they'll get me junk.

Okay. Whoa—not even an argument.

My phone buzzes again—a notification on the Facebook page: *we miss and love you sheri.* I put it down. Pretty soon, though, it's humming with every post and comment, and I already regret my decision. I can't leave the group without looking suspicious, so I turn the sound off and ignore it.

The dog looks up at me. "I know, Ollie. It's annoying, isn't it?" He gives a little whine.

It's Day Four since she went missing and it seems like we've gotten nowhere. The police don't seem to have anything and our search didn't find any clues. They don't seem to have found anything today or we would have heard. I don't get it. She had no enemies and this place always felt safe—until now.

I hear a car in the driveway, and Mom walks in with groceries and fast food.

"What time did you get up?" She puts the food on the counter and a grease-soaked bag in front of me.

"Twenty minutes ago. Where are Dad and Heather?"

She ignores the question and starts pulling vegetables out of the grocery bag. "You must be starving."

"There's a Facebook page for Sheri, Mom."

She pauses as she pulls out a container of strawberries. "Did you join it?"

"I wasn't sure if I should, but in the end, I decided to." She nods, and I know she's weighing the pros and cons. She goes back to the groceries to hide her contemplation.

I dig into my very unhealthy breakfast and unwrap the burger, spilling fries onto the paper. I can't wait to sink my teeth in. That's when I notice the extra bacon spilling out the sides of the bun.

"Where's Dad and Heather?"

Mom's face tells me everything.

"Did you guys go back? Were you helping them search? Why didn't you wake me? What's wrong with you? I should've been there! I should've been there more than you or Dad or anyone! I loved—dammit—I love her. I *love* her."

The tears come again and Mom comes around the island to hug me and I fall into her shoulder and she shushes me like when I was little. I can't stop crying. My head hurts, my muscles ache, and I'm so full of pain now that it won't stop spilling over.

22

It's Monday morning and I should be at school, but I'm not. I'm driving the car and even though I haven't put thought into where I'm going, I know.

I park a block away from Sheri's school and get out and walk. I want to keep a low profile. I feel the longer the search for her stretches out, the more people are going to start looking for someone to blame, and I'm quite certain that I'll be at the top of their list.

I head towards the student parking lot, hoping to stay unnoticed. Although I've played basketball here a few times and picked Sheri up after class occasionally, almost no one should recognize my face. I cut between the few cars parked in front of the student entrance and move across the grass.

I'm sure security is tighter now, but it's early enough that the buses haven't dropped off their loads of students and it's nowhere close to the five minute bell. It should be just me and a few teachers. I'm thinking that if I steer clear of the office, I should be fine. My feet brush the dew on the grass along the backside of the school, and when I turn the corner towards the shop, I'm hoping my gamble coming here will pay off.

It does. The guy with the blond, shaggy hair

who was digging in the dirt the other day stands by the roll-up doors. He's beside another kid who wears a hoodie, and I see him handing over an empty baggie. They look at me and freeze. I feel like I just busted them. I slow to a halt.

The dirt-digger nods. "You're back."

I say nothing.

"No luck last time?"

I shake my head.

He reaches into his jacket and offers me a cigarette.

I shake my head no.

"Suit yourself." He nods to the kid in the hoodie. "This is Robbie."

I nod and say, "I'm—"

"We know who you are. Everybody in this school knows who you are."

Shit. I should've never come.

"It's cool. I get it. I'd be here too if I were in your shoes."

I watch Robbie slowly pull a glass pipe out of his pocket. It's got a thin crust of black residue at the bottom of the bowl and he slides it into the plastic bag. He squeezes out all the air, rolls it up, and pulls the zip top shut. He stares up at me.

"Problem?"

I feel tall next to the two of them. "Nope." I shrug as nonchalantly as I can.

Robbie glares then turns to Dirt Digger. "I've done my part. Now I need your help."

Dirt Digger nods and I realize I still don't know his name.

"I got messed up this weekend and, well, I lost

the brother's car." He fishes a rolled cigarette out of the other side of his pocket and turns to Dirt Digger. "You got a light?"

Dirt Digger pulls out a well-used Zippo from his jacket and hands it over and Robbie lights up. After a deep inhale, he blows it in our direction. I realize he's definitely not smoking a regular cigarette, and I definitely wouldn't normally hang out with this sort of crowd.

"So, did you crash it?"

"I don't think so, but that's not my problem. I can't remember where I left it."

Dirt Digger watches Robbie, waiting for more information.

"I remember waking up in my bed. The car is missing. Everyone is pissed at me. Can you help me out?" He takes a deep drag on his cigarette.

Dirt Digger shakes his head. "You seriously smell like a Pink Floyd fan bus. Stand downwind, man."

Robbie shrugs.

"What's the year and model?"

"2001 blue Civic."

"Any other distinguishing details?"

"I broke its back driver side tail light?"

Dirt Digger nods but I can't help but laugh.

"You sure it's worth it?" Immediately, I realize that I've crossed the line.

Robbie turns on me. "Go to hell."

"I'll see what I can do about your ride, but until then get rid of the skunkified hoodie. You wear it to class and you'll be busted and out of school for sure. It's like you need a damn babysitter. Or do you want to get kicked out of this school too?"

Robbie smiles.

The warning bell rings. Five minutes to class.

Dirt Digger looks over at me. "Hear that? I think it's time for us to go."

"Where?"

Dirt Digger gives me a look of annoyance but doesn't answer the question.

"Follow me," he says. And with reluctance, I do.

23

We leave Robbie at the door. He still doesn't seem smart enough to clue into good advice. I feel sorry for his family to have such a dumb kid.

We move along the side to another windowless wall at the back. Dirt Digger pulls out his set of keys, thumbs through them, and unlocks the door. We walk along a dark, tight corridor with pipes running overhead. We pause at a corner.

"The caretakers lock themselves in for coffee for about fifteen minutes every morning. They wait for the herds to flock to class before they come out and start their routine. If you don't want to be seen, this is the best way in. You don't want to be seen, right?"

"Yeah, that's right." We move around the corner. Sure enough, there's a door with "Maintenance" on it, the faint smell of coffee mixed with garbage, and the sick, sweet odour of recycling bins. We walk quietly past.

The door to the hall is propped ajar with a wooden door stop.

"This is the only entrance without a camera. The head janitor, Mr. Hill, sits at the surveillance monitors every free minute."

I look at him. "Who are you?"

Dirt Digger ignores the question and pushes the

door open without a sound.

"The janitor, Mr. Hill, is so busy staring that he doesn't see who's staring at him. Sick bastard. I'm not sure if he's looking for trouble or if it will find him."

We step into the hall and he taps the wooden door stop away. The door quietly latches behind us.

"You've gone to her locker?"

I nod. "I was thinking of checking her gym locker."

Dirt Digger shakes his head. "What for? Just another dead-end the cops have likely covered."

"What else am I supposed to do?"

"If you don't know what you're doing here, then why'd you come?"

I stare at him, lost.

He points. "The second door on the left is the gym. Ms. Francis has prep in the morning. There's a room with the washer and dryer if you need to duck out, just beside the girls' change room. No one goes in there. Consider yourself helped." He walks away.

I look at the double doors to the gym then back to him.

"Wait."

He ignores me.

"Dude?" I don't want to shout, but he doesn't stop.

I chase after him and grab his shoulder. "Come on, man."

He turns and I think he might swing a punch.

"Listen, All Star, I'm going to be late for class."

This guy doesn't care about class. He's here for something else.

"Where's your binder?"

I stand in front of him and he looks up at me, but I know he's not the least bit intimidated.

"I can't do this alone. I need your help. You've stepped up twice and you didn't have to."

"I don't need any trouble, All Star, and I sure as hell don't need any attention. You are headed for both. You go down this path, your mommy and daddy will get you a really expensive lawyer and bail your ass out. My mom might, just might, give me a monthly visit in juvie."

He turns and walks away again.

"I want to find Sheri. Don't you?"

He stops.

I feel angry, but I don't have any fight left. The thought of Sheri missing and that I'll most likely never see her again hits me, and I know I'm about to cry.

I choke it all back as I say, "She meant something to you, didn't she?"

He stands there with his back turned, not moving. Suddenly, he turns and walks right up to my face. "Here's the deal. First, stop with the bitch tears. Second, if anything happens, I don't know you." He looks up and down the hallway and then turns before moving away quickly. I have to sprint to catch up.

"And third, my name isn't dude or man." He looks over at me, shaking his head and offering me his hand. "It's Charlie. Charlie Wolfe."

PART TWO

24

He wakes in a sweat.

He's been sleeping well and dreaming deep and last night was almost no exception. The dream was the same one he'd been having over the past few nights. He would walk in fields of yellow with blue skies above him and the bright sun against his face. He feels the warm wind blow and sees it shake the long stalks of grain. None of the nagging, twisting, wanting thoughts that have gripped him over the past few months seem to disturb his rest. Almost none, except—

Over the past days, the news has been covering the missing girl. At first, he tried not to notice the television, to feign disinterest, but he noticed that others had become invested in what the reporter called "a tragedy," so he began to pay attention, to slip amongst the sheep, and follow the script. The time spent has earned results—the lead detective, Gekas, is struggling with the problem he left her, leading the others further away from him and the answers she's seeking. He watches with particular interest as the parents gather their friends and family to search the running trails. He's certain that he's taken the proper precautions but he needs to be sure. He knows that the police won't reveal what they know and the reporters are too stupid to notice the important details that lie in front of them, but he watches nonetheless, scanning the background of every shot.

What wasn't on the news, what was amidst the rumors spoken in the hallways before class, was that the most serious suspect was the girl's boyfriend. His alibi seemed tight, but it didn't stop people from trying to bend reality to fit their own preconceived prejudices. He was the scapegoat, the sacrifice to appease the angry gods, the answer to the question: "Who did it?"

He knew that if he waited long enough, the people would make the boyfriend pay. He knew no one suspected him.

Except—last night's dream. He walked in the fields and felt the sun and the wind and he was alone. He opened his eyes and it was night and the moon was high above and he still felt safe. Until somewhere in the distance, somewhere across the plain, prowling beneath the surface of the fields, an animal howled. And the boy knew he needed to hurt someone again.

25

I follow Charlie through the school and into the library and watch as he takes a red binder from a pile off the counter. We move through the stacks and he quickly grabs a couple of books off the shelves. We go to a table at the back and all of his actions seem arbitrary.

I can't stand it anymore. "What are we doing here?"

He points. "Reconnaissance. Now, sit."

I take a seat, my back to the entrance of the library, and he sits across from me.

"Open them." I look at him, and he nods at the binder. "Open."

I flip the front cover and find neat, colorfully penned notes on Shakespeare. All of the *i*'s have perfect circles over them. I'm definitely thinking it's a girl's writing.

"The textbooks too."

I stare at him.

"For being an All Star, you are really slow on the uptake." It takes me a moment but I realize I'm supposed to look like I belong here. I shrug and comply.

Charlie looks over my shoulder, studying the space. "The librarian teaches English this period. The assistant doesn't get here until 9:00." He leans and looks past me to the front desk. "We're good. Give me your phone?"

"Why?"

"Just give me your damn phone!"

"Why don't you have one?"

Charlie looks directly at me. "Give. Me. Your. Phone."

"Alright." I take it out of my pocket, unlock it, and put it on the table. Charlie takes it, scrolling through my messages.

I'm staring at him when he looks up.

"What? Do your homework. I'll be right back." He tosses my phone back as he leaves.

I stare at the wall and twist around, but Charlie is gone. I look down at the books he's grabbed from the library stacks: a collection of Edgar Allan Poe stories, a book about building the national railroad, and an atlas. I push them aside and flip through a few pages of my brand new red binder to discover it belongs to a Jenny. I find a pocket at the back of the binder and unzip it to find a red pen, a blue highlighter, and a pencil with a broken end. Whoever Jenny is, she came very unprepared. I try to make the pencil look usable and hold my hand against my head, hoping to conceal my identity while appearing to study.

It feels like an hour before Charlie returns but my phone barely shows five minutes have passed. He's brought Jessica, Sheri's best friend, along with her boyfriend, Paul, and a girl I only know as Katie. They all grab a seat at the table.

I haven't seen anyone since Sheri disappeared, so it feels good that they came. Although Jessica is way more girlie than Sheri, she's always been there for her, so we've spent lot of time around each other. Paul is an alright person but rarely tags along with his girlfriend, so I barely know him. Katie is friends with Sheri, too, but pretty low key, and I only know her from the occasional party.

"Hey, Tony." I can hear the strain in Jessica's voice and I can tell she's barely keeping it together. "Any word?"

I shake my head.

Charlie plops himself down across from me. "Why do you think you're here? For a long missed chit chat?" His interrogation begins, "Who here's talked to the cops?"

We look at each other. Jessica raises her hand. Paul and Katie do too. I follow.

"Cool." We all look at him. "Figure out if they asked you all the same things. I'll be right back."

He's off again and I realize I need to get used to his style.

The four of us sit silently for only a moment, when Katie starts: "They asked about the last time I saw her. Or if I knew about any fights she had with anyone." She pauses and I know everyone wants to look over at me. Thankfully, she doesn't linger too long and pushes through, "They gave me a card and asked to call if I thought of anything else."

We all share similar stories. Cookie-cutter questions that no one can provide answers for. It seems like no one is being accused of anything based on how they've questioned us, but I can't help but feel that I'm their best lead. I'd like to think that we're all being treated equally, but as her boyfriend the finger is pointed straight at me, and I hate it. I'm guessing we're all sad about her disappearance, but I just can't help but thinking I feel it deeper than the rest.

Charlie returns, this time with Sheri's ex, Dillon, and I feel instantly uncomfortable.

Dillon nods in my direction. "What's he doing here?"

My anger bubbles up but Charlie stares at him like he's an idiot—which he is.

Jessica comes to my defense. "Shut up, Dillon. As Sheri's boyfriend, he's got more right than you to be here."

"Yeah, Sheri's boyfriend who fell off the radar the minute Sheri never made it home." His accusation is a punch in the face. Any sense of unease is gone—now, I'm just pissed.

"And where were you the night she disappeared, you jealous prick?" I realize I'm standing and he's standing and my fists are up and bunched tight.

Before I get a chance to swing, Charlie steps between us and pushes me back, knocking me hard against a bookshelf. "Calm down." Every muscle in my body is tense and Charlie holds Dillon back like a referee in a ring. "You calm?"

Paul stands now and his arm holds me back, but his body is turned towards Dillon, ready to fight. I size Charlie up—he's small and strong—and I'm still not sure whose side he's on yet, so I decide not to carry this any further. I relax to let Paul know the moment has passed, and he takes his seat.

Charlie turns to Dillon. "Stop being a dick. We're not here to fight."

Dillon's fists drop and the rest of us sit back down.

Charlie leans in. "I want you guys to think about what the cop asked you. All the normal stuff right?"

We all nod.

"Now, think—is there anything else? All the things that seem weird or don't seem normal. All the things an adult or a cop might overlook. Texts? Picta-bombs? People? Things in the school? Things out of the school?"

We sit in silence and my mind runs through every single day, minute, and hour, right up to Thursday when Sheri went missing but nothing is coming to me. I look over at Charlie and he stares back at me with a stony poker face. He's not judging me but only waiting for answers. I'm not sure where he's going with all of this, but I feel like he's the best I have.

He breaks his stare and looks back at the others. "Another thing—you're going to stop texting—"

Katie cuts in, "Are you kidding?"

He looks at her impatiently. "Don't interrupt. You're going to stop texting anything about Sheri. If you stop cold turkey, it's going to look suspicious. You can even say some basic stuff about Sheri but you've got to assume people are watching. Make sense?"

No one seems to like the idea but they nod.

Charlie checks his watch. "It's almost 9:00. Get back to the routine."

Everyone gets up and leaves except for the two of us. I look over at Charlie. He's smiling.

"That went well!"

"What are you talking about?"

"I told you—reconnaissance." Charlie's phone buzzes in his pocket but he silences it. "Jessica is definitely on your side and Paul seems like he'll go wherever she follows. Obviously, Dillon thinks you're guilty, but the interesting one is Katie. She's our ordinary Joe Public. Knows you but doesn't know you. She tells me that most people are still on the fence, so we're going to have to keep an eye on that."

"It was a test?"

"Well, no. It's good to get everyone to quit using their phones. Who gives a teenager a phone, anyway?"

"What are you talking about? All that stuff about the cops listening—?"

"What do you think this is? CSI?"

"Then, why did you do all this?"

"I needed to know if people thought you were guilty. So I could decide."

I stare at him.

"I think I'm at a solid 99%."

"You were only deciding—?"

"If I could trust you? Yes. Among other things."

"Like what?"

"I also needed to figure out Dillon. He's definitely up to something."

The librarian comes back into the library.

"Time for us to go." He stands. "Come on."

"Where?"

"You're taking me to the scene of the crime."

When I stand, I can still feel where the bookshelf hit me. What have I gotten myself into?

26

We step out of the student entrance.

Charlie's got his phone out but he seems to be struggling with the password. "Where's your car?"

"You know there's no real proven crime yet. She's only missing—"

"Keep telling yourself that, Junior. Where are we going?"

I point and he moves across the parking lot. Students are still driving in, kicking up gravel as they pull to a stop.

Charlie continues, "Not everyone around the school thinks you're innocent. Katie was waiting to see Dillon knock you down, so having you lurk around Sheri's school won't help our cause."

Charlie cuts towards the nearest yard and goes through the back. Across the lawn is a big patio door, with the curtains open. An animated raccoon is on the TV. I freeze at the gate.

Charlie looks back and sighs. "If we're going to work together, you're going to have to quit this bull-shit. Grow a pair and let's move."

I follow, scooting behind him. He goes between the garage and fence and I am tight on his heels. I hear a dog barking inside the house and someone yelling at it to shut up. We move across the driveway and onto the street, only a few houses down from my car.

He's still wrestling with his phone and gets out his wallet.

"Is this why you hate teens with phones? Because you're technically inept?"

He doesn't even look at me as he pilfers through it. He goes back to his phone.

Charlie shakes his head. "What an idiot! His own birthday!" He swipes the screen a few times and hands it over to me. "Ah, see, look at that. The day she disappeared, Sheri got three texts from Dillon."

I look down at the phone, "What are you talking about?"

"It looks like he's been trying to rekindle things with your girlfriend. I knew he was a sneaky bastard—"

I stop beside my car. "What—? Whose—? Is this Dillon's?" I reach for the phone but Charlie pulls it away.

Charlie smiles. "Yeah, while you provided that great distraction trying to fight him, I grabbed his phone and wallet."

"What the hell—?"

"I'm guessing he's already figured out they're missing, so it won't be long before he locks it down. Or tracks it on GPS," Charlie scoffs as he continues to scroll through Dillon's texts.

"Looks like Dillon is a busy, busy boy. He got texts to and from 'the X'—that'd be your girlfriend, Sheri—but there's also texts to 'gf for now.' Man, this guy's a piece of work."

I'm not sure what to do. A part of me wants to know what Dillon and my girlfriend were texting about. Yet, it doesn't feel right, the whole invasion of privacy thing. Then there's a part of me that's willing to do almost anything to find Sheri.

"Should you be reading those?"

"Who's Mia-ow? Sounds interesting," says Charlie without looking up.

I'm curious to know what he's reading but it feels like poison. I need to convince myself that I have to trust him, to trust his process. I need to be objective and focus on the bigger goal of finding Sheri, so I let it go, deciding not to ask questions.

He taps the text stream. "Dirty, dirty Dillon."

Damn, he's not making this easy.

"Mia-ow is definitely the tease. *I'm full of all sorts of surprises. You want to know what? Then you'll just have to come and find out yourself.* Now, I know why he calls her Mia-ow!" He holds up the phone. "Whoa, check this out!"

Ugh. It's sensational and terrible. Charlie's found a selfie of Dillon smirking in his bathroom mirror, sans shirt, his pants pulled down to the low V cut of his obliques. It's one of those things I can't unsee.

"I wonder if there are any selfies of Mia-ow."

"Are you insane?"

"Hey, this is all useful information. It's either Dillon or it's not."

"Right? And when he tracks us down with the GPS, it'll be all of us."

"Ah, quit whining. We'll toss it long before and he'll never know. Speaking of which, let me take a couple of photos with your phone for reference later."

Every move he makes seems to come with such ease. No nerves, just actions. Maybe he's done it all his life. Maybe he just doesn't care. But for me, it's all new territory.

27

We jump in my car and drive away from the school.

Charlie immediately opens the glove box. He doesn't ask, just starts rummaging.

"Dude?"

He doesn't look over. "What did I say? My name's not dude."

He rifles through the registration, flips through the owner's manual, and pulls out every information pamphlet the car dealership has jammed inside.

"Your dad's got an oil change coming up."

He lowers the visor and flips open the mirror a couple of times. On the last time he holds his gaze longer than is necessary, and the expression of mischief on his face slips away. He slams the mirror on the visor shut and looks around some more.

He goes through the console and checks the slot under the radio, jingling through the spare change. He leans back in his seat, tilting the back down, then up again, then down. He sits forward and wipes the dash with the flat of his hand and studies the little coat of dust on his fingers. I feel defensive and turn on the music to distract both of us. Tom Petty sings "You Don't Know How It Feels." It's my dad's guilty pleasure and I'm embarrassed.

He looks at me.

"What?"

"The music. It's a classic. Nice!"

I stare at him, waiting for him to reveal sarcasm but he's already moved on, looking relaxed in the passenger seat, grinning. He opens the window and hangs his head out just enough to let the wind mess up his blonde, shaggy hair. It's like I'm taking my dog, Ollie, out to the country for a run.

"Where exactly should we go? On the trails, I mean? Everyone's searched there—the cops, her family, friends."

He rolls up the window and reaches into the side pocket of his baggy cargo pants and pulls out a piece of paper. I glance over as he unfolds it. It's the running map from Sheri's locker.

I grab Charlie's jacket in my fist. "Where the hell did you get that?"

"Pay attention to the road."

I squeeze my fist tighter.

He leans in, smiling. "You are a serious snapcase man. You need to gear down."

I let him go and he leans back. "Sheri's locker. The day you came by the school. Remember? You pussied out and went to the bathroom and I stepped in and took what was needed before the cops got there."

I'm dumbfounded. This kid's either got balls or is seriously stupid.

"You saw me?"

He nods slowly. "And you should thank me because I was able to finish what you never could."

My lips tighten. I know I should be grateful for

this, and I am but I'm also pissed.

He smiles. "Besides, what's a freakout going to get you? Answers? Nope. You asked for my help and here we are."

Damn, I wish he wasn't speaking the truth.

"Now, if you can cool your shit long enough for me to explain, I think we can get somewhere. Think you can do that?"

I lean back in my seat. I'm frustrated with myself and my inability to keep calm. It's not like me, I've always been able to do this. On the court. At parties. But now I'm slipping and Charlie is the only one of us that's holding it together. Or he's the one messing me up. I'm still trying to figure it out.

He holds Sheri's map between us.

"It looks like Sheri was doing a longer run that day, according to this. We'll start there and check things out."

He folds the map and hands it to me and it feels as a peace offering of sorts. I take it and put it in my pocket.

I drive on and Charlie opens Dillon's wallet, leafing through the contents. He pulls out a twenty-dollar bill. "Can we stop for an iced cappuccino?" He waves the money near my face. "Dillon's buying."

This guy is too much but I laugh and find myself turning into the nearest coffee shop. At this point, I figure we both deserve it.

28

We arrive at the trails and I pull into the parking lot. The place is empty and all signs of the search are gone. All of the wire flags have been removed and the litter has been cleared away. It's like the place has been abandoned for weeks. It's unnerving.

I sit in silence while Charlie works away at his beverage.

"Are we just going to sit here?"

He doesn't answer and peers at the entrance to the trail, past the barricade that keeps motorized vehicles off the footpath. The path runs east-west, and his eyes trace the flat horizon leading to prairie fields. I try to figure out what he's looking at.

"Is this where Sheri parked that day?'

"I don't know. The car was gone when I showed up—"

"Right. For the search." He rolls his eyes. "But when you two ran, this is where you parked?"

"I, uh—"

"You ran this trail before, right?"

"Yeah."

"With Sheri?"

"Uh, no."

"You've never gone running with your girl-friend?"

"I have, just not this trail."

He looks at me, shaking his head. "You are so weird." He looks back out at the path. "Have you done the whole loop?"

"Yes."

"It's good, huh?"

I look at him, trying to understand his meaning. Charlie Wolfe seems like the furthest thing from a person who would go for a run for fun out here.

"What? You think running is for rich people?"

"I'm not—"

"Don't. Let's not even start that game."

I stop trying to defend myself. "Why do you run?" I ask.

"To know."

"To know what?"

"To know what's out there. To know where I live. To know that I can outrun someone if I need to. Why did you run out here?"

I hear all of it in my head: To see if I was better than others. To keep my body fit. To prove something to myself.

"Cuz."

I see him looking at me and I feel the sting of judgment but I'm not sure if it's his or my own.

He slurps the bottom of his drink until the last of it rattles up his straw.

"Do you have a napkin?" I'm not sure why he asks, because he hasn't made a mess. I shrug and look through the console and hand him one. He pulls out the straw, taps it on the side of the cup, then jams it in his mouth.

"Alright, then. Let's get to work."

29

He climbs out of the car and walks over to the garbage can at the head of the trail. It's empty and has likely been searched and cleaned for clues by Gekas and her team. Charlie wipes the sides of his plastic cup with the napkin, before dropping it into a garbage can.

I climb out and follow him, locking the car behind me. The day is beautiful, but the prairie wind pushes gently against us. He looks out at the trail, the straw hanging out of his mouth as he flicks it up and down. He peers through his messy blonde hair but the wind keeps tossing it into his eyes, so he raises his sunglasses to keep it out of his face.

He looks back at me, his hand out. "Map?"

I reach into my pocket and pull it out. I never noticed the shape it was in until now, folded and wrinkled—not from Sheri but from Charlie. It's one of the few parts I have left of her, so I open it carefully. I catch Charlie watching me before he takes a step closer to look at it.

He digs in his pocket and pulls out another piece of paper. I realize it's the calendar that was stuck underneath it.

I look at him. "Really?"

"When are the things that I do going to quit surprising you?" He points at the date she disappeared. "She went for a long one that day. So that means…" he traces his finger along the map before continuing, "it means that we have a run ahead of us."

Before I know it, he's left and trotting down the path at a slow pace. I take off after him, following a step behind. He speeds up. I am pretty sure he's doing this to challenge me but I keep up easily. After a while, he eases back beside me, pulling the half-chewed straw out of his mouth.

"Ah, look at that. We ran this trail together. Something you didn't even do with Sheri."

"Are you naturally a dick, or does it take practice?"

"At last!"

"What?"

"You quit whining and had a bit of backbone there for a moment."

"Screw off!"

"Excellent. You might be useful to me yet. But let's not overuse it."

He falls back into silence, looking left and right along the trails, and all I can do is shake my head. This guy enjoys pushing my buttons and although I know it's intentional, I can't figure out what his reason is.

He twists his body around and continues shuffling backwards, looking at where we came from. I look over my shoulder, trying to figure out what he's looking at.

He turns back around, sinking the straw back between his teeth. "A little bit further." He picks up his pace and I have to sprint again to catch up. I'm barely feeling it and know I've got energy to spare, but I can hear him trying to regulate his breath. After we run around a small hill and a bend, Charlie spins backwards again.

"Almost...almost...and there." He stops.

I turn, trying to find out what he's looking at.

"I don't...see it."

He pulls out the straw and points with it out past the hill.

Then, I realize. The car is no longer in sight.

"Do you think...?"

I don't have a chance to ask. Charlie pulls out a cell phone and takes a photo.

I can't figure out where he stole that one from.

"Whose is that?"

"It's mine."

"You have a cell phone?"

"Yes. What'd you think? I'm Amish?"

No, just that he looks like he can't afford one, I think to myself.

I catch him glaring at me. I hope being a mind reader isn't one of his many mysterious skills.

30

"Everything after this point is fair game."

I stare at him, trying to catch his meaning.

"The hill provides cover. There's plenty of trees, shrubs, and low spots—all good places to hide. Another kilometer and it crosses the end of a grid road." He nods and we can see the glint of a truck cab travelling half a mile away. "Easy to avoid being seen by anyone in a vehicle, even if they were looking."

"But the search parties covered this area."

"And they found nothing. Because…?"

At first, I wait for him to finish his thought, but when he leaves it for too long, I start to speak, "Because—"

He interrupts me, "Because, it isn't the right place."

"What does that mean?"

"Whatever—no—whoever happened to Sheri, chose somewhere…"

He trails off again. This time I wait, but he doesn't finish his thought and continues walking down the trail. We carry on in silence until we hit the end of the grid road where it stops at the creek.

"Did they search the entire trail?"

"Not on the day I went out."

"You didn't go the entire weekend?"

"No—"

"Why not?"

"There were…problems."

"What? You forgot your baby blanket to keep you warm?"

"No—!"

"Then, what?"

"I—"

"What?"

"Forget it."

"No, don't. Don't forget it." He's in my face, fired-up, and all of it's making me feel intimidated, "Don't forget. Don't forget her. Don't forget how all of this makes you feel. She's your girlfriend. We are the two people who are going out of our way to make sure she doesn't just become—" His eyes look out past me, out past the horizon, searching. And then he's back. "Just don't. Let's keep looking. Okay?"

I know he's intense. I know he cares. Because he's here. And now I know that there's layers to this kid. I'm freaked that he's given me shit like someone who's lost something, but he's also fired up something in me and I'm primed and promise myself I won't stop until we catch whoever did this.

We move past the grid road. Charlie asks for the map and I hand it to him. When I feel the paper slip out of my fingers, I realize that I've let go of this small piece of Sheri, but it's too late to grab it back without seeming crazy.

He looks at it, turning it around. It flaps in the breeze. He folds it and hands it back.

"This second half is the longer part of the loop. Four miles. There are two farms at each end," he points first to the east, then to the southeast, "but still plenty of cover to do something discreetly."

There's a small makeshift footbridge that's been assembled out of 2x4s and wood planks. He crosses to the south side of the creek and walks slow, scanning the landscape, tilting his head, studying the ground. I don't know what he's looking for, what clue he expects to come across. We wind along the creek, a play structure coming into view in the distance.

Even though the breeze is keeping me cool, the sun is shining and my mouth is dry.

"You guys got along well." It's a statement, not a question.

"Yeah, we did. We do." I latch onto the word. It gives me hope.

"Girls in their teens can be such drama queens. They look for shit to make them sad. They overreact to everything." He looks back at me. "Sheri wasn't like that. And she was even less like that when you started dating. Wasn't sure if I was a fan of you at first." He stops and looks at his phone for a moment. "I am getting to be though."

"Look, man, I'm not looking for a fan or a friend. I just want to find Sheri."

Charlie looks up from his phone.

"Yeah, I definitely think you're alright now."

31

We carry on down the trail towards the playground, and now I can see the hunched concrete structure of the washroom ahead. Even though we aren't far from civilization, it feels like we're in the middle of nowhere—eerie and isolated.

Charlie stares at the washroom for a moment, then climbs to the top of the monkey bars and scans the horizon. I secretly hope he starts verbalizing what he's doing. I look in the same direction, but stop because I don't know what I am looking for. He hops down and lands softly like an athlete.

He walks towards the women's washroom. I wonder if it's unlocked this late in the season. With a closed fist he pushes the door open.

I step in behind Charlie. Sunshine from outside fills the space. The door's hydraulic hinge exhales shut. Light pushes through the dirty, frosted skylight above us and softens the edges of everything in here. There are two stalls with working doors, a hand dryer that looks like someone beat it with a hammer, and a mirror of polished metal. Small bathroom tiles line the walls and form a sink. Drawings, swear words, and a phone number of someone named Chelene are graffitied throughout the bathroom.

I watch Charlie step into the first stall in the corner and close the door.

"You gotta go?" I joke.

He comes out quickly and walks over to the sink without saying a word. It looks like he's counting steps but who knows. He turns around and moves to the other stall. This time he shuts the door and locks it. There is a faint echo. He stays in there for a moment.

Click—he steps out. I'm starting to feel useless. I don't know what he's doing and I don't know what we're looking for. I'm absolutely lost.

"Charlie?" My voice echoes and breaks the silence. It's louder than I expected and it startles me but it doesn't seem to faze him.

He stands there for a moment. "What's in the garbage can?"

I lean in to look. "Nothing. Not even a bag."

"Can I see your phone?"

"Why? You have your own."

"Come on. Quit arguing. It's lunchtime and I'm hungry."

I sigh and grab my phone. I hand it to him.

"What do you listen to? Hip hop, no doubt." I shoot him a look, but I see him scrolling through my playlist. "Ha, knew it. Nothing Top 40 and nothing old, right?"

I need to learn to ignore him but I don't. "Right, because I listen to good music."

He scoffs, "Do you have headphones with you?"

"Yeah?"

"Hand them over."

"Charlie—?

He doesn't even say anything and gives me a look. I dig into my pocket and pull out my earbuds and hand them to him. I feel like this was an elaborate plan to take me into the middle of nowhere and shake me down. Except, I asked him to do it.

He unravels the cord and plugs them in. He hands me the earbuds. "Stick them in."

Once I have them on, he hits play.

"Can you hear me?"

I nod.

He turns it up. "How about now?"

Yup.

He cranks it a little louder. I see him say something and I pull out one bud. "What?"

"Nothing."

He motions me to put it back in. As I do, he turns me so that I'm facing the mirror. I see his hazy, distorted reflection moving behind me, indiscernibly, like a creeping ghost.

He steps beside me and pushes the tap on. The water runs and he walks back into the stall.

"Do you think she was in here?" I yell.

I don't see him and I turn. "Hey assh—!" Suddenly, he's there, beside me and it scares the crap out of me. I pull out my earbuds. "What the hell are we doing here?"

"Lay down."

"What's wrong with you? I'm not laying down."

He stares at me, chewing on the corner of his lip. The beat of the music pumps through my headphones but it's distant and far away.

"What are we doing here?"

He shushes me. "Lay down."

"Are you trying to help or is this you messing with me?"

"Down."

"No."

He sighs and flips on his phone flashlight and shines it on the ground beneath the sink. He crouches, looking under the cabinet, illuminating all the dark nooks and crannies of the space. He stands and aims the light at the mirror, then turns it so it shines beneath his face, illuminating him like a ghoul. He stares at himself for a moment and I watch.

"Spooky." He turns and smiles. "I think this is good for now." He shuts the phone light off and walks past me.

I stare at the space, taking a long look around, trying to figure out what the hell we just did.

"Shepherd?" I turn and Charlie is standing at the door, holding it open with his sleeve-covered hand. "Let's go."

32

I step out of the dark washroom and squint in the outside light.

As my eyes adjust, I turn and ask, "What now?"

He's already heading back down the path from where we came.

"Where are you going? Shouldn't we go that way?" I point out towards the distant fields.

"Nope."

"Why?"

"Because, we're done."

I look at him.

He sighs and comes back towards me. "Take out Sheri's map." I take it out and unfold it carefully.

He points to the map and then down the path. "This leads onto the railroad. Then there's a farm and then there's another farm over there. After that, nothing. Just the path."

I nod.

"We're just wasting time going that way. If I was going to do something to Sheri, this would be the place."

"What do you mean if *you* were going to do something to Sheri?"

"Stay calm, man. Quit thinking with your heart. I'm just saying that if someone were going to do something, it would have to be secluded, or else they'd be seen or heard. This place is sheltered, it's concealed, and it gives whoever a place to do it."

I stare at him and I feel the next question rolling out of my brain and hanging deep down, lodged in my throat before I can finally say the words, "Do what?"

He looks at me and he shakes his head. "I don't know, man. I really don't." He hands me back the map, and looks across the fields to the south. "But whatever it is, I don't think it's good."

33

We're almost back at the car when I hear *bzz...bzz*.

Charlie pulls Dillon's phone out of his back pocket and looks at it.

"I thought you we're going to dump it?"

Charlie shrugs his shoulders like it's no big deal. "Do you recognize the number?" he asks turning the phone to me.

Dillon's phone continues to vibrate in Charlie's hand as I try and figure it out. The *bzzz* seems so loud in this quiet place. The number looks familiar but my heart is beating too hard to recall who it belongs to when I hear that phone ringing in my presence.

"Wait." I reach into my pocket and pull out Detective Gekas's card.

"It's the same number? The cop?"

I nod.

"Cool."

Cool? I'm thinking none of this is cool.

"I guess they'll be talking to Dillon again, huh?"

He is as casual as can be. He walks to the garbage bin where he dumped his iced coffee cup and wipes the phone down with his shirt before tossing it inside. It rattles against the metal for two more rings before finally going silent.

I watch him saunter over to the car and I wonder if I need a little of his "who gives a shit" attitude. He knocks on the hood with his palm.

"Come on, time's a-wastin'!"

I shake my head as I dig the car keys out of my pocket. "You sound like a middle-aged white guy."

He smiles. "Let's move along now, hear?"

I laugh and unlock the door and we both climb in.

As I pull back onto the road, Charlie spends a ridiculous amount of time adjusting the seat. He checks himself in the vanity mirror, drawing back his lips, running his tongue across his teeth, flicking his hair to ensure appropriate shagginess. He catches me staring.

"What?"

"Why are you so happy?"

He scoffs "Why shouldn't *we* be? We know where Sheri—" He pauses, searching his mind, before settling again, "We know the place Sheri disappeared from and we have the profile of the suspect, which I think is a hell of a lot more than Gekas knows."

"Wait—? We have the profile? When—? How did we come across that?"

Charlie smiles. "When they called Dillon."

"They think Dillon is responsible for all of this?"

"No, not him. But he fits their profile, just like you fit their profile."

"What? What are you saying?"

"When we had everyone meet this morning. All the stories were the same. Except yours."

"How was mine different?"

"You're not from her school."

"So?"

"That made you the anomaly. Until now."

"The phone call?"

"Yes. No one else has been called on twice. Something has made him a suspect."

"But what?"

"I don't know and I don't really care because that isn't a part of our investigation."

"If he's a suspect though—?"

"We can't go chasing Gekas's lead. It's counterproductive. Let her do her own work."

"So, what then? Do we ignore Dillon? "

"Well, he's still a suspect. But he's not the only one."

"Who else do we have?"

"Based on what the cops are looking for? A teenager. Most likely a male. Relatively decent home life." He rolls his eyes at me. "Seems to have some connection to Sheri, maybe goes to her school or knows her from parties or some other activities." He stares out the window thinking until I interrupt.

"Earlier, you said *is*.

"Huh?"

"When you were talking about Sheri and our suspect, you said *whatever it is*."

"So?"

"You don't think this is done, do you? You don't think Sheri is the last."

"No, I don't. She may not even be the first. But there's also something else..."

He gets quiet for a moment.

I stare at him, "What?"

He sighs and shakes his shaggy hair and relaxes back in his seat. "Don't know." He points to the car stereo.

"May I?"

"Go ahead."

He twists the dials and Dad's Tom Petty compilation comes on.

Charlie joins Petty at the top of his lungs, "I'm freeeee fallllling!"

He sings all the way back to the school. He knows every word. It's actually impressive.

34

We pull up to the school. Classes are still on and there is no one outside. Charlie sings out the last note of "Don't Do Me Like That" and then turns down the music.

"That was awesome! An in-the-moment moment, you know?" He's right.

At this moment things feel light and sort of right. It's been too long since I've felt this way.

Charlie digs into his back pocket, pulling out Dillon's wallet. He rips it open. "Pfft. Velcro? Grow up," he says to himself as I smile again.

Charlie goes through the wallet and takes the last of the paper bills. At a glance, it looks like about fifty dollars: a twenty, a couple of tens, and a couple of fives. I know it's not right but I don't stop him.

He stuffs the cash in his front pocket and nonchalantly tosses the wallet out towards the side of the school.

Two uniformed Constables walk out of the school talking to the Resource Officer. I straighten in my seat.

"Easy," Charlie whispers not taking his eyes off of them.

They walk across the grass towards a patrol car parked down the street. The Resource Officer stands on the curb as they hop into the car and drive away.

"See, nothing to worry about. My guess—they're just looking for Dillon Ross.'

Charlie and I watch the Resource Officer look down the block, before we turn and head inside. We exchange glances. It's the first moment I actually feel connected to this kid. I look down the street and see the patrol car turn at the stop light.

"We're going to find her, right?

Charlie straightens up, tapping the roof of my car. "Go home Shepherd. We'll talk later." He turns and walks away from the school.

35

I pull into the driveway of my house. It's almost the end of the school day. Although I haven't been to school, I'm exhausted. My body, my brain—I want to close myself in my room and shut the world out. I need some time to process everything Charlie and I did today. Mom's probably still at work but Dad's likely home. I'm hoping if I walk in quietly enough, he won't notice.

I step into the house, slide my shoes off, and set the keys on the counter. The house is quiet, so I'm relieved. I head straight up to my room to be by myself.

"Anthony." I freeze halfway on the stairs. It's Dad.

"We need to talk to you." We? Mom shouldn't be back from work this soon. Could it be the detective? Is she in the kitchen? I don't want to do this. I exhale in annoyance.

"Your mother and I are waiting. Come on now." I'm not in the mood for a conversation, or an argument, or anything. I walk into the kitchen.

The counter is bare, no tea like a few days ago. Mom's standing and her arms are crossed.

I try and lighten the mood. "Aren't you supposed to be at work?"

"Weren't you supposed to be at school?"

I go for one last attempt to save my ass. "School's done?"

"I cancelled my appointments because we need to have a talk."

I cringe.

"We got a call from the school that you weren't in class—at all—today. Can you explain to your father and I where you went and who you were with?"

I quickly run through my day: taking the car without asking; going to Sheri's school without permission; almost getting into a fight with her ex, Dillon, in the library; taking off with Charlie Wolfe —who picked Dillon's pocket; and then going to the last place Sheri was seen. None of this is going to fly with my parents.

"I drove around."

"You drove around? By yourself?"

"Yes." "All day?"

"Yes."

"You expect us to believe that?"

"Yes." I roll my head in a gesture of total irritation and I'm not apologetic about it either. I'm getting fed up and tired and it's making it difficult to edit my thoughts.

"Anthony, it's not like you to disappear for a day and not check in, not return texts, not tell us where you're going. It's just—"

"Get off my back!" I never raise my voice but I need to do something. There's no way I can get into all the messy details with them. They won't understand and they'll get in the way of my search for

Sheri.

"Anthony! Don't raise your voice to your mother."

"Look, I'm tired and I don't need to tell you anything!" I know I'm out of line. I know this isn't typical for me but I also know this has nothing to do with them.

"Yes, you do have to tell us—"

"No, I don't. Just send me to my room."

Ollie barks and I see my parents are speechless. A moment of silence sits between us.

"What? Are you going to ground me?" They've never done—there was never a need to—and I know they won't. "So I skipped. Big deal! So you didn't know where I was for a few hours; you don't need to know my every move."

Dad doesn't raise his voice, "Yes, we do. We're your parents." He's so calm right now it only makes me angrier.

"What do you think I could possibly be doing?"

Mom isn't as composed. "You weren't at school, where you were supposed to be. You weren't with your friends. You're not at the gym. You need to be responsible."

I'm offended because they know I am—or at least I *was*.

"You need to let us know where you are at all times."

"What for?"

My parents look at each other, until Dad steps in. "Since Sheri—"

I don't need to hear another word.

"Things aren't safe for you—"

"I'm done here!" I turn around and head up-stairs.

"Anthony!" Mom tries one last time but I ignore her and slam the door to my bedroom.

36

Practice makes perfect.

The boy had worked hard to prepare for the runner. He had considered the details, rehearsed the steps, and when the time came, he had performed the act perfectly. He never left a thing to chance. The police hadn't found her yet, hadn't figured out what he had done, and he was quite certain they hadn't even considered who he was.

However, the first girl was a misstep. He failed in carrying it out and it sat like a blunder in the later performance. He needed to remedy this mistake.

If at first you don't succeed...

The second time, he planned ahead and didn't act as rashly. When the idea first came to him and he imagined its execution, he staged his plan where things were familiar and safe. He had wandered those halls and moved among the students. He knew the layout and had visited the bathroom prior to his rendition and thought he knew what to expect. Yet, all of this had failed him, so this time he chose a school that was unique.

After rehearsing the act enough, it came easily and smoothly and he no longer had to proceed through it with great effort. He could move through each movement without over-thinking, allowing his body to work with the rhythm of his victim. They could exist together in the moment, adjusting to each step, each action leading to a new and exciting reaction, until they reached the catharsis together, where they could go no higher, and their moment together would come to its resolution.

After the runner, he knew he wanted to restage the first act and rectify his mistake. He chose a new school that had been built in the southwest of the city to accommodate the influx of families that had moved into the neighborhood in recent years. He arrives in the afternoon to get his bearings, but not too early to attract attention. He scouted the location the morning before, watched as the students moved inside, and took notes on how to dress for the role. Jeans and a t-shirt and he would be set. There were also a lot of baseball caps, but it felt like they drew attention to his desire to be inconspicuous. He opted for a hoodie, which worked as camouflage and helped conceal his body type. He copied a schedule from his brother and altered it with names and classes from the school's website in case a teacher asked him why he was wandering the halls.

He slips into the library, and moves to the stacks to grab a book by Cormac McCarthy, before sitting down at a cubicle in the corner to wait. When the bell finally rings, he finds he's read through a couple of chapters and hopes to remind himself to pick it up after he's done. He heads out of the library and towards the gymnasium. Boys' basketball occupies both courts, so he continues along. He guesses there's likely someone in the girl's change room, but assumes he can't move inside inconspicuously without stepping into a swarm, so he proceeds down the hall.

He locates the head office at the end of the hallway, with two teachers standing outside—he's running out of options. Turning down the next hallway, a brunette—most likely a senior—steps out of a room, her backpack slung over her shoulder. She turns off the light, locks the door, and looks back at him with a smile. She turns and leaves, heading down the corridor, and he saunters to a water fountain to wait. She goes around the corner and he continues to follow her. Looking down the next hall, he finds it empty and silent except for her down at the end by an open locker. He watches, hoping she'll be the one. She closes her locker then crosses the hallway and enters the bathroom. He smiles as he moves down the hallway to follow.

37

It's later and the hard work is done. He waits in the darkness of the bathroom because the janitors clock out at 11:00. When he thinks they've moved on to another part of the school, he opens the door and looks down the dimly lit hallway. He waits and listens, making sure that he is alone and that he has all the time in the world.

He goes through the girl's bag and finds a set of car keys.

He rises and moves out of the stall and closes the door quietly. When he scouted the school the previous day, he noticed the shop doors on the east side of the school, so he heads in that direction. He should be able to find something he can use to move the body.

He's still cautious. There is always the chance that a teacher has come back late to work. He doubts the odds of it, but if he is wrong, if his luck goes bad, then he'll have to make a choice. If they're strong, maybe a coach or gym teacher, he'll have to run and hope to hell he can get away. If they're an art or science teacher, maybe he can overpower them and win. Either way, it is not part of the story he's imagined in his head and that unpremeditated moment worries him. It's best to be careful.

He encounters no one and finds the wood shop. The door is locked and he doesn't want to leave any trace of his presence, so he decides not to break the glass window to get inside. He checks the garage next and finds it shut tight as well. He thinks of his options. The maintenance rooms will likely be secure, as well as the gym. He wanders back down the hall towards the library. There's a set of double doors with a wide gap between them and he pulls out his jackknife and slides it in and against the latch. He wiggles it back and forth and slowly pushes the bolt past the strike plate. He swings the door open and walks inside.

Behind the checkout desk is a back room and he discovers the door is unlocked. Perfect—in the back corner, a projector sits on a cart. He lifts it off and pulls the cart out of the library, wheeling it down the halls, back to the room.

He drags the girl out from the back stall and slides her onto the cart, careful to tuck her hair under her so that it won't catch in the wheels. He pulls a blanket out of the backpack and covers her, trying to make everything look as inconspicuous as possible. As he twists everything around and out of the room, he glances at himself in the mirror and smiles. He moves towards the student entrance, still alert for any other people.

He looks outside, knowing that once it closes, he'll be locked out from the safety of the school. Across the street, light fills the windows of cookie-cutter homes. Down the street, though, construction is still in its early stages, the structures caught in the cold, clean radiance of the street lamps.

He presses the button on the car keys and the parking lights flash. He moves carefully and quickly across the student parking lot. He opens the back-door and pushes her body inside. He closes the door and climbs into the driver's seat.

He heads towards the row of unfinished build-ings, where he can take his time and make things right. He turns the lights off and slides among the concrete and wood skeletons.

As he disappears to the edge of the city and sees the beginning stages of new buildings, he feels like he's travelling back into the past. Soon that first per-formance will vanish from view—vanish as if it nev-er, ever existed.

38

I wake up every hour on the hour through the night. I'm off my game. I'm tired. I'm anxious. I have thoughts spiraling, images of the trails, of that echoing bathroom, of Sheri. I miss her so much. I finally give in to the morning before my alarm clock sounds.

I sit up rubbing my face and grab my phone. Just a couple of texts from Mike. He's checking in. I figure I need to play through a regular day to get everyone off my back. Maybe I need a break from the drama of all of this garbage, too. I'm conflicted.

I get dressed and make my way downstairs. Ollie is laying on a mat in the kitchen. There's no sign of anyone else. Although my sister's at school, Mom and Dad are usually around in the morning but not today. I'm curious about where they are but I'm grateful for the silence.

I open the fridge and get out the soy milk. It feels like a cruel joke but I pour it on my cereal anyhow. I notice a note from Dad on the counter while I silently crunch my breakfast. It reads: *Taking Mom's car for an oil change. Here's 10 for the day.* I find the money underneath and realize it's a peace offering of sorts. However, there's nothing from Mom and I feel bad. I'll have to make amends later. I put the money in my pocket and head for the door with the hope for an ordinary day at school.

When I open it, Detective Gekas is standing there. Shit.

"Hello, Anthony."

I smile and it's awkward, yet I feel it's somewhat the same for her.

"Your parents gone for the day?"

"They'll be back later."

She nods.

"You don't have to answer now, but what were you up to last night?"

"Did something happen?" I feel a twist in my gut, a defensiveness.

"There's—"

"Another girl gone missing?"

"No—"

"Then, why are you coming to me?"

"They found a body, Tony."

My stomach twists up sideways inside me and I grab hold of the doorframe.

"No, it's not Sheri. It's someone else."

I look at Gekas. "Another?"

She nods.

My head swirls and I think of Charlie saying that he doesn't think Sheri was the first, or the last. And if they found one body... I shut my mind to the thought.

"I don't think you're the one doing this, Tony. But I do think you're not telling me something. Something that might be important to this case." She stands there, leaving things open-ended and quiet, hoping I fill the gap. I stare back, waiting for her to continue.

"All right... If you think of anything, can you give me a call?"

"I have your card."

She nods and moves halfway down the steps before turning back towards me.

"Now that this body's shown up, there's going to be a lot more rumors going around. Don't let them get to you, okay?"

I nod. She's trying to be nice and I've been completely resistant to her up to this point.

She nods, looking down at her hand as it runs along the railing. For the first time, I see that she's struggling for a lead. She turns and heads the rest of the way down the steps.

"Detective Gekas? If I hear about anything, I'll let you know."

Gekas turns back and smiles. Now, I only hope I can help.

39

Morning at school hits all new levels of crap.

I arrive early to talk to Coach about my absence. He says the team needed me but I can get back to practice when I'm ready. I tell him I'll start fresh on Monday and he's cool but the truth is I don't want him to be nice. I want him to be hard on me, to push me, to be the Coach and not let me be lazy or, worse, scared.

Mike shows up at my locker and encourages me to party with him on Friday. Jessica sends me a text while I talk to him: *Paul thinks u should come out. We're heading to the Coffee House. Maybe the dunes after.* I appreciate the support my friends offer but really I would rather stick my head under my pillow and stay there until everything blows over—or the end of the school year shows up—whichever comes first.

That's when it happens. I see a couple of Grade 10 girls looking at me, whispering, and I know the story of the dead girl has gotten out. Everyone's talking, looking at their phones, and it moves at a supersonic pace through the hallways. TV and radio news crews are on the scene and streaming live. Social websites drone with speculation as details filter out.

The girl's name was Maggie Phelps and she was a senior at Ashworth Comp, the newest school in the southwest of the city. A construction worker found her body in a ditch when he arrived at the site in the morning. Not much else is being said and a make-shift tent was erected, shielding any details from the cameras.

It doesn't take long for the questions to start: "Is there a connection between Maggie's body and Sheri's disappearance?" The police spokeswoman offers no comment. The next question skirts what's on everyone's mind: "Does this indicate foul play in Sheri's disappearance?"

No one says *it*, but now the thought bubbles up out of everyone's brain. The thing that I've been avoiding for so long, even when Charlie and I walked the trails yesterday. The thing I don't want to believe in, the thing Sheri's parents don't want to hear.

Her parents—in no time, news crews will be dispatched to their home and asking uncomfortable questions. All the pain and anguish that had been tucked away during the search will now spill over.

The news of the dead girl moves swiftly through the student body. I move through the hallways and everyone seems to have two reactions: steering clear of me or driving right into my path. I avoid some people, but others collide into me, knocking me into the lockers. I'm pissed and I want to fight but I see judgment in enough eyes—the odds are against me and I'd lose.

By afternoon, the grief counselors are stationed at the office for people dealing with the unknown, unexpressed emotions created by Sheri's disappearance and Maggie's death. When I come back from Psychology—even Ms. Statten couldn't get me out of my funk—somebody has taken a Sharpie and written on my locker: KILLER.

I know everyone's looking but I don't care anymore. I stare at it and I'm surprised that someone would be bold enough in all of this tragedy to be such a dick. I also know that I'm done for the day. I toss my bag inside my locker and slam the door. I'm halfway down the hall when I hear, "Shepherd!" I turn, ready for a fight, but find Charlie's standing there holding a box from the local doughnut shop.

"What are you doing here?"

He looks sincerely surprised that I would question this. "What do you mean? We got a new lead."

"What? When?"

"The girl. Come on."

"Where?"

"To the crime scene."

40

Charlie and I head across town. He's opened his box of sugary treats and is already digging into a Boston Creme. He hasn't offered me one, not that I'd take it, but they sure look and smell good.

"Why the hell do we need to go to the school?"

"As far as I can tell, the cops haven't considered that she may have been killed at the school."

"The body is nowhere close. Why would you even think that?"

"Because that's our guy's MO."

"What is?"

"The news says the last anybody saw her alive was when she was working after school in the office of the student council. They also found her car near where her body was discovered. The assumption is that she left, our guy saw her and attacked her or took her out to the construction site, then killed her."

Again, that word.

"But you don't think that?"

"My sources—"

"Your sources—?"

"Yes. *My sources* say that a janitor says he saw her leaving—"

"But you don't believe that?"

"Hell no! People suck at remembering stuff like

that. Eyewitness accounts are, like, fifty percent accurate."

"And you get this statistic from where?"

He ignores my question and keeps moving on. "The janitors are out of there by 10 or 11 at the latest. That means our killer," I feel myself wince, "needed a maximum of four or five hours to lay low."

"So, what are you looking for?"

"Proof of the pattern, man!"

I stare at him. I'm really not sure I know what he is talking about.

"And why am I here?"

"Because, we're a team!"

This is all news to me.

41

I pull to the side, a block away from the school. The place is swarming with news vans, worried parents, and cops. Lots and lots of cops. The place is in full Code White lockdown.

Charlie stares at the activity. "Shit."

"What?"

"They might mess up our crime scene."

"What? This is not ours? This is theirs. We should let them do their job."

"And how is that working for us? Or for Sheri?"

"This isn't a game."

"No, it isn't. We're trying to stop a killer."

I step in. "Stop."

"What?"

"Stop using that word."

"What? Killer?" He stares at me for a second, then, "Okay, I pussyfooted around it yesterday, but it's time we face this. Whoever did this to Maggie is likely the same guy who killed Sheri."

There it is. The two words, side by side. I've known it all this time but I haven't wanted to say it. I chew my lip, staring past Charlie at the chaos of the school. It had been a similar scene at Sheri's school only a few days ago. I didn't see it but it was all over the news, Facebook, and Twitter.

Charlie keeps going, "The sooner you quit deluding yourself and face that truth, the sooner we can find whoever did it. That is what you want?"

I'm nodding without thinking. "Yes."

"Good. So let's go in—"

"Whoa." I'm upset but not crazy. "I can't go waltzing into that school on a day like today."

"Why not?"

"Gekas may not think I…May not connect me to what happened with Sheri or Maggie, but every angry parent and teenager will be looking for someone to blame."

"Good point." He looks out at the school, mulling it over. "Okay, you stay here and run recon. You see or hear anything that might be valuable, let me know." He shakes his phone.

"What's your number?"

"I programmed it into your phone yesterday. Look up 'Hot Diggity'."

I'm a little less fazed by his actions today. He grabs another doughnut, this time a honey dip, opens the door of the car, and swings his feet onto the pavement.

"Okay, give me fifteen, twenty minutes to get in and out."

I nod.

"And don't touch my doughnuts, okay? You want some, you buy your own, got it?"

I can't help but laugh again at his manners but he doesn't seem to notice or care.

He stares out at the school, likely mulling over the plan in his head. He looks back at me, "You talked to Gekas?"

"Yeah. Why?"

"Just that you didn't tell me. If we're going to be partners, you've got to keep me in the loop."

Then he's gone and I'm left wondering when he accepted me as a partner, or an accomplice.

42

The wait for Charlie is excruciating.

It's already been ten minutes and even though I need to give him another five, I'm ready to call him and tell him to head back. I'm certain he won't listen to me, so I don't know what good it would do. It may even make things worse by drawing attention to him. If I do it, then at least I can say that I was against his actions when the authorities track us down and take us in.

I watch the crowds outside the school. Parents keep swooping in and airlifting their kids out of harm's way. Fear has set in and rational thought is out. Nothing has happened to anyone while they were in class; everything has occurred afterwards. If anything, these crazy adults should be locking their kids up once they get them home from their daily education.

News reporters keep asking the same questions, desperate for some bit of newsworthy tape they can play at 6:00. Moms and dads aren't having it, so every socially needy teen crowds around the cameras hoping to be interviewed. I like being a part of our connected generation, but for every interesting person or story out there, there are a dozen duck-faced poses and angry rants from someone who's desperate for attention.

I keep watching, but the back of my mind keeps drifting to what Charlie said. *Sheri was murdered.* It hurts somewhere deep down in my brain when I think about it. I keep having this memory of her smiling at me—I don't know where it is—all I know is it's sunny and warm—knowing that I won't—no, that I may not—see her again. I want to throw up. I want to cry. But I force it all back, rolling down the window, letting the fresh air in, and breathing deep.

A dark car pulls up to the school and I know I've seen it before. Gekas steps out and I sink lower in my seat. I'm sure I'm far enough away that she can't see me, but I don't want to take the risk. I grab my phone and text Charlie: *Gekas is here. Get out.*

I hold the phone, staring at it, waiting for a reply. Nothing. I peek over the window frame and watch Gekas talking to two officers at the front doors. She's facing my way and I'm hoping she doesn't notice me across the street. A guy sitting in a car by a school where one of the students has just been murdered is suspicious; a guy ducking down, trying not to be seen, in front of that same school is a whole new level of wrong.

I look at my phone. A minute has passed and still nothing from Charlie. Where the hell is he?

Gekas moves inside the school with one of the officers, while the other remains stationed at the door. I text again: *gekas is inside.*

I wait for a response but by this point I'm expecting nothing. I'm considering the possibility of sneaking inside to find him. Where would I start? How quickly would someone realize I don't belong?

When would Gekas come after me? What would happen if I showed up? I realize I might not even make it across the front lawn before reporters and cops will figure out who I am and swarm me.

Bzzz. Finally. I look at my phone, but it's not Charlie—it's Jessica.

FYI - Dillon was dating murdrd girl

What? *How do you know?*

I wait, watching Jessica typing, the little gray dots cycling over and over.

Katie told me. She was interested in him til she heard. Says he still tried to make a move on her.

Ah, classic Dillon. Playing as many girls as he can. It also explains why Katie maybe didn't seem to be on my side. My mind flips to Charlie stealing Dillon's phone. I go to my photos, scrolling through them, until I find the screenshots he took. *Gf for now*—I am guessing that was Maggie. Damn. I look over the messages but there's nothing there: *want to come over? cant. football. later? maybe.* This guy is as boring as 90s soft rock. I have no clue what Sheri ever saw in this idiot.

I text Jessica a *thx* and look at the time. Charlie's been in there for twenty minutes.

I'm stuck. I'd drive away but that would be a dick move and I've thoroughly convinced myself that I'm not going in. My mind tries to put the pieces together about Dillon. Two people he's been with have had…bad things happen to them. Plus, there is a third—Miaow, whoever that is—waiting on the sidelines. Right now, he's my number one suspect, and I want to figure out what the hell he's up to.

"Did you touch my doughnuts?" I nearly crap

myself to find Charlie kneeling beside my driver side window.

"Where the hell did you come from?"

"Ah, I had to take the long way back. Seriously, did you?"

"What?"

"Touch my doughnuts."

"No!"

"Cool. Did you know Gekas is here?"

"What do you think I've been texting you about?"

Charlie looks at his phone. "Oh yeah, I forgot I turned it off."

"What? Why?"

"I figured you'd get panicky and start texting me every second."

"Then why'd you tell me to keep an eye out?"

"To keep you out of trouble." He circles around to the passenger side and jumps in. "Let's go."

I start the car and pull around the first corner I can. Once we are a little way down the block, I hit the gas and make as much distance between us and the school as I can.

43

Charlie opens his box and starts munching on an apple fritter. I'm not a fan but I guess someone's got to eat them.

"Can we stop at a gas station?"

"Sure. You need a coffee to wash that down?"

He nonchalantly pulls his doughnut closer. "That's just gross."

"So, what did you go looking for in there?"

Charlie chews for a bit, pondering the question. "Yesterday, out at the trails, I kept wondering if the place he chose wasn't out of convenience."

"What do you mean?"

"I wondered if it had significance in itself." He points at a gas station on the left and I pull up to entrance. He runs in quickly and comes back with a map.

"You scared I'm going to get lost?"

He ignores me and continues with his thought, "I wondered if he attacked Sheri in the bathroom for a reason." He looks at me, waiting.

"What?"

"You going to act up every time I say her name?"

"I didn't say anything!"

"You don't have to. You just get all weird and

edgy."

I could argue but I know he's right. I've lost all sense of a game face. I resign. "Continue."

He watches me for a moment. "I don't think it's simply the convenience of the attack. You could hang out in a stall, wait until someone comes, then attack."

"But how could he expect—" I pause, then push through, "Sheri to show up there?"

"I don't know. Unless he was stalking her. Or he knew her and this was the end of something." I hate him saying any of this but I also think of the text about Dillon. I'm about to say something but he keeps going on.

"I don't think it's just a pervy thing, like wanting to watch them pee. It's something more..." He trails off thinking and I try not to interrupt. "Anyway, I wanted to see if there was a pattern there, if the bathroom had significance."

"And?"

He gets big grin on his face and pulls out his phone to show me a picture. It's white and gray and has some writing on it, but with all the bumps and potholes on the street and my desire not to make us crash, I give up. "What is it?"

"It says '*A stitch in time*'."

"That's it? No, '*saves nine*'?"

"Nope."

"What's it mean?"

"I don't know. But do you know where I found it."

I shake my head because he's on a roll.

"It was on the floor, behind a toilet in the last

stall of the first floor girls' bathroom on the west side. "

"You think it's from Maggie's killer?"

"You know how many bathrooms I checked in the school? All of them. At least, I think I found all of them. And this was the only one."

"So, a threat? Like, nine people to die?"

Charlie shakes his head. "Nah. My thought is the guy had four or five hours to wait around, pre or post attack."

"So, he either got bored and wrote it or he's getting cocky and leaving a signature."

Charlie nods, excited by the idea. "Better still, do you know what else is on the west side of the school?"

I try and think about the layout of the school and realize after all that waiting around, I barely remember anything except for the reporters, the students, the cops, and Gekas.

"It's only a few hundred yards from the student parking lot, which looks directly at the construction site where they found her body."

It's all circumstantial, but I still wonder if he might be on to something. "Did you just say you went into every girls' bathroom? And no one saw you? In a school on lockdown you never once got caught?"

"What can I say? I'm the Magic Man."

"I thought you were Hot Diggity?"

"That too!" He finishes off his apple fritter and opens up his map.

44

Now it's my turn. "While you were sneaking around toilet stalls, I connected with my own sources."

"It's about time. I can't do all the work."

I try to ignore the shot, but it's true. I'm not really sure what I've been doing to help. "Turns out, Maggie was dating Dillon."

He pulls out a jam-filled doughnut, caked with sugar. "Oh, that?"

"Wait? What? You knew?"

"Of course, I did." He pauses, realizing. "Did I forget to tell you?"

I nod. So much for being partners and sharing all the info.

"Shoot. Sorry about that. After you dropped me off, I decided to follow up on Dillon. He works over at that burger place on Quance—"

He looks at me, as if I should know the place he's talking about.

"You know, Romeo's Burgers—"

"No clue."

"Anyway, he works the drive-thru on the weekends." He pauses, taking a big bite of his doughnut. Sugar sprinkles are everywhere. I look as it falls around him and all over my dad's tidy car. "I could really go for one of their Sloppy Chew special…"

"Dude?"

He looks and I nod to the mess he's making on the seat.

"Oh, sorry." He instinctively grabs a napkin from the glove box like he totally expects them to be there and begins dusting his lap and the car seat off. "So after the new girl showed up dead, I went back and looked through the employee records—"

"How do you even do that?"

He looks at me and I realize who I'm talking to.

"And sure enough, Maggie Phelps worked there, too. I did a bit more digging around, and guess what? Never mind, I'll tell you. They were dating." He looks at me as he licks off a glop off raspberry jam that has ended up on his finger. "I don't suppose we could stop for a burger—"

"No."

I drive in silence.

"What's up your ass?"

"What about 'we're a team' or 'yeah, we're part-ners' or 'keeping each other in the loop'?"

"You're mad because I didn't tell you about Dillon?"

"Yes."

The situation finally dawns on him, "Ah, I see how you could be upset about that."

"You could, could you?"

"Yeah, I think so."

His ability to be this much of a dumbass astounds me. I laugh.

He stares down at the last doughnut in his box—chocolate covered with sprinkles. "You know,

Dillon's at a football game this afternoon."

I look over at him.

"We could go check him out. Of course, Gekas and her homies will make the connection soon enough and likely be on their way."

"Sounds good."

He closes the lid on his last doughnut, saving it for later. "Sweet."

45

We pull into the parking lot of the city stadium. School buses sit at the players' entrance and a handful of cars edge around them. Even though schools play in the stadium of the national league team, turnout is minimal.

I watch as Charlie hops out of the car, carrying his map and doughnut box with him. As he heads towards the main entrance, I follow behind. "Are you ever going to share?"

"Let it go," he says over his shoulder, then realizes I'm talking about his food. "Why should I? You're rich. Get your own."

I jog behind him to catch up. "I'm not rich."

"So says the guy who lives in snob central."

"Whatever."

"What do your parents do for fun? Art gallery openings? Night at the symphony?"

I laugh but know their last date was for a hospital foundation fundraiser. I decide not to comment.

"My mom's idea of a good night is being drunk on the couch watching reality TV."

I'm guessing he isn't lying but I don't know how to reply.

"You and I are night and day."

He shifts the doughnut to his other side, away

from me.

"So why are you hanging around?"

He looks over at me.

"I mean, if we are so different, if who I am seems to piss you off, why are you helping me out?"

He glares, then a sly smile comes across his face. "You know that trying to make me feel like a jerk isn't going to get you anywhere near my doughnut box."

I smile and let it go, but I keep thinking that somewhere underneath there is something more to the story of Charlie than a kid from a broken home and a mother who doesn't care. At least, that's my best guess. His indifference makes me think that if she's around, she's an irrelevant feature of his life.

He keeps poking at my so-called "rich kid" status too, and it's annoying. I'm not the stereotype he thinks I am, but then Charlie definitely doesn't act like a poor kid from the wrong side of the tracks. He's full of surprises. He pulled that cell phone out of his pocket when I didn't even think he owned one and for all I know he could drive around the corner in some souped-up muscle car. If he keeps going the way he has been, nothing will surprise me in the end.

We head inside the stadium and move up to the second level. We decide the seats above the few spectators present will give us a good view. We exit the ramp out onto the shady side of the stadium. The sun is out but a fall breeze cools things off.

Charlie zips up his sweater, pulling it tight. "Maybe I should have bought us some shitty gas station coffee."

I smile. "Would have worked well for the stakeout."

The players are on the field. The game is in the second quarter. Dillon's team has the ball and it's third and one but I can't see where he is.

Charlie points towards the center of the field, "Our boy is the running back."

I see his name, Ross, over the number 27, standing to the left of the quarterback, number 48, waiting for the snap. He cycles around as 48 takes the ball and cuts quick across the back. The quarterback twists and pitches the ball under his left arm into Dillon's waiting grasp. Dillon digs down and runs and I can see the speed in his legs. He's quick but not observant and he's rushed by the safety, who slams him hard to the ground. I admit I enjoy seeing him taken down.

The offensive line moves off the field and Dillon takes a seat on the bench. He pulls off his helmet and pours some sugary electrolytes down his throat. The whole action seems posed, like he thinks he's in a commercial and everyone's watching.

Charlie scoffs, unfolding his map, "He's always announcing how he's an elite athlete in the halls."

"What a douche."

"Couldn't agree more."

I lean forward in my chair. "But what if it's all a show for someone—special…"

The stands are filled with adults, mostly parents, and a few students. Cheerleaders hang out on the sidelines, mingling during plays, the occasional few smiling over at the guys on the bench. Yet, Dillon doesn't seem to be one of them. He appears focused on the game, until he suddenly looks over his shoulder at someone down low in the stands to the left of us. He smiles quickly before looking back at the play.

"Did you see that?" I ask and realize Charlie isn't even looking, his eyes focused on the map. For once, I've seen something Charlie hasn't, and I point in the direction Dillon was looking.

"No one I can see...oh, wait..." he pauses, holding his hand out towards me.

"What?"

"Your phone."

"You have you're own."

"Yeah, but I can't use it for this!"

"For what?"

"Just give me your damn phone."

I stare at him.

"Please!"

"Fine," I say with disgust, but inside I'm laughing. I guess I can teach a stubborn dog new tricks.

He takes it, tapping in my passcode without even asking. I'm guessing it took him only seconds being around me to figure it out. He heads to the browser.

"Why can't you use your own?"

"They always figure out it's me."

"Quit with the pronoun game. Who?"

"School officials."

I react, grabbing the phone and find he's on an admin page for his school. A spreadsheet of teacher's contact information lists names, addresses, and phone numbers. He steals it back and scrolls down the page.

"Oh, snap." He hands me back the phone and points. "See down there? Second row, fifth from the end?"

I scour the crowd and see a pretty, tall, blonde woman, maybe in her late 20s with hair pulled back in a ponytail.

"That's Miss Turner." He taps at my phone.

I search the list and don't see it.

He points. "Mia Turner." I look at him, feeling puzzled, "Miss Mia-ow Turner."

"Double snap!"

That's when we see Gekas walk into the stadium, flanked by cops, heading straight for Dillon.

46

As soon as Gekas hits the field, it's chaos. Refs are blowing whistles, coaches are running out, parents in the stands are yelling. Dillon sees it all happening but doesn't seem to register that they're here for him. He stands in position, waiting for the next play, and it isn't until Gekas beelines past the quarterback that what's going on finally dawns on him. He backpedals a little, but she yells, "Don't do it, Dillon," and he freezes on the spot.

She's talking quietly now, and the coach is yelling and the refs are trying to figure out why the hell this woman has interrupted the game. I look over at Charlie but he's gone. I search the crowd and see him ducking into the nearest exit. I follow.

"Where are we going?" I yell as I catch up.

"As soon as Gekas showed up, Mia-ow took off."

"You think they're in this together."

"Oh, they're into something, alright."

We see her heading down the ramp towards the parking lot and we sprint to catch up. By the time we're outside, she's rushing to her car.

"Miss Turner—"

She doesn't turn. "I don't know anything—"

"Miss—"

"Please, just leave me alone." She struggles to get her keys out of her purse, battling to get the door open.

"Mia-ow."

She pauses and turns, finally looking at us. "Charlie?"

He slows to a halt, hands raised. "I just want to talk."

"About what?" The sight of him has thrown her off and her keys slip out of her hand.

"Dillon."

Her face drops and she begins to cry.

47

When Mia's tears don't stop, I suggest we sit in her car, at least until Charlie and I figure out exactly what's going on.

She unlocks the door and Charlie looks at me. "Shotgun," he whispers, and moves quickly into the front seat on the passenger side. I shake my head at his lack of decorum and climb into the back. It's packed full of papers, makeup, and dusty mixtape CDs.

Charlie ferrets out a tissue—I don't know where he got it from—and hands it to her. She wipes away the tears and snot and groans as she looks at herself in the visor mirror.

"God, I've had better days."

Charlie opens up his doughnut box. "Have the last one."

She looks at it, shaking her head.

"Come on, Miss Turner. It'll make you feel better."

"I think we're a little past the 'Miss' part," she says as she gives into the temptation of the chocolate covered treat.

I lean forward, wedging myself between the seats. "Can you tell us what happened?"

She takes a big bite of the doughnut and sprinkles shower down onto her lap. She stares out the window, running the side of her pinkie along the corners of her mouth to catch any chocolate.

"At the start, it was innocent. Nothing but him hanging around, asking questions. I didn't think anything of it. He was a student and there are some lines you simply don't cross. Then the guy I was dating cheated on me and it hurt. One day, after school, I was feeling like crap and he hung around and I started talking about my ex and he listened. It felt good. He said nice things to me. He said I deserved better. That I was pretty. And then it kept happening. He'd visit and we'd talk. It was always about things he had done or things he wanted me to do and it was never about school or other girls. It was interesting and I knew what I was thinking and how I was starting to feel, but I kept saying to myself *as long as nothing happens, it's all right.* All I had to do was make sure we didn't cross that line."

She's chewing meditatively, and I already know what she's going to say next.

"But Dillon was persistent and kept gently pushing that line. He gave me his number 'just to talk' and I took it and left it for the longest time. Then I had one long, bad week, and I went home that Friday. I felt miserable and I had a drink and saw his number and…"

She holds the last few bites of doughnut hovering in front of her mouth and looks like she's about to cry. She shakes it off, though her face crinkling as she seems to berate herself in her mind.

"We never *did* anything."

"Mia, we read some of those texts—"

"It never meant anything. It was all talk, all flirt-ing, all…"

Charlie finishes her thought, "Foreplay."

She looks at him, shocked by his accusation. She wants to get mad, play the teacher, but knows it's useless—and all true. "Now, he's in trouble, and soon they'll figure out it's me. I'll lose my job and—"

"Wait, you think this is about you two?"

She looks at Charlie, confused, then turns to me. "Isn't it—?"

Charlie shuts the lid on his box. "Oh, Mia, this is so much worse."

48

The last of the parents pull out of the parking lot and only a few buses and cop cars remain. Mia isn't handling the new facts very well.

"But that's impossible."

"I promise you, it is."

Mia protests, "No, he couldn't have."

"Why not?"

"Because—" She's not making this very easy.

"You said you two didn't do anything."

"No, but—"

The nature of their relationship dawns on me. "It didn't stop you from hanging out together."

The pained expression returns to her face. "He showed up at my house one night. We visited. Then we did it again, watching movies. I'd sit on one side of the couch, he'd sit on the other."

Charlie laughs, "The buffer."

I start realizing how much Mia hasn't figured out about life even though she's likely ten years older than me.

Charlie pushes the questions forward, "Was he with you last night?"

She nods.

"What about last Wednesday?" I ask.

She thinks back. "Yes. I think we watched the

new Matthew McConaughey film that night."

I lean back in the seat and ponder the mess Mia has left for herself. "You need to tell the cops."

"What do you mean?"

I'm shocked by her naivety but I persist, "Dillon is the main suspect in a murder case."

"But if I tell them, I might lose my job."

"And he might go to jail."

I can see the gears grinding in her head and I can't believe she isn't even considering helping him. "I like him. He's so sweet. But, I've wanted to be a teacher for so long—"

Charlie interrupts, "You know what, Mia. Don't."

I turn on him, "What?"

"He'll spend a few nights in jail, but there isn't enough evidence to hold him."

"You don't know that for sure."

He ignores me, turning back to Mia. "Wait it out. Go home and think about it. Don't rush your decision."

"Charlie—?"

"I'm sure it's going to work itself out." He puts his hand on the door handle and I know he's about to leave.

I lean forward. "Mia, don't listen—"

Charlie's already getting ready to go. "Thanks for your help. We'll let you go—"

"Charlie! Mia—"

But he's popped open the door and is gone. I want to convince Mia to talk to the cops but I also need to catch up to Charlie.

"Go tell them the truth. Ask for Detective Gekas.

Counios and Gane

She'll be able to help you keep it anonymous. I'm sure of it." Charlie's gone and I can't wait any longer. I open the door and look back at her. "Mia, please, do what's right."

I get out of the car, feeling certain she's not going to listen to me. I see Charlie standing by my car, his hand on the roof, waiting for me to let him in.

"What the hell was that about?"

"You said it yourself. Dillon's a douche. Just let him spend a few nights in jail."

"You can't be serious."

"What's it matter to you?"

"It's wrong."

"So?"

"We don't let innocent people go to jail!"

"Why not? It buys us some time to sort out this case without spending every second trying to stay ahead of Gekas."

"Are you for real?"

Charlie's hand slips from the car. "You know what? You go do what's *right*. You go talk to Gekas and tell her everything. Tell her about everything we've been up to and see what she thinks. Maybe she'll say, 'Oh, thank you so much for all this wonderful information, Mr. Shepherd,' right before she throws your ass in jail for tampering with evidence, obstructing justice, or maybe because you've made yourself seem like a pretty good suspect again. Yeah, that's right, go on, have fun."

He's walking away and I let him.

I can't believe Gekas would really think any of what Charlie's said. She said I'm not a suspect. But I also know that she'll likely be pissed about Charlie

181

and me snooping around the investigation. Except, there's no need to get him involved. Nobody really knows about the two us working together, so I could keep the centre of attention on me. Also, I haven't contaminated any crime scenes, so it gives me deniability. I can't say the same for Charlie. Also, Gekas is moving towards a dead-end right now with Dillon. Letting her know the truth will get her back on track, or at least searching for the right person.

Still, Dillon's an ass and he wouldn't help me if he had a chance. I know it's a false argument though, and I dismiss it as soon it pops in my head.

When I see Gekas and the officers step up out of the stadium with Dillon, his hands cuffed behind his back, I know what I've got to do. When I look in the direction that Charlie went, I can't see him. He's already disappeared somewhere across the tracks.

49

Gekas sits behind her desk, staring at me with disbelief.

She didn't want to listen to me outside the stadium. Dillon was already taken into custody and read his rights. She wasn't going to release him because of some hearsay from a kid. She told me to come down to her office at the station in an hour, but I ignored her and sat on the benches at the front until she would see me. When the officer behind the front desk called to let her know, I could tell by his face that she wasn't pleased. She let me sit there for almost two more hours while I stubbornly waited. My gut just couldn't deal with letting an innocent person be stuck in jail if I knew there was something I could have done about it—even for a douche like Dillon.

"I told you to come talk to me if you had something, but this isn't what I had in mind."

I try to relax in the chair but the sun streams in brightly through the window behind her and right into my eyes. "Dillon's got an alibi."

She pulls a cup of coffee towards her and by the rings I see around the edge I can tell it hasn't been washed in forever. She takes a sip, cringes, and pushes it away.

"I know. He told me."

I didn't think this through enough. Of course he did. He doesn't care about Mia's job when it means his life.

"Except, I can't seem to track down the person he was with."

I'm not sure how much to say. "She was at the stadium."

Gekas smiles. "Of course *she* was." She leans forward, smiling. Shit, how much have I already screwed up. "And how do you know Miss Turner, since you don't even go to her school?"

"I…"

Gekas doesn't say anything, leans back in her chair, and waits for me to put my foot in my mouth.

"Sheri told me."

"Oh, she did." Gekas smiles again. She knows I'm full of crap. "She told you about her exboyfriend's relationship with his teacher."

"Yes." When all else fails, keep on pressing through the bullshit.

"Even when he's trying to get back with your girlfriend at the same time?"

I know she's digging at my emotions, hoping to crack my lie. "Yeah. That's why she told me. I saw a text from him and was pissed. She told me not to worry, that he's just playing everyone. She told me about her, and Mia—Miss Turner, and Maggie."

By now, all I can see is Gekas' silhouette and I can feel the heat of the sun bleeding into the room. Or at least I hope it's the sun, because I know I'm starting to sweat.

"Well, she seems to have told you everything.

Why didn't you tell me any of this when I came to your house this morning?"

"Because I didn't know it was relevant." At least, I hope I didn't. "You never told me the girl— Maggie's—name." I can't remember anything about this morning, so I open my mouth and my brain pours out whatever stories it invents.

Gekas looks at me, smiling, shaking her head. She rises and leaves the room, taking her cup with her. I'm not sure if we're done, so I look out the door behind me and see her down the hall, in a break room, dumping her coffee and filling it fresh from the pot. She comes back to the room and sits down.

"This is all really nice of you, Anthony, helping out a guy who hits on your girlfriend, *dated* your girlfriend, who you got into a fight with the other day at the school of your missing girlfriend."

Shit.

"Oh yeah, I know. You and—," she opens a folder on her desk, "Charles Wolfe had a little visit with some of Sheri's friends, as well as Dillon, whom you had an altercation with." She closes the folder. "Nothing serious. A little pushing. A few threats. Nothing a person could go to jail on." She smiles, holding for a moment, building up for her pitch. "My question is what are you and Charles up to?"

"Nothing." Swing and a miss.

"Anthony, really? You can do better than that."

"I was only asking what you asked the others, to figure out if I was a suspect."

"And you enlisted Charles to help you with this?"

Ugh—strike two for me. I keep going, "Yeah, he knows the place, the people—"

"Anthony, cut the crap."

Gekas is ahead of me and we both know it. The only question is how soon do I admit it.

I come clean. "I want to know what happened—who did this—who..." I look out the window above Gekas at the long shadows of the city's skyline. "I want to know who killed her."

"Do you know the kind of person Charles is?"

I've got a pretty good idea, but I'm sure she's going to tell me anyway. She turns in her chair and grabs a second folder. This one's thicker than the other. A lot thicker. She slaps it down on the desk and opens it up.

"Seems like Charles is a busy boy. On the times we've caught him, he's been arrested for invasion of privacy, gambling, possession of prohibited weapons, public nuisance, public mischief, vandalism, disorderly conduct, theft, breaking and entering, trespassing, arson, criminal negligence, bodily harm, dangerous use of a motor vehicle, identity theft, and attempted escape. He was too young to even get tried as an adult for half of these. He's also suspected of corruption, misleading justice, possession and trafficking, false pretenses, forgery...Do you get the idea?"

My head spins. I knew he was trouble—I knew it—but I don't think I expected this much.

Gekas wheels her chair close to her desk out of the bright sun. I can see her eyes and I know she cares.

"Anthony, I'm going to find out what happened.

I promise. But you need to let me do my job. You and Charles need to quit doing what you're doing so that there are no mistakes. We don't know that Sheri and Maggie are connected. At the moment, these are two separate incidents and need to be treated as such. But when we find out what happened to Sheri and we find the person or persons responsible, they go to jail. You've got to do this for us, okay? You, me… And Sheri."

I nod. I know she's right. But in the back of my head, I'd really like it if she'd sent the person responsible to the morgue.

50

After I'm done with Gekas, I head home. I'm exhausted and all I want to do is to lie down and sleep the night away. I arrive home, pulling into the driveway and head through the backdoor by the kitchen. I'm not sure if I'm ready for Mom and Dad, so I hope I can sneak to my room.

Ollie greets me and shows all the unconditional love I need. I toss my bag on the floor by the shoes and give him a good rubdown.

The house is silent. I'm sure Dad is here somewhere and Mom is too, but I don't want to get into anything. I'm dreaming of the old days when I could make it through a day with some good old uncomplicated teen angst. The normal stuff. Not the parent-fighting-cop-questioning-girlfriend-missing stuff.

Yet, I don't even get a hello and it stings. Sheri's disappearance opened a hole in my life and it keeps getting wider and I feel like I'm going to tumble in and never return.

Maybe it's time for allowing some small semblance of normalcy back into my life. Since there's no supper cooking, I leash the dog and put a plastic bag in my pocket, but before I head outside, Dad calls from somewhere in the house.

"Son?"

"Yeah…" I wait for a moment.

"Where are you headed?" He's so casual, so passive-aggressive sometimes. I bet what he means is 'don't even think about leaving without saying where you're going before dinner.'

I try not to sound defensive, "It's still a bit early. I was taking Ollie for a walk."

Silence. Ollie looks impatient and I feel it too.

"Your Mom's picking up Thai on the way home from the clinic. She'll be home around 6:00."

"Got it, Dad." I look down at Ollie. "Come on, boy. Let's get the hell out of here before he says anything else."

We head for the creek and walk along the path. It's getting cooler out. I pull my hood over my head and settle one hand into the pocket. Ollie walks without pulling and sniffs at everything. He doesn't leave a tree trunk, bush, or leaf unturned.

I mull over my past few days with Charlie.

Damn, he's different. Not a kid I'd hang out with. He doesn't think like anyone else I know and some of the things he does—the way his brain works—he doesn't care or give a crap about what's right or wrong, or what should or shouldn't be done. I worry that one day he's going to cross a line and end up in a whole heap of trouble and I might be around when it happens.

He's lead us—where exactly? He assumes Sheri was attacked in the bathroom on the trails and that Maggie died in the bathroom at the school. But he has no hard evidence to back up either of these things. All we have for it—no, all I have for it—is a huge fight with my parents, skipping school and practice, and dealing with Gekas while we mess up her investigation. He was wrong about her, and every step forward I make with Charlie wrecks everything else in my life. And I don't think we're any closer to finding out what happened to Sheri.

Still, my gut says that I should pay attention and keep him around. And that scares the crap out of me. That seems unstable. Everything in Gekas' file makes him a straight-up sociopath—if Ms. Statten's psych class has taught me anything. Yet, if Charlie is right, maybe it will take someone like him to find this killer. Psychopath, sociopath—aren't they all the same disorder, one's just a little further off the rails?

Charlie's got something on his mind, something going on his head, and I need to trust him. And now that Gekas knows about us, I wonder if I should warn him. Would it even matter? Would it slow him down? Or stop him? Or would it just propel him forward to do more?

I open my phone, and bring up Hot Diggity and send a quick text: *Gekas knows about you.* I'm sure there's more I should say, but I leave it at that.

Ollie finally does what he came out for. I pull a bag out of my pocket and do the good pet owner thing. "All done buddy? Should we carry on a little further?"

I'm not in a rush. The only thing that's waiting for me is take-out and an awkward supper with the parents, followed up with a huge, heaping load of homework.

I walk a little further, enjoying the cool wind, the warm sun, and the auburn trees. I take a deep breath in, the smells of walnut and rich spice spinning my head. I open my eyes. A leaf falls from a tree and lands on the path and Ollie pulls me ahead to greet it.

51

My prediction for an awkward supper is one hundred percent accurate.

Mom and Dad talk about their day. Dad's wrapped up the contract he was working on and Mom's made some calls to hiring agencies for a new receptionist. It's all small talk and dead air fills the room.

I miss Heather. She's out tonight, but if she were here, she could at least share tales of university and make it a little less uncomfortable. It hasn't occurred to me until this moment that maybe she's skipped this family meal on purpose. I know I would have.

None of us bring up yesterday. By now, they likely know I've missed the afternoon at school again. They probably haven't asked how my day went, fearing I might lie—or worse, tell the truth. I'm guessing that if they ever met Charlie, I'd be grounded for sure.

The Thai food is tasty and since there are no dishes, clean-up is faster than normal. Which is good, since all I want is to get out of here as fast as possible.

Once in the safety of my room, I shut the door. I sink heavily into my desk chair and stare at my bag of homework. It feels like forever since I opened a book and did anything. I've got assignments from every class.

I realize the right thing to do is to cut ties with Charlie and let Gekas do her job. I can go back to my ordinary life of school, practice, and having regular meals with my folks. In a week or two, life will get back to normal, and maybe with Charlie and me out of the way, Gekas will find Sheri's killer. I pause on that thought. I have come to terms with the worst possible scenario. I accept that Sheri isn't coming home, and sadly, it's almost a relief.

I sway in my chair, looking at the books stacked high on my desk and sigh. I pick up my phone and see a message from Mike and another from Jessica. Both are asking me to come to the party this weekend. I'm not in the mood to socialize. I'm not in the mood to do much of anything.

I turn off my desk lamp, slipping my room into darkness. I lay back on my bed, putting on headphones and go to my playlist. I cue up some music and open a mindless first person shooter on my phone. I'm in my own little bubble, listening to Run the Jewels, defending the Earth from an alien invasion, letting everything else slip away.

52

"Anthony!"

I'm jolted out of my sleep. My earbuds lay somewhere beneath me, and my phone is nowhere to be found. I look at the clock. It's almost 8 PM.

"Anthony!" Dad yells at me from downstairs.

I walk to the door, not leaving the safety of my room. "Yeah?"

"There's someone here to see you."

I run through my head who it could be, and although I wish it might be Mike, or even Gekas, I'm certain I know who it'll likely be.

"Be right down."

I come down the stairs and take a quick peek around the corner. Damn. Charlie Wolfe is standing in *my* front hall and Dad is standing there, talking to him.

"I read *The Spy Who Came in From the Cold* and thought, 'whoa this is great. I need more of this.'"

"You should read *Tinker Tailor Soldier Spy.* I've found that to be most satisfying."

"I hated that book. I kept waiting for something to happen. It's like Le Carré was being obstinately obtuse."

Dad's quite a bit taller than him, but Charlie holds his own, not seeming to be intimidated at all.

"What about craft and subtlety?"

Charlie laughs, "What about a good story? And the mole? I knew it was him all along."

I can't believe my ears. He's standing in my house, arguing with my dad. I want to ask how he knows where I live but it may be better that I don't. I need to cut in.

"Heh-hem."

They both stop and look at me.

"Oh, Anthony. Charlie popped in to check on you."

"I see that."

"Hey," he says nonchalantly.

I think I want to punch him. I give a nod back, which is then followed by the most silent moment of silence.

Dad stands between us and finally breaks in. "Well, I'll let you two chat. Charlie, it was nice to meet you. If you get a chance try *The Secret Pilgrim*."

"Thank you, Mr. Shepherd. I will."

Dad walks back into the family room where I assume Mom is. I watch him go. Once he's out of earshot, I step to the front door.

"What the hell is that?"

"What the hell is what?"

I don't have time for his bullshit. "What are you doing here?

"Maybe we should step outside."

53

Charlie and I stand on the front step. Getting him out of my home makes me feel a little better, but it's dark and it's cooled off since this afternoon. I shiver in the cold.

Charlie nods at me, "You should have put a jacket on."

"Why are you at my house? What's going on?"

"Your dad seems nice."

"I know he is, Charlie. Now, answer the question."

"I never knew mine." He looks up at the porch light and I think he's genuinely sad.

I soften. "What's going on?"

"I think you should stay in for the next couple of nights."

"What are you talking about?"

"Don't hang around me. Get back to your usual schedule. Go back to practice. Hang out with your friends. Then, come home, do your homework."

"Where is this coming from? Is this because of the text?"

He's distracted, his mind struggling to catch up to the conversation we're having. "Oh, yeah, the text. I figured as much."

"Gekas knows everything we've been up to so

far." I consider if I should tell him everything but he beats me to the punch.

"Did she show you my file?"

I don't answer and he smiles. "It's thick, huh? Every cop likes to show that off when I go in, thinking it'll scare me straight." He shakes his head. "Everyone—school, cops, parents—expects us to want redemption. You know who doesn't care? The kooks out there hurting people who try to play it straight."

His look reminds me of the first day I met him, but I'm exhausted and can't keep up to his thinking. "Charlie—?"

He pulls out the gas station map he bought earlier in the day. He unfolds it quickly and I see he's labeled it with a marker. He points, "Sheri disappeared here. We don't know what happened to her, but we don't think it's good." I know he's avoiding the word "murdered" on purpose and I appreciate him for it. "Our theory—," he looks at me, "okay, my theory, is that whoever attacked her did it in the bathroom on the trail."

He flips the map over to the other side. "Maggie was found here, dumped in a ditch behind the construction site in the new subdivision of the city. Two young women attacked? Most likely the same guy. So, I go on the hunch that he'll stick to his M.O. and check the location where she was last seen," he points at her school, "where I find a marking on a toilet in a bathroom near the student council room where she was working."

He looks back at me. "I know it's all pretty flimsy, but we don't have much else so far. It also seems that whoever our killer is, he's been focusing on high schools and, so far, has been trying to keep his distance from the center of the city."

"But Sheri—"

"I know. There's an anomaly. Both are high school students. Both are women. Both final locations are outside of the city, but I feel certain that Maggie was attacked in the school. Sheri was nowhere near the school, but that isn't to say our guy didn't follow her from the school. All of this goes with Gekas' profile that we're dealing with a teenage boy most likely."

"If he attacks again, I'm guessing it will be up north." He points to the top right of the map. "This is all industrial warehouses and factories. There's only one school and it's more east than north." He points to the other side. "There are three schools up here. One is a Catholic school and two are public schools. If he were to attack anywhere, it might be here. Yet, it's twenty years old and the city has grown up around it quite a bit. It might put him off. But there's also a new mall and a lot of the students wander there for the food court and the movie theatre."

I know his mind is buzzing now.

"So, what Charlie, you going to watch all of them?"

"Yes."

"How—?"

"All I need for you to do is to stay safe and out of trouble for the next while."

"What are you planning on doing?"

"Keep yourself surrounded by people. Friends

are good. Your folks are better."

"Charlie—"

"I think I can catch him, but I need us not to mess it up."

"Catch him?"

"Gekas makes it harder but we just need to keep out of the way."

"Charlie? What are you planning on doing?"

He looks at me and smiles. "Me? I'm going to get thrown in jail."

PART THREE

54

I wake the next morning face down in my pillow. I'm exhausted. It seems the events of the last two days—really, that's it, just two days?—have worn me out. All the conditioning Coach puts me through doesn't seem to protect me from the runaway bus called Charlie Wolfe.

He didn't explain much to me afterwards, taking off into the night to supposedly to get arrested. He always likes to cross the boundaries that lead to trouble. He's just plain crazy. That's the only explanation for his choices. I don't know how his plans will catch the killer but, in my mind, his math doesn't add up. Once again I am left with questions.

Yesterday, I compared him to a sociopath, and with his impulsive decisions and total disregard for the law, I feel that was a fair assessment. He won't care and keep sliding and one day take out everyone in his path. The further I am from him, the safer my family, my friends, and I will be.

I drag myself out of bed and head downstairs. Mom is there, drinking a cup of coffee at the breakfast table. There is no avoiding it: I am going to have to sit across from her. I grab some bran and raisins, avoid the soy milk for the real stuff, and take a seat.

She starts us off. "Good morning."

"Morning." I chew away at the cereal, not sure what to say next, hoping it stops at a short greeting, but I know it won't. And it doesn't.

"Your friend, Charlie—"

"Not my friend—" I'm short about it but the less I associate with him the better. Besides, those were his orders.

"Okay, the boy that stopped by yesterday—" She looks to make sure I approve.

I nod.

"Your dad had a nice visit with him."

"Yeah." I should be more responsive but I don't know what to say. Charlie seems like the kind of guy who would say or do anything to get what he wants. Was he actually interested in what Dad and he talked about? My brain decides to blurt out what I am thinking, "I'm not even sure he's read those books."

"Maybe not, but sometimes we have to give people the benefit of the doubt."

Is Mom defending Charlie now? What the hell is going on around here?

"Is he in a class of yours...?"

I quickly slurp up some cereal and chew the raisins, shaking my head, hoping that if I wait long enough she'll move on. She doesn't, though, so I proceed, "He's from Sheri's school."

"Oh, so you met him through Sheri?"

She's digging. I wonder if Gekas has already talked to her and Dad. "I think he might've been a friend of hers." She catches the slip in my change of tense as quickly as I do. We stare at each other across the table with the realization that we both accept that Sheri is likely gone forever.

She clears her throat and swallows. "So, he's pretty upset as well?"

"Yes. He just wants to know what happened."

She reaches across the table and takes my hand, giving it a gentle squeeze. "We just need to be patient. Okay, Son?"

I look at her. She loves me. I nod. It feels good to kick the door open and let Mom back into my bubble after the past few days.

55

I walk to school, setting my phone on vibrate and stuffing it deep in my bag. I want some silence to prepare myself for what's ahead. After the media got hold of Maggie's death yesterday, the school turned on me, even though there was no evidence to back it up. The only way I was going to survive was to ride it out and stay off the radar. Whether Charlie intended it or not, his recipe of family, friends, homework, and practice were probably the best solution.

By the time I get to school, though, it feels like a wave has swept yesterday away. I open the doors and people are already coming by and giving me nods and an acknowledging "s'up." I'm still getting sad puppy-dog eyes from some of the younger girls, but in general, the whole mood is different. Even my locker door has been scrubbed clean, with not even a hint of marker left on it.

Mike greets me with a solid bro hug. "It's good to finally see you back on your feet."

"I was here yesterday—"

"Yeah, but you looked like crap."

"Thanks. What's going on around here?"

"Haven't you heard?"

Mike fills me in that Gekas had a one-on-one interview with the local paper about Maggie's murder and Sheri's disappearance. She said that despite the many similarities, no evidence of a connection had been uncovered. Dillon's arrest was also replaced by news of his release, stating that "confirmation of his innocence has been substantiated by two witnesses." It seems that Gekas finally tracked down Mia.

She also announced that another team, headed by Detective Ben Waters, would be investigating the circumstances of Maggie's death while she continued to focus on Sheri's disappearance. She expressed her gratitude to "the family and friends of Miss Beckman for their tireless patience and support," and promised that these separate incidents will be each given the Homicide Department's foremost attention. This information is supposed to put me at ease, but I'm not sure if it does.

I go to my first class, history, and grab a seat. I expect the whispers, the looks, but there's nothing. I look around and everyone looks bored or half asleep. No one is looking at me. I look up at the board and realize that the only thing I should be caring about is that King John of England signed something on June 15, 1215 and it seems pretty important. I grab my pen and take notes, trying to figure out what's going on and why the *Magna Carta* was so important. I am finally making the connections between it and the Thirteen Colonies when the bell rings and I realize the last hour has zipped away.

By noon, I am getting back into the groove of things. Whatever vigilante justice swept through school yesterday seems to have been settled by Gekas' words. I sit with Mike and some of the other guys from the basketball team and listen to the stories of last week's game. Again, I'm told I was missed and they hound me to get back to practice this afternoon. I push them off until tomorrow, knowing I need to carve out a chunk of time to deal with homework. Catching up will suck but it's necessary. Who knows? A few hours of running drills with Coach yelling at me tomorrow morning might make me feel like things are back to normal.

It isn't until the 1 PM bell rings that I feel a painful ache deep down. I realize that I am missing the familiar *bzzz* of lunchtime texts from Sheri, so I force myself to think of other things. Afternoon classes fill the emptiness. I discover we've started George Orwell's *Animal Farm* in English. In chemistry, I find myself completely lost trying to understand mole conversion calculations. The last bell rings and I'm absolutely grateful to drag myself out of class and head to my locker.

People fill the halls, talking, laughing, pushing, yelling, making out, breaking up, running ahead, and falling behind. I move among them, with them, between them. Yet, I feel different. I know there's a space between those of us who've only known the ease of life and those who've felt the thorniness of death.

Charlie knows what I'm talking about.

I push the thought away, forcing it into a deep, dark hole. It's time I get back to living—Sheri would want it that way.

56

When I get home, Dad's on the couch reading—this time it's *Better* by Atul Gawande. The aroma of fresh baked bread fills the room.

"You've been baking?"

He doesn't look up from the book and says, "I needed the right sort of something to go with my chicken green chili." It's all for effect. When Dad makes his chili, he starts in the morning and it simmers all day. A meal that Dad puts this much effort into usually means something good has happened in the family. He must know that Mom has made her peace with me.

"How was school?"

"Good." The word comes out without thinking.

"Hope they're not taking it easy on you with homework."

"Nope. I'll be at it until I'm your age—" I drop my heavy book bag.

"Don't say it—"

"What? Old man?"

"I can still throw you over my knee."

"Come on, bring it." We look at each other and smile. I've missed this back-and-forth with Dad..

"Head upstairs and get cleaned up before your Mom gets home."

"Sure thing, Pops."

I hear him grunt as I head up the stairs. I toss my bag on my bed and am surprised to hear Heather behind me as she says, "Ah, the prodigal son returns."

I know things are getting back to normal when I turn around and see her.

"You mean the prodigal daughter?"

"I'm not going to stick around while the three of you fight. You were kind of a dinkus."

I shrug my shoulders. She comes over and hugs me. "But seriously, are you okay?"

"I was until you got all PDA on me." I joke, but it really does feel good to know she cares about my well-being.

She doesn't let go and squeezes tighter, scrunching up her face. "But your my widdy-biddy baby brudder!" I feign vomiting and then decide to play her game.

I clutch her tight and sway her side to side. "Oh, thank you, my big sissy-wissy."

She shrieks with laughter, trying to get out of my big bear hug. We almost fall over with our shenanigans. We turn and see Mom standing at my doorway.

"You two are so very weird." We pull her into the mix and she can't help but giggle as she tries to push us away. "Stop it, you two," she shouts between hysteric breaths.

I let them go and Heather and I crack up as Mom tries to gain her composure.

I enjoy the moment. I feel like I haven't laughed in forever.

57

Dad's food is amazing.

I savour the chili and sop up the leftover sauce with the bread. I don't think I've ever enjoyed Dad's cooking so much and I tell him. I'm certain the unspoken truth at the table is that everything that happened in the last week has given me a refreshed outlook on life. Yet, I could care less about coming through a tragedy, because I'm not worrying what might happen or thinking about what horrible things people can do to each other. I'm enjoying the good things I have in the present.

After we're finished, I offer to clean up the dishes but Mom and Dad send me upstairs to do homework. Knowing the stack of assignments I've got to catch up on is waiting, I reluctantly oblige. I don't want to do any of it, but it's got to get done and there's no way out of it. I drag myself up the stairs and sit down at my desk.

I flip through my assignments and choose biology since I skipped Mr. Harriet's test on Monday. He's giving me a take home test that's twice as long, and I figure working on it might prompt some goodwill. It takes me until almost 7:30. Once I'm done, I put it to the side and open up psychology. I have six chapters of reading and questions to get through and I want to get it done before bed.

As I work, my phone vibrates and I do a quick check. All the usual faces except for one—Charlie. For a brief moment, I wonder what has happened to him. Did he really get himself thrown in jail, and if so, why? I dismiss it quickly and go back to reading about developmental psychology, working my way from childhood to old age.

I surprise myself and get done before ten and get ready for bed. The house is quiet and dark when I wander down to grab a glass of water. Mom and Dad are sitting in the den watching a movie. I say goodnight before heading back upstairs.

I shut the door to my room and climb into bed. If I'm going to show up to practice tomorrow before school, I'll need my rest. I crack open *Animal Farm* and read but can barely keep my eyes open after the first few pages. I set the book down, turn the light off, and fall asleep.

58

I leave the house the next morning and arrive at practice early. The doors are open but the gym is empty. I grab a ball from the supply closet and bounce it, listening to the *thunk-thunk-thunk* echoing in the cavernous space of the room, building my willingness to give into the energy of the space. I pass the ball between my left and right hand, shifting back and forth, building speed, my shoes digging into the court, the rubber squeaking each time I alter course. My eyes are on the hoop and I dig in, knees bending, muscles tightening, until I power into a jump and feel the ribbed, leather surface of the ball solidly in my grip. I roll it off my fingers, ignoring the backdrop, slamming it home. I land rock-hard and it feels good. I feel like I'm me again. I've missed this.

That is, until Coach and the rest of the guys show up and drills begin. By the halfway point, I feel like I've been away from this for a month and I'm dragging behind everyone else.

Mike dashes beside me, chuckling, "Too many bacon burgers on your time off?"

I wipe the sweat from my eyes, ready to argue, but I choke on my breath, which only leads to further razzing. I let him have this moment to gloat. I know myself and it won't take me long to get back in shape. Then Mike will be dodging me and my smart ass comments.

At the end of the hour and a half, I'm done and ready to fall over. My muscles are worn out, I'm soaked with sweat, and I'm only now catching my breath. Yet, I feel alive. The rush is comforting and familiar. I'm grateful I got up early to be here. I'm even grateful for Mike's verbal abuse.

In the locker room, we get ready quickly and head to first period. Mike suggests plans for lunch. He wants to go to the new sandwich place because there's *another* girl, Haley, that he likes.

I roll my eyes. "Wingman extraordinaire. You'd never get anywhere without me."

"You wish." He raises his arm to flex his bicep. "It has nothing to do with you. It's all this." He kisses his muscle. "Who can say no to this?"

I gag and he laughs as he heads away down the hall. Somehow I find myself agreeing to tag along.

I reach biology class and grab a chair just as the bell rings. I make sure my phone is off and tucked away because Mr. Harriet hates distractions. He was good to give me a break on the test, but he's all about order and having things done a certain way. He expects our notes to follow his rules and if we don't, we lose marks. Yet, I force myself to focus not only because I have to, but because I want to.

Ms. Statten's psychology class is perfect for the next step of the day. I arrive early, before the bell rings. The lights are dim, the vibe in the room is quiet, and the projector isn't on yet. I head to her desk.

"Anthony?"

"Hi, Ms. Statten. My missing assignments."

She smiles, taking her glasses out of her hair and putting them on—the guys in my class love this look. She glances down at the small stack of papers I'm holding.

"Thank you, but I'll be taking late marks."

I nod. "That's fair, Ms. Statten." She always says she's preparing us for what's to come after high school, and she keeps her standards high and rigid. I respect that, but I also feel gratitude. I love that she doesn't feel sorry for me, that there are no favors here. Her principles are upheld no matter what and it makes me feel totally normal.

She takes the papers from me and I have a seat. The projector goes on and note-taking begins. Before I know it, the bell goes. It's been another productive hour and even the last class of the morning—chemistry—flashes by. By the end of it, Mr. James has helped me understand mole calculations and I'm feeling almost caught up. That swamp of work I had getting back into things is less consuming, and what I have left to do from these morning classes seems manageable.

59

As I exit the student parking lot doors, I reach for my phone out of habit but tuck it quickly back in my pocket without looking. I want disengagement from the digital world and let myself be present here, now, on this beautiful, warm fall day.

Honk—I look around. It's Mike and he's in a hurry. His arm hangs out of his small, red rust bucket, his over-amped stereo pumping. I guess this sandwich date's got him worked up. I slowly jog up to the truck, feigning to rush over.

"Sorry, man. Just getting more homework in."

"Get in! I've got important things to do."

I hop in. "Like getting the number of this girl, Haley?"

"Hell, yeah!" He kicks up gravel as he peels out of the student parking lot. It's not possible to look more desperate than he does right now, but I like his enthusiasm. I laugh.

"Easy, tiger."

He looks at me and turns up his stereo even louder.

I shake my head and yell over the noise, "Man, you've got a lot of work to do on your style."

He reaches for the volume again and I swat his hand away, surrendering with laughter to his crappy listening choices.

60

We walk into the food court at the mall. I stand behind him while he looks for the new sandwich joint.

"There it is."

He scans the crowd and smiles. "And there *she* is."

I look across from the sandwich shop and among all of the people, there's Mike's new dream girl, Haley, sitting with another friend.

Mike beelines it through the food court. He stops abruptly and then turns to get some food. He orders two drinks, two sandwiches with the works, and two cookies. I hope he's buying.

"No sauce," I chime in as the sandwich is made.

I watch as Mike shifts his weight from left to right—he's nervous. It's pathetic and brave all at once. He has the tray in his hand but hesitates. I look at him and then at Haley and grab the tray.

"Follow me." I meander through the crowd and plunk down beside the girls. "Ladies, two free cookies in exchange for two seats? Or a chance to meet two interesting guys?"

Haley replies, "You can just have the seats."

She doesn't want to talk but I'm feeling confident. "Thank God! Because my friend and I, well, we're really stunted in the conversation department. Really, our goal is to try and speak in complete sentences."

Both girls laugh. The ice is broken.

I hold up my cookie. "You wanted a bite of my mocha chocolate chip cookie?"

Haley shakes her head no.

"Your loss." I take a bite, pretending to savour its flavour. The table laughs again and I know they're warming up to us.

Mike and I banter back and forth with the girls, laughing and being ridiculous. It feels good—real and distracting—that is until I realize the time. "Crap! We've got to go. Ladies, nice to meet you both. We'll have to do this again sometime."

We depart to make it back to afternoon classes. As Mike and I head for the car, I ask, "Did you get her number?"

"No."

"Why the hell not? I thought that was the point."

"Uh, no. The point was to work on my game—and I got it, game that is."

"Like how you got the movie theatre girl's number?"

He scowls, "Listen, I like Haley, but I need to make sure I *like* her before every other lady loses out on this fine piece of man."

I burst out in a big laugh in the parking lot.

"Every other lady? There are that many?"

He glares. "Shut up."

I climb into the car, happy with my day.

61

The afternoon goes as quickly as the morning, and before I know it, I'm sitting in my fifth class, the last period of the day. The intercom crackles and a heavy jolt kicks me in the stomach.

"This is a reminder from Mrs. Tavler to all students of the drivers ed program: tomorrow is the final chance to submit permission forms for in-car instruction. If you don't get them handed in, you will miss your session and not continue on." The intercom clicks off. With that, I feel relief as the heavy feeling dissolves.

The bell rings and I head to my locker. Tonight will be another night dedicated to homework and catching up. I pile the books I need into my bag and sling it—oof, too heavy—over my chest. I move outside and the air is cool, so I pull my hoodie over my head and walk home.

Mom and Dad have supper figured out, as well as some of my time. They get me to walk Ollie, take the garbage out, carry some donation boxes to the front step, and bag some leaves. I don't complain. It's their way of keeping things real, and keeping me busy and distracted.

Heather joins us for supper. Her mid-terms are done. She's completely relaxed "for a day or two."

Afterwards, I negotiate to do my homework in lieu of dishes, since I've already done a bunch of chores. Heather empathizes and volunteers.

I beeline upstairs and close my door, shutting out the noises of the kitchen. I pull the heavy books and binders out of my bag and stack them on my desk. I'm ready for another mini-marathon of homework and I don't mind. Being in top shape mentally is as important as it is physically. I stay up until 10:30 finishing the last of my homework and then head to bed. I lie there, peacefully, eyes closed, the tension of my high school responsibilities slipping away as I drift into a pleasant coma of sleep.

62

It's Friday and the end of a long week.

I wake and head downstairs to the kitchen where Dad's pouring coffee. Ollie barks a friendly hello.

Dad shushes him. "Heather's still sleeping, Ollie. Be nice."

I grab a bowl of Sticky Nut and Raisin Os and grab a seat. Ollie moves over and sits on my foot for his morning pet.

"How'd you sleep?"

"Really good."

"You look rested."

"I feel rested. Where's Mom?"

"Already gone for the day. Big game coming up?"

"Not until next week."

"Think you'll win?"

I know what he's up to—settling us back into the routine—so I go with it. "Hope so."

He smiles and pats me on the back in a fatherly way and heads off to work. I take my bowl to the sink and head upstairs.

I glance down at my phone—plans are already underway. Mike's found a party that Haley's going to be at. Paul and Jessica send separate texts letting me know their plans. A couple of guys from the basketball team check in to see if I want to go to a show. I figure my plans will shake out in the end and I'll do what I'm supposed to, so I put the phone down.

I get to school and the day flies by. The last bell rings and we're released, gushing out the doors, flooding into the streets, mentally escaping a week of drudgery. I am more or less caught up and see this weekend as a breath of fresh air.

As I walk home, I feel the phone buzzing in my pocket. I'm sure some study somewhere says this is going to cause penis cancer in the future, but I keep the phone in my pocket anyhow. I check—looks like plans are falling into place and people want me to make some decisions, but I feel no urgency.

Back in my freshman year, a teacher always said, "If you're cool, they'll wait for you," when we herded at the door at the end of his class. I've always thought it was a good mantra.

I ignore the messages for now.

First home, then supper.

63

When we're done supper, I get up and put my arms around Mom and Dad. "You two have a date night?"

Mom giggles. "Maybe? Why? You want us out of your hair?"

"No, I just figure you deserve one. I'll do the dishes and then I'm heading out, probably with Mike. I may meet up with Jessie and Paul. Not sure."

Mom looks at Dad, and I can see the relief in their faces. It feels like everything is back to normal for the most part, but she gives me the look.

I laugh, "Yeah. Yeah. I'll let you know when I know for sure. Sound good?"

She takes her wine glass and looks at Dad, smiling. "So what are we going to do?"

Dad checks his watch. "How long are you going to be gone?"

"Dad, seriously? Gross!" My reaction is just for show—I'm happy my parents love each other and show it.

They leave the kitchen, wine in hand, laughing. I quickly clear the dishes, jamming them into the dishwasher. By the time I'm wiping the table, I hear the familiar sound of Mike's arrival—*hooooooonk*. I race upstairs, give myself a shot of cologne, and rush out to his car. "What's your hurry? We've got all night."

"You, maybe, but me? Not so much. Word is Haley's at PJ's with a couple others from her school and then they're headed to a farm party."

I send a text to Paul and tell him what I'm doing and that he and Jess are welcome to join. I have a feeling they will.

We get to the restaurant and check the place out. There's a couple of Mike's friends from a different school. He questions them on Haley and her friends. They were there and are headed to the farm party just west of town around 10:00. That gives us some time to kill. Mike has a few drinks that he buys with a fake ID, no doubt trying to calm his nervousness over seeing Haley. We eat pizza and play a game of pool. I let him kick my ass and he gloats, but I let him have that too. After a couple of hours, it's time to get to the party, so we head outside.

I have Mike's keys and we climb into his truck. He turns on some crappy early 2000s rock and roll and grins.

I look over at him. "I'd say something—"

"But you're too much of a nice guy?"

Sometimes the wingman's job can be a drag, but tonight it feels worth it.

The radio DJ announces the next song and it's Tom Petty's "I Won't Back Down." My smile fades. I haven't given Charlie a thought in these past few days of blissful normalcy. He just told me to be with my people and faded out of my life. I haven't re-ceived one message from him—nothing—and I feel unsettled. I look over and see Mike sitting in the passenger's seat singing along but it's not the same.

Where is he? Where did he go? Is he in trouble? Is he in jail? I feel a strange urge to text him. I talk myself out of it, shaking off this bad feeling, reassuring myself that there has to be a reasonable explanation. If anyone can dodge a bullet, it's Charlie Wolfe.

To distract myself, I change the channel. Mike looks annoyed until he realizes it's now Lynyrd Skynyrd's "Sweet Home Alabama," and he rolls with it like a distracted puppy as we carry on down the country road.

We pull up to the farmhouse. The yard is full of cars and a bonfire burns high. Mike races off looking for Haley, and by the time I'm mingling with the crowd of people, I've nearly forgotten about Charlie.

64

I'm face down in my pillow and my eyes are still closed because the light is too bright in my room. My head pounds ferociously, in a rhythm I don't like. I drag myself up and wipe the drool—gross—off my cheek. I have my clothes on from last night. My phone is gripped in my hand. I tap to turn it on but the battery is dead.

I swing my legs off the edge of the bed. My ears start to ring and I'm dizzy. This is terrible. What happened last night? I reach into my jacket and take out my wallet. Well, at least I wasn't robbed. That's something.

"So much for you listening to my advice."

I look over. "Charlie?"

He sits at my desk chair, staring at me.

"What are you doing here?"

"Gekas wouldn't let me stay in her jail anymore."

"No, I mean, what are you doing *here*? In my bedroom?" Then I realize what he just said.

"What? Wait! You were in jail? That's horrible." He shrugs, like it's no big deal. "Were you in the drunk tank or cells?"

"Temporary holding." He looks at some papers on my desk, unconcerned as I try to imagine what his night was like.

"Were you alone? Were you with criminals? Were you scared of getting the shit kicked out of you?"

He's ignoring me, still reading whatever is on my desk.

"Charlie!"

He looks at me and sighs, "Fine. Your folks are off at the Farmer's Market and I let myself in."

"You broke in?"

"No, I figured out where you keep the spare key."

"We don't have one.

"How can you not have a spare key? What happens if you get locked out?" He stares at me blankly and I don't break. "Yes, fine, I broke in. Happy?"

"You need to get out. Now."

He stands and pauses at the door. "Out of your room? Or your house?"

"Out."

He tosses his hands up, as if him standing here is no big deal, before leaving the room.

After that start to the day, I'm awake—really awake—but I want to resist getting out of bed, worried what I'll find next. However, I drag myself out of bed, throw on some clothes, and assume Charlie isn't done with me.

Sure enough, by the time I get downstairs, there's a bowl of cereal on the counter and he's finished brewing himself a pot of coffee.

"These are nice beans. Is this your Mom or Dad's thing?"

I assume now that he's back in my life, there's

no getting rid of him. "Dad's."

He smells the brew. "Nice. We don't get this in the trailer park."

I never really considered where he might live, and yet I question whether he's telling the truth or dramatizing.

"Charlie, what are you doing here?"

"I told you—Gekas kicked me out of jail."

"Seriously?"

"Yeah. She questioned my motivation. Thought I was doing it on purpose. Can you believe that?"

"Yeah, I can believe that, because the last time I saw you, you said you were going to get yourself thrown in jail!"

"I did? Hmm…"

"How?"

"What? Get sent to lockup? After I saw you, I went to the closest convenience store, walked over to the candy bars, took one—a Ziggernut, if you must know—made sure the clerk was watching, opened it and ate it. When he just threatened me, I walked out of the store and sat on the step. He still didn't call the cops on me, so I went back and got myself an energy drink, which was a bad choice for a night in jail, and went back outside."

I stare at him in disbelief. "Why?"

"For an alibi. Why else?"

"From what?"

"From the murders, man. Aren't you keeping up with our investigation, at all?"

I don't usually have the urge to cuff someone in the head, but I sure feel like doing it now.

"Anyway, it's a minor offence. I admitted to it

and they kept me for the night."

"But then, that means you were out on Wednesday."

"Yeah, so I go back out and had to do it again, which really sucks, because I had to really commit myself the second time."

"Why?"

"Well, my old buddies from the jail the night before couldn't figure out who'd be so stupid to steal a chocolate bar and drink, except someone planted by the cops. They thought they should stick a shiv in me and let me be an example."

"How'd you get out of it?"

Charlie sits at the counter digging his spoon into the very large bowl of cereal and crunching away. I wait patiently for him to swallow.

"Stayed awake for most of it. I couldn't convince them I wasn't a rat. At some point, I started thinking I should let them cut me and if I survived, I'd be in the hospital. The thought of risking an infection or bleeding out kept running through my mind, though, so I decided to wait them out instead."

He's seems to be really enjoying his healthy granola crunch. He adds some more soy milk to it. I shake my head, but I try to look expressionless. He carries on.

"And you went back in?"

He nods. "I went back in, scared I wasn't going to sleep again but the second night was easier. Mostly drunks and druggies. There was a guy who was coming off something bad with some mental health issues, but he was in a cell at the far end."

"By Friday night, Gekas was on to me and

wouldn't let me stay. I found the nearest all-night restaurant and just waited the night out."

This is really unbelievable.

His spoon hits the bottom of the bowl—*clink*—and he moves to the cupboards, looking for mugs. I point and he pulls down two cups, pours us coffee, and hands me one.

My head still pounds and the first sip seems to ease the pain. "So, why are you here now, Charlie?"

"Haven't you heard?"

65

Charlie pulls out his phone and scrolls to a news site. On the front page: "Second teenager found dead. One still missing."

"Shit."

He takes his phone back. "I know, right?"

He doesn't seem sincere.

"Did you see where they found her?"

He sounds excited and it bothers me, but before I can say anything, he grabs the map out of his back pocket and unfolds it. He lays it out on the kitchen counter and points. "Right here—Lone Pine Mall."

I realize it is one of the places, along with the schools in the northwest part of the city, that he pointed out. "You were—"

"Right? I know. Get used to it."

His cockiness again—

"I read this guy. Best of all, we've got him."

"What do you mean?"

A grin spreads across Charlie's face. "After I left you at the stadium, I kept building my map, figuring it out. I saw what looked like a pattern. I knew I could take a gamble and try and get there before him and set a trap."

I don't say anything—I don't want to encourage his enthusiasm.

"I pulled some trail cameras—you know, the type hunters use—and duct taped them in the bathrooms—"

"You what?"

"Chill, we're not being pervy peepers—"

"But that goes against all sorts of people's privacy—"

"Yeah, yeah. Moral, ethical, blah, blah…"

I get in his face. "Charlie, a girl died. You get that, right? Someone's daughter, sister, friend…and girlfriend. Not just once, but three times. So you cut this shit about it being a game and acting like we are some boy detectives. Because we aren't. We're nothing like that. Sheri died, then Maggie, and now this girl, by some weirdo who has some sick ideas about women. So, cut it out, okay?"

He's quiet. He's never quiet. He doesn't move, but he sinks a bit in his seat. I wait until he says something.

"Okay."

That's all he's got. *Okay.* I don't move, inches from his nose.

"Tony—?"

"What?" I snap, realizing he's never used my first name before.

"Let's get this guy."

66

Charlie and I are in Dad's car, heading to the northwest end. My head still pounds from my bad choices the night before. The coffee and the pain relievers haven't helped, so I've got the music on low. It's some vocal pop guy singing about love and loneliness and being far from his girl. I try not to latch on to it, but it's hard not to be affected in this moment. The whole thing with Charlie is bad business, and I don't like digging up the dead for clues. The past three days of peace have been wiped away by his presence and me yelling at him didn't help. I don't feel bad about it, because he was acting like a jerk.

"You don't think I care, but I do," says Charlie as he stares out the window. "Sheri was a good person who didn't deserve to die. I didn't know Maggie or this other girl, but I'm sure they were decent people."

He's quiet for a moment and I think he's done, but he continues, "But they're strangers. I have absolutely no connection. Sheri was nice to me in school. She didn't whisper behind people's backs, she wasn't a snarky bitch. But we were from different worlds and we didn't mix. I don't know how to feel sad about people I don't know."

"Then why do you do this?"

"Because you've got a problem that needs solving."

I look over at him. "That's it? Really?"

"For now, sure. That works for me." That answer is not good enough for me.

"Charlie, did something like this happen to someone you knew?"

He watches out the window and then opens up his phone and flips through apps. He leans over to show me his screen. "This new girl's name is Bonnie McCallum. She lived in the neighbourhood, went to the Catholic school there. She had a night shift at the Citrus Shack, which stayed open late to catch the late night movie crowd. She was supposed to close with another girl but disappeared at the end of the night. The other girl looked for her, thought she flaked out, and went home. She didn't think anything of it until Bonnie showed up in a dumpster behind the mall."

Nothing—that's all he gives me, something about the victim. Whatever's going on in that head of his, whatever past he's hiding, he's locked it away and shoved it deep down, never allowing it to the surface. I know pushing him won't help, so I focus on what's ahead. "What's your grand plan?"

"We get to the mall. I think Gekas will start clueing into what's going on soon enough. Too much has been happening around bathrooms for her not to search them. We'll have to get there quick, then get in and get out. The place will be busy, but they'll be looking around the Citrus Shack, points of entry, and all points in between the store and the dumpster. I'm hoping the place isn't on full lockdown and some of the stores are still open. That way, you won't look conspicuous."

"Wait— Me?"

"Yeah. If I'm sighted at the last place Bonnie was seen, it'll start looking weird. Almost 30 percent of killers return to the scene of the crime."

"Where do you get this stuff?"

He ignores me. "If I show up again, they'll probably pick up on it. Crime scene photographers are documenting the crowd half the time, just in case they get a guy who likes to revisit his handy work."

"Again, how do you know?"

"Come on. You do realize there is a thing call a com-pu-ter, right?

I give him a look to stop messing with me.

"Oh right, you're going to get all up in my face again." He grins, happy to get a reaction out of me. "It's good to see you growing."

He's edging towards being an asshole again. "Charlie—"

"No, I mean it. The sooner we face what this person does, who he is, the sooner we quit fooling ourselves and stop him from doing it to someone else."

I stare at him in dismay. Of all the things I think he'll surprise me with, sincerity is the least I expected.

67

We pull up in front of the mall and, of course, it's surrounded with police cars and news vans.

"Here we go again," I say out loud, not on purpose: it just comes out. Charlie looks straight ahead, acknowledging what I have just said.

"Yup."

"So I just walk in there…and?" I feel mentally stunted that I can't keep up with Charlie's process.

"Yup." We sit in silence for a long time. I really think he's going to answer my question because I'm not sure what to do, yet the silence drags on a little longer than I'd like.

"And…?" I repeat still staring ahead at all the vehicles and officials and officers that stand in our way.

"Go," he instructs. I put the car into drive and go away from the mall.

"Where am I going?" Charlie gestures without saying a word. I drive forward slowly. He points to a small street nearby and I turn.

"Park."

I pull over to the curb and park the car. The action is now behind us. I glance in the rearview mirror. No one is in a panic but I see consistent movement among the cruisers of uniformed and civilian dressed people. I don't feel as calm as they all look.

"When a burglar is about to break into your house, you know what he does?" Charlie finally speaks.

"I have no idea, Charlie."

"He finds a place he likes. One that looks nice. Curb appeal. Something worth entering. Then he parks a block or two away.

"Yeah." I'm wondering what his point is but he always seems to have one, so I give him time.

"Then he walks right up to the front door and rings the bell. Just like that. He's all full of balls and rings the bell. And if someone comes to the door he just makes something up like he's lost or looking for so and so, or selling something. Pretty good huh?"

I glance up at the rearview mirror.

"We can't ring the front doorbell at this place. They'll know we're not selling cookies," I add.

"If no one answers, then he goes around back and tries the back door, or the window or the garage. They don't care about alarms. Neighbours ignore those. Cops don't get there in enough time."

I look at him hoping I will be less confused in a moment or two.

"Ever locked yourself out of your house?"

I nod.

"Well, how many ways can you think of to get in without a key?"

He waits and I realize he actually expects me to come up with an answer, so I go through the options I've considered every time I've lost my key.

He asks again, "How many?"

"Three."

"Times three."

"Pardon?"

"If you know three ways to get into your house without using your key, then a burglar knows nine. Into your own house!"

He sounds so impressed, but I don't want to know how he knows this information. I really hope it's from the internet.

"They walk in and do a sweep in around eight minutes. They get what they need and walk out calmly through the front door to their car. It's pretty seamless."

"Thank you, Charlie Wolfe, for that mini lesson on B & E's. What's your point?"

Charlie smiles. "You're in and out in eight minutes."

I cock my head trying to understand what he just said. "Sorry. I'm what?"

"You're going into the mall, through the backdoor, getting what we need, and getting out."

My eyes widen and I realize what Charlie is telling me to do. He sees my expression. My brain flashes an uncontrollable fast-forward to a night in jail with some druggie with mental illness or Charlie's buddy from the gang, and then it jumps to my parents paying bail. None of these are good options.

"Don't panic. You've done this before."

I give him a look.

"My school, remember? You're a pro. And you're better at it than you think, Uptown Boy." He pats me on the back. It feels both patronizing and reassuring.

"Remember, there is more than one way into

every single place."

Charlie unbuckles his seatbelt and gets out of the car. I shut the car off and follow. We walk a little further down a side street, out of view from the scene at the mall.

"I don't believe the entire place will be shut down. I think they'll have police caution tape to keep people away unless they find something solid." Charlie walks beside me. We turn a corner and head back towards the mall, but from this street I see we're coming up along the back where deliveries are made.

"We'll just hang out here for a bit. Something will come to us."

Charlie is so certain. I admire that about him. I don't know his life or what it looks like but he puts such an optimistic spin on everything, even this—even jail. He feels some opportunity will present itself. How does he know? Is it from practice or is it simply patience? I'm not sure he'd be able to tell me if I pressed him for an answer.

"When the opportunity comes, go inside. Go in like you're supposed to be there. Like you work there or you own the place. Go to the bathroom, not the one near the food court but the one away from the main square, down the hall by the music store. Walk straight in."

I listen and then it occurs to me. "Wait, you want me to go into the women's bathroom?"

"Yes."

"Charlie, I'm not sure if you noticed, I'm a six foot tall dude."

Charlie lifts his sunglasses over his head to hold

back his hair and looks me up and down. "Oh, I noticed." He puckers a kiss and smiles.

"Man, how can you be joking, right now?"

"Look, if you act like you're supposed to be there nobody actually notices you. If you act nervous and out of place, and—well, like you—people see that kind of energy."

"What if someone catches me?"

Charlie tilts his head. I can feel his annoyance. "Wow, man, do we have work to do." I know he's thinking that I'll never be a part of his world, that he and I are in completely separate time zones.

"If someone walks in on you, apologize and act embarrassed. Swear, act stupid—that'll be easy— and ask where the right washroom is, then leave. People make mistakes all the time."

It makes sense, but my brain panics, worrying about police asking me what I'm doing.

"Stop thinking. Go in and get out. Once you have what you need, you can stop by the deli and get me a Italian classic."

I look at him. "What?"

"It gives you an excuse. You're there buying a sandwich."

I give him a second look.

"Oh, and no sauce."

I shake my head. Besides trying to figure out what happened to Sheri, no sauce might be the only other thing we have in common.

"You're something else, Charlie Wolfe."

I run through the scenario in my head, visualizing it like Coach gets us to do with plays, while we hang out in silence. Sure enough, a back utility door swings open moments later. I tap Charlie's shoulder.

Charlie looks towards the door. "There."

"Should I go?"

"Wait."

We watch as a woman exits with a cart full of garbage. She props the door open so that it doesn't slam shut behind her.

"Nice. Business as usual. Some things keep going no matter what." He looks over at me. "When you think it's right, get up and walk in."

That's all he says. Nothing specific. It's all up to me now. I feel my heartbeat speed up as I watch the woman pushing the cart over to the large bin. I get up and cross directly to where she works.

She's almost done and I'm thinking I won't make it, when I hear a phone ring. My breath catches for a second until I realize it's her phone. As she turns and answers, I speed up and walk right behind her and through the back door of the mall.

68

The hallway stinks from piled up garbage that hasn't made it to the bin. I hold my breath as I move to the end of the hall before exiting to the mall courtyard.

There is a police presence on the one side. The Citrus Shack has barriers around its front, with an officer to keep people moving along. I look over briefly to see if Gekas is around, but I don't see her. I keep moving, putting space between me and the law. As I move into the retail area, I slip behind a lottery kiosk to obscure my view.

The stores are open. There are a few customers and I do my best to become one. I walk, trying to window shop, but it feels awkward and forced. I think about what I would normally be doing when I come to the mall and my mind goes blank. I decide that if I wanted something, I would go directly to it, so I head towards the music store.

I step inside and see two employees working the early morning shift busy stacking shelves. I force myself over to a bin of two-for-one movies and flip through it.

"Can I help you?"

Shit! I look over and see one of the workers looking at me. My head spins, trying to remember what I would normally say in a moment like this. "Uh, nope. Good." I'm happy I almost got a complete sentence out.

"Well, let me know if you need anything."

I nod and force a smile and move around the bin, so my back is to them. I work the next step through my head, trying to imagine myself getting into the women's bathroom. Coach would be so proud that I'm using his visualization exercises—but to what end?

I step out of the music store and move around the corner to the other set of washrooms. My head is no longer pounding—my heart is outplaying it. No one is down this hall. On the right is the men's washroom and on the left is the women's. It hasn't been taped off yet. Charlie is one step ahead. Again.

I walk to the door. This is a really bad idea—no, dammit, this is a good idea—for Sheri. I listen for a split second.

I hear nothing. Good. I walk inside.

69

There are eight stalls in a row and a very long counter with four sinks. Two hand dryers are on the wall beside me. I realize I'm frozen in place and I force myself to move.

I kneel down under the first sink and look. Nothing. The twists and turns of plumbing and the dark underbelly of the countertop offer plenty of places to hide the camera. I realize I'll have to check every sink. Why didn't I ask Charlie where it would be?

I move over and look under the next sink. Nothing.

I hear a shuffle of feet behind me and I freeze. I realize there's someone in the washroom and see a pair of black heeled feet at the end of the row of stalls. Dammit, what if she comes out and finds me here. My nerves shake. I've got until she decides she's done. The motivational voice inside my head is solid, and I propel myself to finish what I came to do.

I squat at the third sink, feel around, and then move to the last one.

There! A piece of duct tape hangs down and I pull on it, but there's no camera. My heart speeds up even more. This is worse than the final minutes of a tied game. I look underneath and see nothing. The toilet flushes behind me—shit!—I move. I hear the stall door unlock as I exit the washroom and move down the hall to lose myself amidst the shoppers.

70

The whole thing is a bust. Some cleaner or maintenance worker must have found the camera and yanked it out. Hell, they probably have a security camera of their own, waiting to find the sicko who taped it there. With everything going on around here, they'll see me going in and think I'm the perv. Or, worse yet, they'll make connections and think I'm the one who killed Bonnie.

I'm pissed off at Charlie for getting me into this mess. The whole thing was a disaster from the beginning. I reflect on the past few days, how nice it was to get back to a normal life, and how quickly Charlie has turned my life upside down all over again.

Suddenly, I feel the piece of duct tape in my pocket—something hard and thin, like a small MP3 player, is stuck inside. I peel back the adhesive and find a small SD memory card embedded in the tape.

I exhale. It feels like the first breath I've taken since I walked into the mall.

My mind races.

Somebody left it for us—no, the killer did. My heart skips a beat—he knows about us. But also—Charlie found him.

No matter what I think of Charlie, no matter

what sort of stuff he gets me into, he did it. He found the killer.

I pull the duct tape off the memory card and slip it into my pocket. My heartbeat falls back into a normal rhythm, something my body is more used to.

I walk to the grocery store deli and order an Italian classic because today my man Charlie deserves a sub, with no sauce.

The man behind the counter assembles it as the radio plays "The Kid's Aren't Alright." I smile.

"Anything else for you today?"

You have no idea, mister.

71

I walk out of the mall after paying for the sub, a sports drink, and a couple of bananas. I head down the street away from the police, Gekas, and the crime scene.

I plan my route back to where Charlie and I started and I notice I'm not worrying about how I'm acting. I've moved into my natural nonchalant swing. I still feel the rush of the moment, but the remnants of adrenaline that had me shaking have burned off the last bits of my hangover. I'm not sure if it was the experience of cutting it so close to getting caught or breaking the law, but either way, I'm feeling something very new.

I walk around back and Charlie's nowhere in sight. Now, where the hell is he? I feel a little kick in the gut.

I move to the edge of the parking lot and scan the entire place and can't see him. What am I supposed to do now? What do I do with this memory card? I sigh and walk back to where I parked the car.

The Saturday morning streets are still quiet. The buzz I'm rolling with is gone and my hangover is coming back. A few hours with Charlie equals one bad night of drinking.

He sits on the curb by the car.

"Hey," he says casually.

"Hey?" I question.

"What took you so long?"

I throw the bag with the sandwich at him as hard as I can.

He catches it. "Easy, man."

"Why'd you leave?"

"There was just too much action. It was better over here and I knew you'd find me."

His answer doesn't make me less angry. "Come on. Let's get out of here."

Charlie unrolls the paper wrap around his sandwich. "No sauce, right?"

I shoot him a look over the vehicle.

"Okay, okay. Gee wiz, dude." He takes a big bite and nods approvingly.

"Did you get the camera?"

"Sort of. It wasn't there."

"What?"

"The only thing was this." I hold up the memory card.

"Where was that?"

"Stuck to the tape, under the sink."

Charlie gets that distant look on his face and a smile crosses it. "Looks like someone wants us to come out and play."

I grin because for the first time since I've met him we're on the same page.

72

Charlie digs into his backpack and pulls out a card reader and plugs it into his smartphone. I wonder what other sorts of spy toys he's got hidden in there. I also wonder how much of it he actually bought.

The card loads and thumbnails pop up. They're small and hard to see.

"Once it transfers over, we can look at it as stills or time-lapse."

I realize what I'm about to see and the idea of watching something horrible happen to this girl is too much for me. The excitement of catching this guy melts away. "Wait. If he knows about the camera, how do we know we'll see who this guy is?"

Charlie watches each image appear. "Yeah, he's probably onto us. But I'm hoping he'll screw up and leave us something we can follow."

I feel our lead on the murderer slipping. His phone signals that loading is complete.

Charlie scrolls to the start and pushes play.

A view of the bathroom pops up, the top eighth of the screen cut off by the sink cabinet. At the bottom is a date and time stamp that begins on Tuesday evening after Charlie left me at the stadium. Nothing happens on the screen for a while. Legs zip back and forth across the bottom of the screen and the lights wink on and off, yet even in the dark the stall and floors are illuminated.

"See that? Night-vision. That feature costs extra."

"You bought all these in a store?

"Pshh—no. It needed to be liberated from stores." My suspicion is confirmed, but I feel he may have said it just to mess with me.

The time-stamp skips forward another day. Women's feet shuffle across the screen and the lights flick off periodically. Nothing out of the ordinary. I know we should speed ahead to the time the attack likely occurred, but I'm tense, keeping an eye on the time, waiting uncomfortably as it moves towards yesterday. Charlie's sandwich rests on his lap as he waits. When it switches over to Friday, we both sit quietly, watching the screen. The clock zips past noon, then three, then six.

"Soon," Charlie says quietly.

I look at him, expecting anticipation, but am surprised to see sadness. On the screen, there are more feet, then something on the floor, then the image freezes on an empty room.

I'm confused. "What happened?"

Charlie taps the rewind button step by step until he and I are staring at the swollen, red face of a girl that I assume is Bonnie McCallum. I never knew what to expect, but it wasn't this. Tears running down her face, ruining her makeup, her eyes wide, but relaxed, her face calm. I realize it's because she's already dead.

Charlie doesn't reverse it immediately and I

look away, staring out the window. A man rakes leaves across the street. A pink bike lies in the driveway. All of these ordinary things in front of me make me feel sick at seeing poor Bonnie.

"He's choking them."

I look back at Charlie.

"It looks like a piece of cloth or fabric. I can't get a good look." He's tapping the image backwards and forwards and I'm not in the mood to watch. Our sensationalized world has not desensitized me.

"Dammit, there's only a few images." He must realize what he's said, because he continues, "It's hard to see him." He turns his phone to me, but I refuse to watch.

"There's this one of her, post-mortem." Sometimes I wonder if he really thinks he's a crime scene investigator. "Then, this one, but her body's turned around and he's kneeling. Then, here are her feet and his knees and hands. Then, him standing behind her. The last one is her feet, standing at the sink."

He's quiet. I look over at him, and he's studying the image.

"Wait. Look."

Reluctantly, I do. I see her feet—she's wearing jeans and running shoes—halfway down the sink. "What?"

He points. I don't see it.

"That's him." Then it registers—caught on the edge of the screen in the distance, are a pair of feet, standing in the stall.

"What's he doing?"

"Waiting for his prey…"

73

I stare at the pair of sneakers in the corner stall. Charlie skips the image backwards and the feet disappear. He skips forward and they reappear, and then the killer is behind her before he pulls her down. I remember back to the day at the Trails with Charlie and my mind fills in the blanks. He waited in the bathroom for Sheri, hiding in a stall until she arrived. He likely stood on the toilet seat with the door cracked open, and when she was at the sink he lowered himself down and moved up behind her. He wrapped something around her throat and choked her until—

I keep seeing Sheri staring at me, smiling, and I swear I can smell her.

Charlie interrupts the memory, "Something doesn't make sense."

"What?"

"Well, he's here behind her and he pulls her down backwards. And she struggles against it."

"So?"

He clicks it ahead to the image of her face in the camera. "How does she end up here?"

"What do you mean?"

"How does she get here. He's got her. She's on her back and he's got the full weight and force of his body wrenched against her. Unless…" He doesn't finish and starts skipping backwards through the frames. I know he may finish—maybe—but he's got to do it on his own time. He keeps flipping backwards, until he stops.

"There."

The camera is in infrared mode and in the corner stall are the splayed out feet of the killer.

"He waited in the corner like he did in the school. If he sat low enough, long enough, then maybe… maybe…" He seems to have forgotten I'm here.

"Finish your thought!" I yell.

He jumps. "Geez, Shepherd, relax." He sighs and smiles. "Maybe he saw the camera. Maybe it made some sound and he heard it. Either way, he knew we were there. And he left the SD card for us to find."

"So?"

"He's performing for us."

74

I watch the footage again, moving frame by frame, watching the steps of the action. I'm aware that I've tuned Bonnie out of the image, knowing that it helps me deal with the horror of the situation. "He did this on purpose?"

"Not the murder. He planned that long ago. But once he knew we were watching, he made sure we saw her."

"And him killing her?"

Charlie nods.

"We need to take this to Gekas."

He grabs it out of my hands quickly. "What? No way. We're not going through that again."

"You have something that could directly help her case."

"That I did illegally and you helped to retrieve. Don't forget, you're an accomplice now."

"You did all this on purpose."

"No—well, maybe—but that's not the point. We show this and they'll toss us in jail." He drops the phone into a pocket inside his jacket. He doesn't seem to notice that he's left the reader with the memory card on the console between us. I set the bag with the energy drink and bananas on top of it.

"Besides, it wouldn't help with the case. The

same reason we'd get tossed in jail is the same reason they couldn't use it. It's inadmissible evidence."

He's got a point, but it doesn't stop me from grabbing my energy drink and knocking the memory card into my other hand beside the console.

"The only good that comes out of this is we work through the other days and see if he makes an appearance and shows his face."

I think about it. "Wait. What about those time stamps? Are they accurate?"

"Yeah, of course. Why?"

"What if I call and tell Gekas to check surveillance cameras around the bathroom at those times?"

"She's going to have questions. She's going to want to know how you knew and why."

"Who cares? She knows we're snooping around. I'm sure she didn't think we'd both stop. She might say we're obstructing justice, but in the end, we're only helping her. She can't get mad about that."

"All right, Shepherd, let's go with your plan." I knew brazen disregard of the law would win him over. "Let's just hope you're right about her."

Yup, you and me both.

75

Charlie wants us to swing by the mall at the time I make the call. He hopes to see her outside and get a reaction. I think it's childish, but the fact he's doing what's right and not serving his own pride makes me go along with it. I find a spot close to the entrance where the forensic truck is parked and pull in.

I find Gekas' card in my wallet and dial. She picks up on the second ring.

"Anthony?"

I'm a little surprised she knows it's me. "Detective Gekas."

"I wondered if you'd be calling."

"Uh, really...?"

"Every time there's another attack, either you or your new friend Charles Wolfe seems to turn up."

I look over at Charlie, uneasy with all she knows. "Detective—"

"Anthony, relax. We know you aren't a part of this. I've already talked to several people that were at the party you were at, and I'm sure Charles has told you all about his adventures." She pauses, letting me process. "But, I have a feeling you haven't been listening to my advice."

"Uh, no, not really."

"You need to bring this to a stop, or else I'm going to charge you with a felony—"

I take a leap of faith with both eyes closed. "Detective Gekas, you need to check mall surveillance."

"Anthony, stop. We're doing—"

"Our guy, the one you're looking for, was in the women's bathroom by the music store last night a couple of hours before the murder."

She's silent for a beat, and then the questions start, "What do you mean *our guy*? How do you— wait, do you know what he looks like? Have you seen him?"

"No." I want to tell her about the images we have of Bonnie but it will only make it worse.

"How do you have this information?"

I know it's time to get out of this conversation but I'm not sure how.

"Anthony—?"

I see Charlie gesturing at his phone.

"Anthony—?"

I muffle the speaker and look at him. "What?"

Charlie whispers, "It's my camera. The one the killer took."

"What about it?"

"The GPS just turned on."

That's when I hang up on Gekas.

76

"Are you kidding?"

Charlie shows me the indicator on his phone.

I feel a rush. This is too much. Charlie holds the GPS to where the killer might be and I've just hung up on the lead detective on the case.

"What do we do?" I feel like it's not a dumb question and I think Charlie is thinking the exact same thing—*what do we do*?

My phone rings. Gekas again.

"No," Charlie says in a strong, non-negotiable way.

I play it in my head. She's got the training and an entire force behind her. They could catch this guy, bring him down, take him to jail. Also, it could be a trap.

Yet, we don't even know if this is the killer. How did we get here? How did we get to Charlie ducttaping stolen cameras in washrooms after finding a clue at the likely expense of contaminating two crime scenes? Oh, and there is the little matter of me withholding evidence from Gekas while also messing up another crime scene.

Or am I after something else? Do I want to be one of the guys that catch him? Am I that much of a self-absorbed ass?

Then I remember Sheri—and her smile and how it catches me off-guard when I close my eyes before I sleep. Most of it I remember, but some things, like the way her cheeks look, or the color of her hair in the sunlight, slip into a shadow in my mind. I struggle to connect it all together and hold onto it, but the more I think of it, the more it falls away.

It's been less than two weeks. Only. What happens in a month? Or a year?

The phone quits ringing and I know it's gone to voicemail. I put it down while Charlie continues to stare at the screen.

"It's the construction site."

A small breath escapes me and I look at him. "Where Maggie died?"

He nods.

I see the tent surrounding Maggie's body. I see Bonnie's dead face staring at me. I try to remember Sheri, but I just can't see her clearly enough.

I make the decision.

"Let's go."

77

I drive and Charlie navigates.

"It should take us about 15 minutes to get there." He's focused on the map on his phone.

I kick around the idea of calling Gekas again but I keep the thought rolling right out my head. With Gekas comes questions and a long sit-down in her office. We don't have time for any kind of sit-down, long or short. If he's there—and I hope he's there—this isn't the time to wait around, wasting minutes trying to explain ourselves. We need to go now and sort things out later. If we get a face, or, better yet, we get him, then we have all the time in the world to answer Gekas' questions.

The radio plays quietly but I can't recognize the song. We turn onto Lewvan Drive, leaving the residential neighbourhood behind us. We pass by the big box stores, over Ring Road, and skirt the edge of the city. Traffic gets busier. People are heading to their Saturday shopping, brunch, all the ordinary things normal people do. I think about my parents, likely down at the Farmer's Market, heading home, making lunch, maybe wondering where I am.

A plane flies over the highway, coming in from the southeast for a landing at the airport.

Yesterday, for a brief moment, I was a student

again, not the boyfriend of a missing girl—a lost girl—a dead girl.

A new thought forms: Sheri's body, dead, cold, gray, laying in dirt and worms and her eyes gazing milky white at me. I can't remember the way my girlfriend's smile looked or how her hair fell across her face but this thought, this damn thought, stays.

"Turn at these office buildings."

I follow his instructions.

"Keep going 'til you hit the edge of the city."

I nod. "Do you think he's waiting for us?" It's a legitimate question. The camera didn't end up there by itself.

"Probably."

"So, when we get there—?"

"I don't know."

"You're kidding! You don't have a plan?"

"No!" Charlie snaps. "I don't have time to run all over the city, investigating every damn crime scene!" He's still cool but this is the first time I've ever seen a sliver of nervousness.

Yet, I'm nervous too and I need some assurances. "So we don't have a plan?"

"No. No, we don't, Shepherd." He rubs his hand over his mouth, looking out the window. "We're going to play it by ear, okay?"

This doesn't assure me, but the only thing that's kept me on this course of action is that Charlie hasn't led me astray—yet.

We hit the end of the road and I take the last street. Charlie shuts the radio off, taking a deep breath in. He does a slow exhale and leans ahead in his seat, watching the construction site as we approach.

"Keep driving along here."

He watches out the window as we move past a temporary blue fence that runs along the premises. The shells of houses rise before us in different stages of assembly. New ones with siding and yards of dirt give way to plywood shells and exposed roofs followed by wooden skeletons coming up from open cement forms.

"Kay, slow along here..."

We cruise in silence, searching around the corners of buildings and empty lots, but it's the weekend, so there is no sign of anyone. No truck, no car, no person in sight. If the killer is here, he didn't drive, or if he did he did a damn good job hiding his car.

We come to the end of the road, circle around, and pull to the side. I stare out the windshield, waiting for the next move, when Charlie climbs out of the car. I undo my seatbelt and follow.

The place is quiet and there is nothing discrete about the two of us wandering around here. I look over at him. "So, in the front, like we own it?"

"Yup."

I shoot Charlie another look. Whether he got my dig or not, he doesn't care—he isn't going to hide. I sigh and lock the car door. It chirps.

If the killer is here, he knows we've arrived.

78

Charlie checks his phone.

"It's somewhere inside there, halfway down the road."

We walk across the road and across the sidewalk to a gate with a heavy chain holding it shut. A big sign—KEEP OUT—hangs above it.

"After you." Charlie gestures.

"Do you think there are guard dogs?"

"If there are, you should be extra quiet."

I bend and wiggle my frame through the space in the fence, hoping not to rattle the gate. Charlie follows and slides in much easier than I did.

We walk between the two rows of houses, in what looks to be the backyard. It's an eerie, sound-less space, and although I try to shake it off, my imagination gets the best of me. I can't help but think of the crime scene just beyond the last row of build-ings, where they found Maggie. Charlie says the killer grabbed her at school—but what if he brought her here, for some ritual or tendency that we aren't aware of. What if we are the next victims?

I'm sure whoever brought the camera out here is waiting for us, hiding in one of these buildings, waiting for us to pass. He seems to kill people at close range—the news said Maggie was strangled and we know Bonnie was—so he doesn't seem the kind who would shoot us with a gun. But, he is a killer—I'm guessing once you've done it a couple of times it doesn't really matter how you do it.

The reality starts to set in on how stupid what we are doing is. "We should call Gekas."

"Wow, Shepherd, it's a new record how long it took you to chicken out."

"It's common sense. We step out of this now, we call her, we wait, and make sure no one leaves."

"Fine, head back to the car."

He keeps walking ahead.

"I'm not leaving."

"Good."

"How can you be so indifferent about this?"

"What's he going to do? Attack us? If he's here, he's trying to figure us out as much as we are trying to figure him out. Sure, he might attack, but he likely just wants to know who he's dealing with."

"And do what?"

"Toy with us. Get inside our heads. Then, maybe kill us."

"Oh great—"

"Relax, Shepherd. This is a meet and greet." He stops.

"What?"

He stares at his GPS, looking at the two nearly finished homes in front of us. He turns towards one and then the other.

"The camera is here, right?"

Charlie gives me a solid nod. "It is. But this is about as close as I can get us." He slips the phone into his pocket. "From this point on, we'll have to use our astute powers of observation."

I glare at him and he shrugs. He kneels down and picks up a rock and pockets it.

"Which one, boss?"

I point to the left and we climb up on the rear balcony of the first house. The patio door is locked.

He smiles. "I guess your powers of deduction need some sharpening, huh?" He jumps over the railing and moves around the side of the house. I follow.

When I get to the front, he's already working at the lock to the garage. He slides what looks like a key into the keyhole and bumps it with the stone he picked up. It pops open like magic and he heads inside. I follow, well aware I just added unlawful entry to my list of recent felonies.

The interior of the house is half-finished. The drywall and wiring is installed, but there's no paint or flooring. Signs of the construction crews are everywhere—tools, extension cords, water bottles, empty coffee cups, and a plaster-spotted radio litter the place. We move into the kitchen. It opens to a dining room that wraps around into the living room. Everything is open and spacious and our feet echo between the walls. We do a quick inspection of the kitchen cabinets and find nothing.

"You check the second floor and I'll check the basement," Charlie offers.

"No, we are not splitting up."

He gives me a look and dismisses me, "Fine." He heads up the stairs to the second floor landing that overlooks the kitchen.

"What does someone do with all this space?"

Charlie asks. It's a sincere question.

"People like big houses. They don't like to feel crowded."

He walks to the edge of the balcony and looks down at the stovetop island. "I could spit in my mac and cheese from here."

I shake my head. "That's just gross."

"So's the mac and cheese at my house."

I follow him into an empty bedroom, wondering how anyone could screw up such a simple meal. The doors haven't even been installed, so we move down the hall. A quick look tells us what we need to know. No one except carpenters have been around here. We head down to the basement.

The stairs are still only boards and lights hang by extension cords from the roof. The basement is unfinished walls, studs, and cement. Light spills in through the basement windows and we're able to see to all the back corners easily.

Charlie turns and heads back up the stairs. "This place is a bust."

"What if the person who took it—"

"The killer."

"Okay, the killer—what if he only tried hiding it out here. You know, tried to get rid of the evidence."

"Well, if we find it, then maybe you can take it to Gekas for fingerprints."

"And if not?"

"We'll search for a bit and leave it at that. Back to square one."

I step into the garage. "But judging by your tone, you don't really believe that?"

Charlie follows, turning to lock the door behind

him. "No. I think it's been turned on for us to find."
"And for what purpose?"
"That's what I'm here to find out."

79

We move across the dirt lot to the other house. This time, we skip the balcony and go straight to the front of the house. I don't like being so exposed to the street and the rest of the city, and I hope Charlie gets the lock open quickly.

He turns towards me and nods. I look and see a small scratch along the wood of the doorjamb.

"Someone's been here who wasn't invited."

He unlocks the door with his bump key and lets the door swing open. We both stay on this side of the doorframe, listening for movement. After a moment, he moves inside and I walk behind.

The house is a mirror of the other one and we move into the kitchen, careful to not bang around too much and announce our presence. There's a piece of wood in the hallway and Charlie picks it up, holding it like a club.

This time, we move towards the basement first and look down. Again, the steps are unfinished and it's open, but in this house there is drywall up along a wall. Charlie takes the first step down and the wood groans. We wince at the sound. Not much we can do now—we continue our way down, remaining cautious and ready for anything.

We reach the bottom and the smell of rot hits us

hard. Something nasty is down here. We check the corners and move into what will likely be a den. A hallway runs off one corner of the room, leading to several closed doors.

I hate this—the whole thing feels like a trap—but I know Charlie's going into every one of those rooms whether I'm here or not, so I better stay as backup. We move to the first door and the smell gets worse. Charlie doesn't even wait for me to be ready and opens it quickly. Nothing—it's empty—and he's onto the next.

"Wait—"

But it's too late and he swings it wide.

"Shit, stop," I whisper, but he ignores me and moves to the end of the hall. The smell is horrible and I want to puke. I'm pretty sure I hear buzzing but it doesn't stop him and he opens the door—and it's bad.

A dog, at least what I think is a dog, lies cut open against a wall, its guts spilling out. I can't handle the sight and a move back around the corner and down the hallway into the den. I take deep breaths and try to stop my lurching stomach but it isn't working. I vomit. I want to get out of here.

"Shepherd!"

I hear him call and wipe my mouth. I look down the hall and can't see Charlie, but I realize that he's opened the door to the last room. "What?"

"You need to come here."

"Can't we just go—?"

"No, you need to come here *now*."

I don't like the way he says it with an urgency I have never heard in his voice before, like taking a breath is second to pushing the words out. I inhale deeply and move down the hallway, keeping my eyes from looking at the dead animal, and head into the room where Charlie is.

80

Charlie stands in the center of the room, staring at the wall behind the door. I can hear the buzz of the flies that swarm the dead dog and I wish it would go away.

I turn to see what he's looking at. Suddenly, I'm not breathing and a cold sweat runs down my neck.

Us.

He's looking at a collage of us—made from newspaper clippings and photos—circled and coloured with red marker—or what I hope is red marker. Underneath is written: *A good beginning makes a good ending.*

"What's the hell is this?"

Charlie leans in, inspecting a particular image. "I don't know."

"Why are there pictures of me?"

"Something's not right—"

"Hell yeah. He's got pictures of me. He knows who I am."

"I'm in a few too—"

I point. "Look, that's my address. He knows where I live."

"I see that."

"Why does he know where I live?"

Charlie shrugs. "He looked you up in the phone

book?"

Like a switch flipped, I punch him hard in the cheek. He stumbles, taking the blow. I yell, "You think this is funny?"

He charges me, pushing me, and we collapse backwards. He's short and strong, but I'm mad. He rolls over me, struggling to get on top, like a stupid wrestler. I grunt and push him back, kicking against the floor, swinging my arms at his sides. He fights to hold me down, but I'm long and wiry and throw him off balance. I climb on top and he rolls me over again. I'm face down and his hand pushes my face into the cement.

"It doesn't make sense, okay? I agree with you. Calm down."

I'm breathing fast and hard and I don't want to listen. It's like all my anger from the last two weeks is pouring out right now.

Charlie twists me in a hold. "I'm going to let you go but you have to calm the hell down. Okay?" I don't give in but he gets off, releasing me. I kick back but he's too far away. I drag myself to my knees.

"Don't you get it? It's too neat. Too clean." I stare at him, still angry, but start to listen to what he's saying. He continues, "When did he do this? This weekend? Workers probably were here until Friday. So he came in, dumped the dog in that room, and put the pictures up in here. For what reason?"

I wipe the sweat off my forehead and catch my breath. "So, what? It's all a setup?"

"He's trying to scare us. And right now, it's working."

I stare at him and see the red mark on his cheek, knowing it will probably bruise.

"I mean, honestly, it's good to see you got some fight in you, Anthony Shepherd. Who knew?" He looks at the wall. "But the proof ain't in the pudding."

I stare at him before looking at the wall and my senses finally come back. I feel good—not about hurting him—but about knowing I have the ability in me if I need it. I stare at the picture of me in a news clipping taken sometime during the search for Sheri last Saturday. It seems so long ago. I don't even remember seeing anyone from the press around.

I look over at my address. Having it up there doesn't make me feel safe for me—or my parents and sisters.

"Do you think he'll come to our houses?"

Charlie's left the room, though I didn't even notice. I step out of the room to ask again—

And I come face to face with the killer.

81

He stands in the middle of the hallway wearing a hoodie pulled around a white, smiling mask. I can see Charlie on the ground behind him, facedown.

He rushes me, plowing hard into my chest. We stagger backwards and he slams me hard into the wall. The plasterboard cracks—or maybe it's my bones—and I fall to the ground. He stomps at my head and I try to deflect but it's useless. I take a couple of kicks to the face and before I realize it, he's on top of me, slamming my forehead into the cement. I'm seeing stars and I struggle to get my arm out from under myself to stop him. He drops his knee full force onto my back and it knocks the wind out of my lungs. He swings, fighting like an animal, and I can't get my arms up to defend myself. My vision blurs and I must have gone limp because at some point he's off me and moving away. I hear Charlie yell out as he gets up on his knees. I try to call him but it feels like my mouth is full of cotton. I push up with my arms but the hallway spins and all I see is darkness.

82

"Shepherd."

The cold cement feels good on my face and I'd rather not open my eyes and let the bright sun in.

"Shepherd?"

I smell the rotting flesh of the dog and I hear the buzz of the flies. I feel my whole body rebooting from some distant place.

"Tony!"

"What?" I mumble, not moving, waiting for the pain to go away.

"You alive?'

"Maybe."

"Well, you look like shit."

I open my eyes and Charlie leans against a wall beside me. He's got a fat cheek, most likely from me, and also a bloody lip and a cut above the eye.

"So do you."

"What…?" He rubs his face with the back of his hand and sees the blood.

"Oh."

"He must have hit you pretty hard to knock you down."

I drag myself off the ground and everything hurts. If I had almost cured my hangover before, there's no hope now. My ears ring and my whole head throbs. My face feels like someone took out my skull and used it as a basketball—I will definitely be a shade of purple mocha tomorrow.

"Actually, he pushed me down the stairs," Charlie says so matter-of-factly that I wonder how many other times it's happened. "He was waiting for us."

"That surprise you?"

"No. But it sure felt like he knew how to take us out."

"Well, he's been watching."

"Yeah…"

"What?"

"Some of what he has about me in that room…"

"Yeah?"

"It's like he knows me."

"I know what you mean."

"No, I mean he's someone close."

"Goes to your school?"

"Yeah…" He sneers, knocking his head back and forth between answers.

"It would explain why Sheri was the first victim."

"But it doesn't make sense."

"Why?"

"Everything he's done—the places he's attacked, staying on the edges of the city—has always been like he's trying to cover his tracks."

"You said he likely followed Sheri home."

"Maybe, but—

"Doesn't seem the kind of guy to work in his backyard?"

"Yeah."

We stare at the crack where my body went

through the wall.

"You took some good hits, Rich Boy."

"Can you quit with that, please?"

"Fine."

I'd never been in such a fight before, so hearing the compliment from someone who's likely been in a few more brawls than me feels good. We sit in silence for a little longer.

"I tried chasing him."

"Yeah?" I can't help but be impressed that he got up after being thrown down a flight of stairs.

"Almost had him at the start but he was too fast."

"Did you get a look at him?"

"Not good enough."

"What was with that mask?"

"Not sure."

He grabs a man purse from beside him and dumps it on my lap.

"His?"

Charlie nods as I open it. "It doesn't tell us who he is, but—"

I pull out a book—*Bluebeard* by Kurt Vonnegut—and a map. I unfold it. All the victim's schools have been circled.

"Holy crap."

"Yeah."

"It looks exactly like yours."

"Yup. Exactly—" He points.

On the right hand side, south of the industrial area, is a circle around the other school Charlie considered.

He drags himself up the wall and it looks like

he's hurting more than he's letting on. "Do you need a doctor?"

"No. How about you?"

"Probably, but I'm going to give a day or two and see. The less I have to explain to my folks, the better."

"Just tell them I beat you up."

I laugh and it hurts.

"You sure you're okay." He actually seems a little concerned.

"Yeah, I think so." I can't let him be the only tough guy. "He really pushed you down the stairs?"

Charlie nods as he helps me up.

"Seriously, what is your head made of?"

"I drink lots of soy milk."

"Really?"

"No, it tastes like chalk. Now, let's clean up our tracks and get the hell out of here."

83

We gather up all our pictures first and spend the next half hour searching the house for the camera. We head to the top floor, getting away from the smell, and work our way downward. We move slowly, looking like a couple of grandpas as we try to climb up the stairs. We search the bedrooms and find nothing and descend to the main floor.

This takes a little longer, checking all the kitchen and bathroom cabinets and reaching to the back of all the closets. When the camera doesn't show up, Charlie checks his phone again to make sure it's still around. A big blue circle surrounding the houses signals that the GPS is still close, so we move back down into the stench of the basement. We check the den, opening the ceiling tiles and looking in the rafters, before moving onto the rooms. By the second room, we've already guessed where the killer left the camera.

"Who's doing it?"

Charlie holds up his hand. Looks like were doing it democratically.

"One…Two…Three."

I do paper and Charlie plays rock—I win.

"Damn." He takes a deep breath and heads to the room with the dead dog and goes inside. I don't want to watch, staying back as far as I can from the smell. Moments later, Charlie rushes out of the room, gagging and retching with his hand covered in blood—but he's holding the camera.

Once clear of the room, he mouths, "Upstairs," and we get as much distance as we can from the nastiness.

Charlie finds a leftover paper cup of coffee in a corner and takes it outside to wash off. As he pours it over his arm, an old cigarette falls out.

"That is all-around disgusting."

"This day couldn't get any worse."

By the time he's washed off and scrubbed dirt over his arm to get rid of more of the stink, it's mid-afternoon. While we head to the car, Charlie studies the map and I open the killer's bag to see if there's anything else.

"The fact that he's plotted them out like this still doesn't make sense."

"Because of the connection you think he has to your school?"

He grunts, not looking my way.

I search all the pockets and find nothing. I toss it over my shoulder and flip through the book.

Charlie looks over and smiles. "It looks good on you."

"Shut up—" Something falls out of the book, catches in the wind, blows across the road. I race after it, Charlie standing in the middle of the street watching. The thing catches in the tall grass that rises at the end, flickering like a playing card on a bicycle spoke.

"What is it?"

I pick it up and flip it over. It's a picture of a pretty brunette with a big smile.

I look at Charlie. "Do you think—?" I point towards the map he holds.

I see Charlie's mind working and know he's already there.

"We have to take this to Gekas."

"Agreed." I look at him, surprised and relieved.

"Look, we got our asses kicked today, but you've got to do it."

"Why?"

"She's got too much on me. I don't need her finding my fingerprints on this thing."

I nod.

Charlie looks up and sees two seagulls flying overhead. "If I get shit on, I'm just going to find a bird to punch."

I laugh as we hobble towards the car.

84

I sit in Detective Gekas' office, once again waiting for her to see me.

I hear people shuffling around behind me but I don't turn to look. There are a lot more folders piled on her desk since the killer has claimed another victim. Whatever BS she said in her television interview, she's shouldering both Sheri's missing person's case as well as every other girl's death. I can also see a stack of papers with reports and tips from nervous citizens or wannabe cops about every kid walking down their street with a hood up.

I'm nervous and I can't stop wiggling my foot. Somewhere behind the cushion of the chair there's a hard bump, like a loose screw, that digs into my back.

I think about how only a couple of weeks ago I was sitting in that uncomfortable plastic chair in the principal's office waiting for Gekas. I wasn't really aware of the messed up things people were capable of. I believed Sheri was still alive and the world was safe. But now, nothing is the same—not the office, or the chair, or me—except for the weird, uncertain twist in my guts. And maybe Gekas' unwavering hunt for answers.

I feel someone step into the room and unconsciously sit up straight. It's another detective, a man, dropping another file on the shaky heap.

"You waiting for Gekas?" He says absently, not really caring for an answer, but I give a him a nod anyway.

"Do you want anything? Water?"

I try to say, "No, thanks," but he's already gone, leaving with as much apathy as he came in with.

The whole department must be under pressure. Listening to the chaos of the ringing phones, the whirring fax machines, and the quiet chatter of clerks behind me, I'd think I was in the office of one of Dad's clients. This police station isn't like the movies. There's no excitement, no eureka moment that moves the case forward. They are doing the groundwork of gathering the pieces of evidence, hoping that something will push the case along. I hope that what I'm about to tell Gekas will help her, but I know it could also blow everything up. My offering is, unfortunately, complicated.

I shift in my seat to reach into the pouch of my hoodie. My muscles hurt from the throwdown Charlie and I had as I pull out the picture of the girl.

I flip it over and stare at her, this girl I don't recognize. My memory kicks me in the head, reminding me of the disgusting remains of that poor dog in the basement of the half-finished house. Immediately, I think about Sheri. I don't like how these two thoughts run together and I try to push them out.

I contemplate how to proceed. Do I tell Gekas about my run-in with the masked killer? Or do I only tell her about the construction site and the dead dog and the room full of images of Charlie Wolfe and me. Maybe I keep it simple, tell her that I have a hunch, or that I somehow came across this information, or that someone left it anonymously on my locker with some cheesy note with "FOR SHERI" written in red marker.

I scoff, knowing the answer. I've placed myself into the center of the most ridiculous cliché. For every lie I'd make, there would be too many questions that will have to be answered. It's all or nothing.

"Anthony."

I jump.

Gekas comes around to the other side of her desk. "Did I startle you?"

"No. I was just distracted." I slide the photo back into my pocket, hoping she doesn't notice.

She sits down and leans forward in her chair. The sun isn't in my eyes this time. Although I feel like Gekas and I should be on a level playing field, I don't feel at ease.

"You hung up on me this morning." She looks tired, but it seems like she's trying to soften her face with a slight smile.

"I know." It's not my style to be rude and I feel bad, but then again none of what I've been up to is my style. "I just really thought you should look at the surveillance cameras."

Gekas nods. "What happened to your cheek? And your eye?"

I'm really grateful I'm not a white kid right now because the bruises don't look as bad as they actually are.

"I had a little too much to drink at the party. Dumb. I know." Crap—the lies begin.

She watches me. And I see the edges of her lips tighten and the smile disappear.

I try to move it along. "So the cameras at the mall?"

"We're going to look into it. It's all procedure. Why did you hang up so suddenly?"

"I apologize. It was rude."

"I'm not looking for an apology, Anthony." She sits back in her chair and glances over at the mess of paperwork sprawled over her desk.

"I'm concerned. You see, you have an alibi and so does your new friend, Charles Wolfe, but your recent decision to stick your nose around crime scenes has me worried."

She's still gentle, but I can feel her firming up.

"This isn't a game, Anthony."

Really? I must have missed that while worrying that my girlfriend's missing, likely dead, that my life's been turned upside down, and I've recently been shit-kicked by the killer!

"I know it's not a game." It comes out much more subdued than it feels.

"And I know you're not a suspect. So, what brings you here?"

I fall into silence. My finger runs along the edge of the photo. Do I tell her the truth or do I lie?

"Anthony do you see this?" She gestures to the files on her desk. "I'm busy. If you're just here to hang out, you need to go somewhere else to do that. Try home or the gym."

I pull out the photo of the pretty brunette with a big smile on her face and put it on her desk.

85

Gekas looks down at the photo.

"What's this?"

"I think it's the next victim."

"Pardon me?"

"I think this is a photo of the next victim."

She doesn't pick it up. She looks at the girl smiling back at her.

"Do you know her?"

"No."

"Does Charles know her?"

"No."

"Are you sure?"

"Yes. I'm sure."

She opens a drawer and pulls out a blue crime scene glove and slips it on. She picks up the photo by the corner, turning it over to look at the back.

"How do you know she's the next victim?"

I don't answer. Silence is better than lying.

"Where did you find this?"

"In a book."

"In the library?"

"No."

"Anthony—?"

"Charlie and I were messing around a construction site."

She drops the photo as she looks at me. I can see the upside down face of the mystery girl I'm trying to save.

"Anthony, you didn't…?"

I sheepishly shrug my shoulders but then interject, "We didn't go into the crime scene."

"Everything out there could be a potential crime scene. Why do you think we put a fence around it?"

The whole thing dawns on me and I realize how deep I'm back in it. "We didn't know."

She sighs, trying her best to move through this. "So you found a book?"

I nod. "And a dead dog in the basement of a house. Guts were torn out. I've—I've never seen anything like it. It wasn't normal."

"And this?" She turns the image toward me.

"That fell out of a book."

"You've lost me."

"We found a book inside the house, near the dog. I picked it up and a photo fell out of it."

Gekas leans back. "Just like that, huh?"

"Yes."

She lays it down and picks up a pen. "Did you find anything else?"

"No." Lying to a cop, especially Gekas, who's really trying to help me, doesn't feel right, but I can't imagine telling the truth right now.

"There was nothing else at that house?"

She's testing me and the lies I've spun. "Nothing."

She points at my face. "And that?"

"Like I said, hurt myself at a party. You know how dumb us teenagers can be?"

"Yeah, absolute fools." She leans back in her chair, fiddling with the cap of her pen, watching me. I know she doesn't believe me, but I also know that she doesn't exactly know what the truth is. I'm sure she can't believe we had a run-in with the killer, but she's smarter than I'd like her to be at this moment, and I can't be certain she isn't already suspecting the truth.

"And where's Charles in all this?"

"He's at home, I believe."

"I mean, does he know about this?"

"Yes."

"He knows you came here, to give me this?"

I nod. "Actually it was his idea. I mean, we agreed on it."

She smiles. "Well, isn't that chummy of you two. He wasn't the one who happened to do that to you?"

"No." I say it too quickly, too easily, before I realize it only narrows her list of suspects even more.

"So, why isn't he here then?"

I try Gekas' tactic and lean forward in my chair. "Because you don't like him."

She inhales and shrugs her shoulders in agreement. "He makes it a bit of a challenge."

I smile—you and me both, lady!

"You bringing this to me, saying she may be the next victim—if she winds up hurt, or worse, it may put the suspicion back on you."

I hadn't really considered this possibility but it's too late now to dwell on it.

"Detective Gekas, will you help me, please? Will you find her? Keep her safe?"

She nods. "Anthony, you can trust me. And when he comes looking for her, we'll get him."

This is the best thing she's ever said to me.

86

I'm sitting in my backyard—it's cold but the sun is shining—when Charlie comes through the gate. Ollie gets up to greet him, his tail wagging.

"You used the gate. I guess I've housebroken you."

"Who says I didn't break into the front and help myself to your dad's wall safe."

I shoot him a look and he smiles. "Well, now I know your family has a wall safe."

Charlie hands over a to-go coffee cup and grabs a leafy lawn chair, plopping himself down, not clearing it off beforehand. It's the little things like this that I find strangely interesting about Charlie Wolfe.

"Thanks man." It's hot and sugary, and I appreciate it.

"Don't thank me. After the soy milk you gave me, for Pete's sake, it's the least I can do." He takes a loud glug of his own drink.

"Your face looks better."

I smile. "So does yours."

Ollie comes over to me for some attention and I scratch the back of his neck deeply.

"So, how'd it go? Are we going to jail, or just me?" He savours the warmth of the coffee between his hands. "I'm guessing, since we're both sitting here, enjoying this tasty beverage, you're no longer a righteous boy and told a few lies?"

"Actually, a little bit of both. Sometimes the truth can be just as good."

"I'll maybe have to try it sometime. And did my name come up?"

"Yup, but I think you're good. You're not really her focus anymore."

"For once. Did you tell her about our masked friend?"

"No, but I wondered if I should."

"Nah, our psycho Marcel Marceau will probably announce himself soon enough."

I don't get the reference but Charlie seems to think it's funny and snickers at his own joke. I'm getting used to him and the things he says, what he does, and how he does it. I shift in my chair and wince as a pain shoots through my body.

"Man, I'm sore."

"You'll be okay. Give it a couple more days. Our masked friend just likes to play a little rough." I can see that Charlie has had different experiences than I have, especially given the way he defines what happened to us. "Playing rough" is a grand understatement.

We sit in silence for a moment. It's my time to relax but I can't. I don't feel like things end with the girl in the picture. It's just a feeling but it's solid. I try and shake it out of my head. Gekas is on her way to find her and she'll be taken in and made safe.

Yet, something's not right. I turn to Charlie. "You don't think he's done yet, do you?"

Charlie shakes his head. "No, I don't."

87

I put my coffee down and turn to him. "What's on your mind?"

Charlie stares in a daze at the remaining leaves in the trees, his finger flicking the edge of his lid. I wait, quietly. He sets his coffee on the ground beside him and reaches over and rubs the dog's head. Ollie follows the love and sits his butt down on Charlie's toes.

Charlie continues to rub behind Ollie's ears, until his train of thought leads him to ask, "Why?"

I don't answer because I know if I give him enough time it will come.

"Why her?" He looks over at me, like he's actually waiting for me to answer, but I know better. "I mean, who is she? Why choose her instead of another? And why that school? Why plan so specifically? Were all the other girls chosen?"

He pauses and I step in. "You said he tracked Sheri from the school."

"Yeah? But am I right?"

He's never questioned himself and it surprises me.

"He can't be from around my school."

I follow his train of thought from earlier in the day. "Because it's too close to home?"

"Exactly!" I answered his own question with his own answer. "And that's the other thing: A photo of me? At my school? If he's not from there, then why'd he follow me there?" He shakes his head.

I feel where Charlie is coming from and I'm in agreement—it's not lining up. He falls into silence, so I pick up the thread, "So, if the pieces don't fit, then what are we missing?"

Charlie leans forward, smiling. "Three girls. Gekas can only confirm two."

"But all are connected based on a hunch."

He looks over at me and I can tell he doesn't like to be challenged, but then he nods and says, "True. If I'm wrong about Sheri, then what else am I wrong about?"

"Two murdered girls, possibly connected, and Sheri, who's still missing—and possibly dead." I hover over my statement before continuing, "And now a potential fourth one."

"Right. Not that we know, but all the attacks seem connected to bathrooms. But for what reason?"

"You don't think it's some weird fetish?"

Charlie shakes his head. "It's weird, I'll give you that. And the intimacy of strangulation sure puts it there, but it feels like something else…"

He trails off again and I can see he's frustrated.

"It's like I'm missing something in front of my face, that I can't see."

I change the question, "Why the mask? Is it just to remain anonymous?"

Charlie lets go of his own thought and pursues mine, "It reminds me of those masks like you see in a theatre."

I nod in agreement as he grabs his phone out of his pocket and does a quick search. "Here it is. They represent the Ancient Greek muses. Melpomene is the Muse of tragedy, and the one our dude was wearing is Thalia, the Muse of comedy."

"Comedy, huh? Not funny."

"I don't think he's trying to be ironic. That video of Bonnie—he was performing for us."

"So, what? Do you thinks he's making a movie?"

Charlie doesn't answer. I look over. "What?"

"That first day, when we walked the trails, we went into the bathroom…"

"Yeah?"

"I went through the motions, like I tried to kill you."

At least he was only pretending. "So?"

"I could see myself in the mirror the whole time. I saw you and I saw myself and I could have watched me kill you."

"All the bathrooms—"

"Had mirrors."

"He wasn't performing for us—"

"He was performing for himself."

88

Bzzz.

My phone hums on the table between us. I look down at the number.

"Gekas."

Charlie looks at me with sincere interest but I hesitate.

"Answer it." I hear a sliver of impatience in his voice, just a sliver.

I pick it up and shoot him a look. "You've got to be less bossy already."

The phone stops ringing.

"See! You took too long."

I feel a little bad that I took a moment to tell Charlie to back off rather than to answer Gekas' phone call. I bluff. "Don't worry. She'll call back."

Immediately, the phone rings again and I feel I won a tiny victory against Charlie.

"See," I say nonchalantly while he gestures frantically at the phone.

I pick it up.

"Hello?"

"Anthony?"

Charlie leans in to listen.

"Yes."

"Is your buddy there?"

Charlie shakes his head but I ignore him. "Yup."
He shoots me a look.

"Put me on speaker phone."

I ignore Charlie's further protests, push the button, and put it between us.

"Hello, Charles."

His face scrunches up at the sound of her voice but he follows through, "Hello, Detective."

"I'm calling to let you two know that we've found her. We found the girl."

A tension that I hadn't realized had been gripping my heart releases. "You did?"

"Yes, we did."

Charlie leans back in the chair.

"I wanted to call you both personally and let you know."

For a split second, I wonder what her motivation is but I immediately shift to gratitude. "Thank you."

"You're welcome."

I should be happy that we may have protected her, but after everything Charlie and I've been talking about, I feel a strong wave of doubt.

"Detective, who is she?"

"I can't tell you that, Anthony—"

"I know what she looks like and I know she goes to Greenville High. It won't take much for a couple of resourceful guys like us to find out." Charlie shoots me a look, wondering what I'm up to. I don't like pushing against Gekas like this—in fact, I feel way outside of my comfort zone—but I'm as certain about my actions now as I am on the court.

"Her name is Tamara Seller. She graduates this year."

"How did you find her?"

"Contacted people at the school board office, talked to the principal, and tracked her down."

"Was she at home?"

"Where are you going with this?"

"Was she at home or at work? Does she have a job?"

"What—?"

"Please, Detective."

"We went to her house. She doesn't have a job."

I look at Charlie, expecting him to know where I am going with this, but for once, he has no clue.

"Is Tamara safe?"

"Yes. She's at home, with her parents and two officers."

I feel relief for her but it's too easy—everything else has been a struggle. I'm silent for too long.

"Are you okay, Anthony?"

"Yes. Thank you for letting me know."

"Anthony—?"

"Thank you, Detective Gekas."

"Don't you dare hang up on me—!" she yells.

I turn off the phone, "She's not the one."

"What do you mean?"

"It's Saturday and she doesn't have a job."

"So?"

"Where is he going to get her? He's never gone to a house."

Charlie picks up on my line of thinking. "He needs a public space—especially a bathroom—"

"With a mirror—"

"Because he needs to see himself—"

"Performing."

299

He stares at me. "She's not the one."
I nod.
"So, what then? Until he makes a move—?"
"I hate to say it, but we have to wait."

89

The boy sits in his car, looking down the street at the police cruiser parked outside the house.

He was proud with how he directed the scene, moving the players around his stage, doing what he wanted them to do. Everything had happened so quickly and he had to improvise so much, yet he was able to make it all work.

When he realized the tall one was the boyfriend of the first girl, he was able to put things together quickly. He had been gathering the newspaper clippings and found some of the photos from the internet. As for the other loser, simply breaking into the school yearbook office gave him all he needed. He had kept the dead dog in a heavy-duty garbage bag in the garage, and once he had his car back from the impound, he loaded everything up and headed to the construction site, appreciating the symmetry of his actions.

Yet, until he saw them move across the space between the houses, he never realized how tall the boyfriend was or how solid the loser was. He knew he'd have to take them down separately, knocking the one down the stairs and keeping tight and close to the other.

The clue that had led the two boy detectives and

the police to this girl's house had been a series of fortuitous coincidences. Early on, after moving to the new city, he had found the book and picture in an upscale coffeehouse on the east side. He held on to them both, unwilling to sever their connection. It had only been serendipity that the school he'd circled on his map had aligned with the girl's school.

The body in his trunk rattled back and forth and he knew it was time to move on.

He thought to himself, Flash the house lights; everybody take your seats. The performance is about to begin.

PART FOUR

90

I wake the next day with a heaviness in my chest. It's not the same pain as my sore body. That hurts too. It's a thick and unsettling feeling. Waiting is horrible. I'm afraid that what I'm waiting for is another tragedy. I inhale deeply and stand in front of the mirror in my room in my boxers. There are deep bruises on my lower abs. A few weeks ago, I was vain about my body and now I have a strange respect for what I know it can take. I turn and look over my shoulder into the mirror at the visual condition of my back, but it aches to do this.

Tap. Tap. "Tony." It's Dad.

I snatch my shirt and pull it on as fast as possible, not wanting him to see me like this because he'll tell Mom. She's a doctor and a mom and is going to freak out way, way more than Dad.

"Yeah," I say as casually as I can even though my heart is pounding.

The door opens. The blinds are down. My room is dark.

"Are you okay?" Dad asks as he inadvertently looks around my room. I can see he's assessing everything. Nothing is out of order so I don't worry about his curiosity. I do, however, turn my back to him, covering my face, pointlessly moving my stack of schoolbooks from one pile to another.

"Are you on your way down?"

"I was going to do a little homework first. I'm almost caught up."

"Good. I mean, I'm glad. It just makes things easier on you later if you take care of business now." He smiles and nods.

"Come down." He's gentle but firm. I can't say no. I shouldn't say no. Things are slowly sliding towards better. He looks at my face and says nothing. Can he see the bruises? Did he notice?

"I'll be right down."

"Your mother made some seriously unhealthy but delicious buttermilk pancakes." Dad walks away, leaving my door open.

The fragrance of pancakes, coffee, and bacon waft up into my room.

I need a lie. I can't avoid them until my bruises are gone. I'm going to have to come up with something.

I head down the stairs with more noise than I normally would to make my entrance a little jollier sounding. It's just the three of us. Heather is out with friends. The table has a great spread of a Sunday brunch on it. I wonder what Charlie's Sunday morning meals look like. I sit down at the table and pour a glass of orange juice.

"Good morning, sunshine." Mom says as she walks by me and sits down with a stack of pancakes.

We settle in. I fill my plate with pancakes, fruit, whip, and bacon, and just as I am about to start eating, it happens.

"Detective Gekas called this morning." I feel like

Mom and I are having a 'casual-off' in trying to out-do our understating the present situation.

I pour syrup on my food.

"She said you went to see her."

I nod.

"About?"

"Just checking in." I highly doubt she'd give my parents information about a case and complicate things, so I risk the lie.

"She's concerned."

"Oh?"

Then she sees it. Her fork clinks as it drops to her plate.

"Anthony. What happened to your face?"

I have a mouthful of breakfast and although it should be delicious, I don't taste one morsel. It's all just mush in my mouth. I chew as I plan my piece of fiction and finally swallow.

"I don't want to sound like a jerk but you may have noticed that my life has recently fallen apart?" It comes out harsher than I expect. "And I decided that after all this garbage I needed to cut loose a lit-tle, so I went to a farm party with Mike on Friday."

"That doesn't explain the bruises on your face." She looks directly at me.

I wonder how they'd respond if I answered their question like this: Well, Mom and Dad, I was wan-dering around with a guy from the wrong side of the tracks and we found a death shrine to us and a dead dog and a photo of a potential victim. Oh, and we were both completely beat up by the masked killer. Thank you. Have a nice day.

"I drank too much." This is not going to go well.

I have made it to grade 11 without any incidents. My parents stare at me from the other side of the table. "And I think I fell off the porch there. I'm not sure. I can ask Mike." I stuff a large amount of pancake in my mouth.

I wish Heather were here. Even for a little back up.

They wait and silence hangs between us.

I swallow. "It's not as bad as it looks." And I take another drink of juice. I wish it had whiskey in it. I laugh inside at the irony of this thought.

"And drinking is a good idea?" Dad steps up when I really thought Mom would take this one.

I shrug.

"The answer is no. Drinking is not a good idea. Drinking in excess is never a good idea. Drinking where you don't even know exactly how you hurt yourself is the worst of ideas." My heart starts beating a little faster.

"How did you get home?" Dad continues the questioning.

"Mike…I think."

"You think?" Dad carries on. I really don't want to cross him. Mom sits with her arms folded.

"I guess if you didn't hear me stumble up the stairs, I couldn't have been that bad, right?"

Mom's face twists in a disparaging smile—her perfect son has taken a turn and is heading for a smack in the head.

I try to save face. "Look, I know it's a bad idea. All of it. I do it so little that it was completely unintentional." I feign defensiveness. "I really just need you to back off for a while and trust me."

They grill me with their silence.

"I won't do it again. There. Happy?" I have never fought so hard over something that never happened. "Are you going to ground me?"

"We love you. We're all trying to get through this. You understand that?"

I nod.

"Grounding you won't solve anything, but can you promise to be more responsible and take care of yourself?"

"I'm sorry. I mean it. I'm really sorry." The tension between us vaporizes.

Dad takes a sip from his coffee. "Detective Gekas asked us to keep you close. She cares."

I want to laugh but I keep it inside. I nod.

"Do you want me to look at your bruise?" She's being more mom than doctor right now and knows that my face is just the tip of the iceberg.

"I'm fine. For real."

"If it doesn't start improving in the next day or two, I'm looking at it whether you want me to or not."

I roll my eyes and sigh, "Fine."

I hope this is the end of the conversation. I just want to go back up to my room, but I need to stick around and make it look like I am trying.

"No turkey bacon, Dad?" He shakes his head and grins as he gets my loving dig at his healthy ways.

91

The rest of Sunday passes peacefully. I stick close to home and tend to my broken self to keep my parents happy. I send Charlie one text message to check in.

His reply is delayed and brief: *Kay*.

I imagine his Sunday is quiet too, perhaps a different kind of quiet than mine. I do some homework and watch an old movie with my parents about a guy stuck on an island with a volleyball.

Monday morning I pop in to see Coach Davies. I am in no condition to train. My back is stiff and bruised. My right hip is black and blue. My face is a wreck. I stand in the door of his office for a while waiting for him to finish what he's doing.

I clear my throat. He looks up.

"Hi, Coach."

"Shepherd."

Then I see him focus on my face. It feels better but looks worse today. Mom told me that's how bruises heal, making their way to the surface. Charlie said it would make me look a little more badass.

"Your face?"

"That's what I wanted to talk to you about. I was doing some work with my dad in the garage. We were building a shelf and it fell." The more I open my mouth, the more I twist my own lies.

"Anyway, I'm pretty sore and think I need a day or two to rest up. I can get my parents to write a note if you need—" *Shut up, Tony! They'll never write you a note.*

"That's fine, Anthony." Coach trusts me—we have a long enough history so the bluff works.

"If you've got plays or something you want me to look over, I can do that."

He nods his approval and hands me a file folder.

"You'll know what to do with this."

"Thank you. I think I'll be good to go by Wednesday."

I force myself to walk away stoically from Coach Davies' office, pretending my body doesn't hurt as much as it does. With books in hand, I head to my first period class knowing all too well that whatever my idea of normal was it is now forever changed. It feels like something is always lurking in the periphery of my sight. Corners hold menace. I never know whether I'm going to see the killer again, coming back to finish the job.

Slap—Somebody strikes me hard on the back and it takes everything I have to not crumble. I turn, ready to fight back, when I realize it's Mike.

"Hey, man! Good party Friday night!" He has a huge, innocent smile on his face. "Whoa! Whose fist did you run into?"

"Long story—"

"That's cool. I got Chrissy's number."

I fake my enthusiasm. "Great. Who's Chrissy?" I don't really care but figure I should try.

"Remember the super cute brunette from the

movie theatre? She's also a cheerleader!" He elbows me in the way a dad would after telling a barely dirty joke. He opens his phone and proudly shows me a selfie of him with yet another girl. She's cute— a long pony-tail and a big smile.

"Good for you."

"You got a little tanked, huh?" He takes another friendly swing with the palm of his hand to tap my shoulder. I step out of the way.

"That I did. How did I get home?"

Mike pauses and shrugs. "Dunno. I was busy wheeling Chrissy."

"What about—?"

Mike ignores me. "Yeah, yeah! It seems there's enough Mike around here for all the ladies." He shifts gears. "Where were you Saturday? I sent you a couple of texts. Figured you were nursing a hangover."

In seconds, my memory flashes images like fireworks popping in my head: the strangled girl, the buzzing flies, the beatdown in the basement, and my third heart-to-heart with Gekas.

"I took it easy."

"Panty," Mike teases.

The bell for class rings.

"Catch you later!" Mike yells with infectious enthusiasm from halfway down the hall. I'm left thinking how different he is from Charlie.

Second period history class comes and goes, and I go through the motions. My phone remains relatively silent. I'm waiting for Charlie, but I can't help thinking of when it used to be Sheri.

I miss her.

It's time for english in third and I settle in. The teacher starts by handing back our assignments for *Animal Farm* and I get mine. A low D. I'm not surprised. I'm going to have to negotiate a rewrite at some point. The notes come up next. We all start writing from the PowerPoint on the projector screen.

Bzz.

My phone startles me. I discretely pull it out of my pocket and look. I have a notification for a Pictabomb message from—shit—*comedymuse.*

I raise my hand.

I cut my teacher off mid-sentence, "May I go to the washroom?" He nods his permission and I exit the class, leaving my books behind and step into a stairwell. I take a big breath and swipe open the app.

It's a girl—bound and gagged in the trunk of a car. I feel sick to my stomach. Her eyes are wide with terror, her face dirty and bruised. That's when that feeling in my gut rushes in and, even worse, I realize it's Chrissy, the girl from Mike's selfie.

92

I take a quick screenshot before the image disappears.

I bring up Charlie's "Hot Diggety" and text him: *It's go time.*

What?

Message from comedymuse. It's bad.

I'm almost out of the school when I realize I need information. I text Mike.

Meet me in the commons.

dude. in class.

now

He doesn't respond. I text again.

NOW

Minutes later, I see him heading down the hallway towards me.

"What's with you?"

I'm not sure how to approach it, so I barrel in because there is no easy way about this. "That girl you met at the party—?"

"Chrissy?"

"Yeah. Where does she go to school?"

"Man, what are you getting at? You trying to get something on the side?"

"Mike, I need to know."

"What is with you?"

"Mike!"

He stops and stares at me. "You know, ever since Sheri, I've been trying to help get your mind off things—but you're not you. You're never around, you're skipping practices. It's like you've just given up."

I hear him speaking but I can't comprehend what he says through the thoughts buzzing in my head. Frankly, I could really care less, and if I did, I'd likely punch him in the face. I hold it all in, trying to calm myself and focus on what's going on.

"Mike, I'm sorry you feel that way, but I think something's happened to Chrissy."

"What are you talking about?"

I don't want to have to explain myself and I sure as hell am not going to show him the picture.

"Tell me what school Chrissy goes to."

He's watching me, squinting like it's going to help him see the reason for my craziness.

"Mike, I think what happened to Sheri is happening to Chrissy." I hope I've expressed what I'm getting at enough for it to mean something to him.

"Why would you…? What makes you…?"

I let him wind himself down.

"Guthrie."

Sheri's school.

"What's her last name?"

"McIntyre."

"Thanks, Mike. Don't worry. I'm going to do my best to keep her safe."

93

I realize what I said and how it may have sounded, but I don't care. I meant it.

I leave him behind and exit the school. I've got my phone out.

Girls from your school.

It doesn't take long for Charlie to reply: *Wat?*

I start typing but Charlie interrupts: *How do u know?*

I erase my message and type: *Long story. Gekas?*

The typing indicator bubbles, then: *Yes*. I'm pretty sure he went back and forth on that. Charlie texts again: *I'm there in five*.

I didn't know he had a car. Or worse yet, he doesn't but he'll find himself one. Either way, he's not at school because no one gets across town from the East End that fast.

I bring up Gekas's number from my recents—it's been used far too many times as of late. She answers on the second ring.

"Anthony?"

"He's got another one."

Silence but I don't have the patience to wait. "Detective Gekas, can I send you the picture he sent me?"

"He contacted you?"

"Yes." I need her focused and on track. "I'm sending it now."

I put her on speaker, click attachment, and go to my photos. It's the first one and I can't even look at the thumbnail. The idea that I have something like this on my phone bothers me.

"Sending it now."

"I need that phone, Anthony. Maybe we can trace it."

"He sent it through one of those self-destructing photo apps. There'd be no trace."

"Maybe a bit of code, something to find him?"

"Sure, Detective." I doubt it though and I think she does too. "You get it yet?"

"It's still downloading…"

"She's from Sheri's school."

More silence. "How do you know? Did he tell you?"

"No. A friend of mine met her." I think about my home address on the wall of the house. "Detective Gekas, do you think he went after her because of me?"

She doesn't hesitate. "No, Anthony. It isn't your fault—"

"But—" I'm ready to tell her what I didn't tell her before—about the pictures and the run-in we had with the killer.

"Don't think that way. It's just bad luck." I'm sure she'll investigate it anyway.

She's quiet now and I assume she's got the picture. "Her name is Chrissy McIntyre."

"Thank you, Anthony. Anything else?"

"The last person I know who saw her was my

buddy, Mike."

"I'm going to have to question him."

"Okay." At this point, I have to do whatever it takes. "He met her at a farm party on Friday."

"Is this the one you where you hurt your eye?"

Crap. "Yes."

"You really have lousy luck, Anthony."

"I know, Detective Gekas. I know."

94

Charlie is outside my school three minutes later. He's got two coffees in his hand and what I can only guess is a bag of doughnuts.

I look around and ask, "Where's your car?"

"I don't have one."

"Then, how did you get here?"

"I was at the coffee shop down the street."

Why do I ever assume Charlie lives a normal life. I wonder if he even goes to school. I hand him my phone and show him the text.

"You say he sent it to you? Text?"

"No, a Picta-bomb." I don't mention that it seems like he and Gekas are joined at the brain.

He stares at it, not moving, taking it in.

"It's pretty bad, huh?"

He looks at me, shaking his head. "No. I know who the killer is."

95

Charlie has me in the car before he says another word.

"Drive."

"Where?"

"My school." He stares out the window, chewing on his first doughnut, mumbling to himself.

"What?"

"I said it's a stupid day to have missed school."

"Why? What's going on? Who is it?"

He grabs my phone and shows me the picture. I can barely look at it.

"What do you see?"

"Chrissy—?"

"No, the car. Blue Civic with a busted driver's side tail light."

"So?"

"It's Robbie."

"Who?"

He looks at me like I should know these things.

"Robbie. The dude I was with the first day you came and asked for my help."

It slowly starts donning on me. The kid in the hoodie with the baggie and the glass pipe. And the lost car.

"Robbie?"

"I know. It doesn't make sense. The kid can barely tie his own shoelace without falling over. But…?"

I think about the beatdown we got in the house, trying to match my earlier impression of Robbie up with the figure in the mask. It still doesn't work.

"You really think he could've pushed you down the stairs, taken me out, then was able to run away?"

"No. That's why we've got to find him before Gekas does."

96

"Is he at school?"

"He has a worse track record than me for showing up."

"Don't you have someone you can text?"

Charlie looks at me. "Unfortunately, most of my connections are superficial. It's easier that way."

I can't help but feel a little hurt, so I stick it right back at him. "That's why it pays to have friends." I hand Charlie my phone as I drive. "Here."

He grabs it out of my hand. "Who do you want?"

"Look up Jessica's name."

He doesn't even pause as he types in my password and scrolls through my numbers.

"Text her and ask if Robbie's been at school."

"Would she even know?" I can hear the edge in his voice.

"Despite what you may think, she pays attention."

He sends the message off and we wait for a response. I consider pulling over to the side of the road, but we need to head to that side of the city, so I keep driving.

"It really doesn't make sense how Robbie could be a killer."

I look over at him, musing as he stares out the window, sipping on his coffee.

My phone buzzes.

"She says, 'No.' Do you think she'll know where he might be?"

"Doubt it. You have any ideas?"

He pulls out his phone. "He lives just off Prince of Wales Drive. Let's start there."

97

We pull to the side of the street a few yards from Robbie's driveway. No other cars are there and the place looks empty.

It's a big house, probably built in the late '80s, with the garage on the front. A few small saplings on the lawn have only begun to dream of being real trees. The grass is green and manicured, even in this dry fall. Not a trace of leaves have found their way onto the property.

We step out of the car and this wide-open street doesn't give us much to try the subtle approach. Also, if this turns into a *thing*, which I expect it will with Charlie around, there's no real place for us to avoid being seen by nosey neighbours.

We stay close to the edge of the attached garage, walking along the wall. I hope it blocks us from view, at least a little, but I know that's just wishful thinking. Charlie puts his face to the window of the garage, cupping his eyes to get a better look and block the reflection from outside. I follow his lead and now I feel like the nosey neighbor.

Daylight illuminates the space and we see the car.

"We need to get inside."

Charlie rattles the knob of the garage door, but

he doesn't take his eyes off the car. It's locked.

"Now what?"

He looks around, and I hope to God he's not looking for a rock to throw through the window.

Charlie heads up the front steps. I follow and he pounds on the door. So much for subtle and quiet, but at least it wasn't a rock through the window.

No answer. No Robbie and no parents. Charlie hops down off the step and heads into the tight, narrow gap between houses. At the end is a seven-foot fence that splits in a T between the two properties. He grabs hold and jumps, wedging his feet between the stucco of the house and a fence post. He pulls up from the cross brace and drags himself the rest of the way over the top.

"You coming?" He asks from the other side.

I weigh my options. Either I have Charlie let me in the front and be seen by someone across the street, or I risk the B & E and follow him through the back.

"Hold on!" I yell as I drag myself not so gracefully over the other side. I still hurt from Saturday but suck up the pain.

"I'm going to assume it's because you're being a pussy that you made that look as awkward as you possibly could."

"Shut it."

"I mean, I thought you guys could jump—"

"Shut. Up." I don't know if he's trying to be offensive but at least it's good to see he wants to mess with me, even now.

We cautiously move around the outside of the deck, but Charlie breaks off and heads toward the patio door.

"You aren't going through that way?"

"The lock sucks and there's too many eyes around to watch me toss a brick through the window." He catches my look. "I know you're thinking I'd do something like that."

"You wouldn't actually do that though, would you?"

He smiles but doesn't answer. He proceeds to a back door but hesitates.

"Charlie?"

His hand slips in his pocket and comes out again, empty. "I don't know. Just…give me a chance to talk to him, okay?"

I nod.

He bangs on the door. "Robbie?"

Silence.

He knocks again, waiting. After all the times Charlie has walked right into a place where he's not invited, this time he wants to watch his manners.

He's about to try knocking a third time but I stop him.

Charlie stares at me. "What?"

"Really?"

He chews his lip, glaring at me. I know he's pissed but I'm sure it has little to do with me. Still, if he decides to take his anger out on me, I'm ready.

Finally, he sighs and smiles and pulls out his ring of bump keys, dumping them in my hand. "You want in? Then have at it."

Unfortunately, I have barely any idea how to use them, except for the time I watched him. I find a key that seems to match and I slide it in. Charlie hands me a screwdriver and I rap the back end while turning the key. Nothing.

I try it again and again but nothing happens. I'm ready to kick the door in.

Charlie sighs and, without a word, shows me the trick. He slides the key in and then while twisting it, pulls the key back gently so it no longer is flush to the lock. He pushes it back in and lets me try.

I push it in, twist it, and pull it back gently. I feel a slight click through my fingers and hit the key with the screwdriver. The doorknob turns and I've now officially committed my first break and enter.

I motion to the door. Charlie swings his long, curly bangs out of the way and raises an eyebrow, moving inside. I follow silently, closing the door gently behind me with a small, quiet *click*.

98

We step into a back entryway, but it's devoid of any pairs of shoes or the clutter of jackets hanging from hooks. A small set of stairs leads us to the kitchen. It's open but filled with black surfaces and stainless steel. Charlie stares at a large glass bowl full of fruit on the center island. He picks an apple up and squeezes it.

"It's fake."

"Sure looks real."

"I bet they paid extra for real-looking fake fruit."

He opens the fridge and assesses its contents.

"What are you doing? Don't you have your doughnuts in the car?"

"What's in a fridge says a lot about someone."

"Anything interesting?"

"Too many condiments. Not enough real food."

He shuts the door

I stare at the bare fridge door. A magnet for a pizza joint holds a couple of receipts under it. "Also, what's on a fridge says a lot about a family."

"Hey, they only moved here recently." It feels like he's apologizing for them.

A cat comes around a corner and meows, rubbing itself against Charlie's pant leg. He doesn't kick it away but doesn't pay it any special attention either.

We walk into the dining room where a large picture, if that's what you'd call it, hangs. It's a field of color—orange—that nearly takes up half the wall. I barely give it any notice, but Charlie stares at it.

"Does it speak to you?" I ask.

He ignores me and moves on into the living room. It's as beautiful as it is hollow, with absolutely no personality. The sofas match the chairs and the white walls are only an extension of the white rugs and white curtains. The paintings on the walls are more ugly deco store designer art, something Mom has strongly voiced her dislike for. There are no photos in this house to indicate who may live here.

"Charlie, this family has no soul."

He sighs and nods as he heads up the stairs towards the bedrooms. The cat follows behind him.

I pause. "Wait, why aren't we going to the garage?"

"Don't you learn anything I teach you, Shepherd?" I wasn't aware I was supposed to be learning. "Let's case the joint quickly, gather whatever we can, then move on."

"But—"

"What?"

"What about the girl?"

He looks at me, his face empty of expression. "What about her?"

"She could be in the trunk of the car."

"So?"

His answer leaves me cold. When he's on the trail of something, he doesn't let anything stand his way, but he's ignoring a person's life. Then I realize what his priorities are. "You're not here for her. You're here for Robbie."

He sighs, like he has no time to deal with me. "He isn't our guy."

"But what if he is?"

I can see he doesn't even want to consider it, but he takes a step towards me. "So, what then? Think you'll get to the trunk and she won't look any different than that dog?"

The image of that poor animal flashes in my mind and I'm not sure I want to face it. Yet, I push ahead, ready to argue, but he cuts me off. "Look, you go be the hero and go save the damsel. I'm going to do what needs to be done."

He turns and heads up the stairs. I stand at the bottom, watching him head down the second floor hallway. I turn and look down another dark hallway, certain that it leads out to the garage, but I can't get myself to move as my brain rushes with thoughts. If Robbie is our guy, I'm certain I could take him. However, whoever went after us on Saturday almost took us both out and I realize this scares me. The idea that this is happening pisses me off, but until I can get a hold of it, I have to back away and follow Charlie's lead.

By the time I get upstairs, he's already moving on from the first room. I peek in as I walk by and see it's the master bedroom. Heavy, dark curtains keep out the light and the room is spotless, with no clothes on the floor or the chair.

Charlie sees me but keeps moving to the second room.

"All done?"

I hate showing my weaknesses to him and try keeping it short, "No."

He stops outside the next room and nods. "Good. Whoever is behind all this laid a shit-kicking on us last time, and I'd hate for us to split again so he can finish the job."

I smile, not sure if he's telling the truth or simply doing it for my benefit. "Hey, what can I say? We're partners."

He looks at me and smiles. "We are, aren't we?"

He uses a sleeved hand and opens the door.

It's the bathroom, and it's huge. A double sink is along one wall and a large standalone tub stands close to a shower.

Charlie stares at it. "Why is there all this stuff?"

"If you don't want a bath, then you can have a shower."

"Then just have a tub with a shower in it." I can see he really can't understand why anyone would want it any other way. "Rich people are stupid."

He closes the door and moves on to the last two doors at the end of the hallway.

"Do you even know where you're going?"

"No."

"Haven't you been here before?" I'm betting he came over for some pot party, but the way he makes friends I wouldn't be surprised if he'd never been here before either.

"Once, but only in the basement."

I pause. "Is Robbie even a friend?"

Charlie turns to me, his eyes looking sad. "Not really. But if we don't take care of the rejects of this world, who will?"

He opens the next door and we find a bedroom. It's another soulless room, like the master, but this one is to the extreme. It's scarce. There is a made bed and a small bookshelf filled with books arranged in order of height. The curtains are open and symmetrical and the light shines on the closed closet door. A chair sits in the corner. The room is empty. It reminds me of when my oldest sister Jodi moved away for college and she slowly took all the stuff out of her room over the years.

We shut the door and move on to the last room.

Rr-wow! A grey streak zips out of the bedroom between our feet.

"Another stupid cat?"

"That scared the crap out of me." I lean in to look at the room.

Chaos.

I don't even question that this disaster is Robbie's room. A makeshift curtain over the window is made of a Skrillex banner. The bed is unmade and clothes are everywhere. A stack of LPs are ready to topple off his dresser. A vaporizer sits next to an autobiography of Henry Rollins and a copy of *Rolling Stone* that has Howard Stern on the cover. There's a book on hydroponics facedown and half-read on the dusty dresser. At least he attempts to be well-informed. The room has no focus, no order. It's mayhem. It smells dusty, musty, skunky, and sweaty. I'm disgusted.

I move an empty pizza box a little to the left with my foot. "Wow, your buddy's a cliché."

Charlie holds up an LP of Deep Purple. "Well, at least he doesn't have terrible taste in music."

I shake my head—we'll never see eye to eye on this stuff.

"It's gross."

Charlie shrugs. "I've seen worse." I hope he's not referring to his own room.

"This is not the room of a killer."

"I agree. Can we go look at the car now?"

Charlie nods. He closes the door to the room. Both cats sit at the end of the hallway, staring at us. I'm glad they can't talk. This is the first time in my life I've entered a home that I haven't been invited into. Or broken into for that matter. My worldview is shifting.

We leave all the doors in the hallway as we found them and head downstairs. I'm at the garage door when Charlie takes a quick turn into the kitchen.

"Just a minute."

I wonder what he's up to when he returns with a can of iced tea.

"Are you kidding?"

He looks annoyed.

"You're not even thirsty."

"How do you know?"

"You just had a coffee. It's in my car."

"So, I want some iced tea."

"Sometimes I think you do things just because you can."

"He'd give me one if he were home!"

"Yeah, well he's not home,"

I'm raising my voice as we head into the garage. Perhaps it's a case of nerves from snooping around someone else's house, even if it feels like a soulless showhome, or the thought that Chrissy's life may depend on us, but I feel frustrated.

"You want me to get you one?"

"No!" I shout.

"You need to loosen—"

Thunk.

We look at each other, my heart pounding so loud I can hear it.

Charlie moves towards the car. "Hello?"

Thunk.

"Holy shit."

"The trunk."

I catch my breath and fly into action, running to the driver's side and popping the trunk. I scramble to Charlie, who stands speechless.

Inside is Chrissy, bound with rope and gagged. But alive!

99

She's terrified.

Without missing a beat, Charlie has his pocket knife out and works at the ropes behind her back that bind her hands.

"It's okay." He sounds gentle.

"Chrissy?" I ask.

She nods.

"I'm going to take the tape off your mouth. It's going to hurt for only a minute, okay?" Her eyes go wide with fear and I wince before I yank.

She whimpers.

Charlie moves to the rope around her feet. "One more." He pulls the cord away and helps her sit up.

"There you go."

She's distant, not focusing on us. He kneels down and places his hand on her shoulder. "You're safe. We're not going to let anyone hurt you." He turns to me. "Call Gekas."

I nod.

He looks back to Chrissy. "Are you okay?"

She's a long way from the selfie Mike took at the party. Her clothes and face are dirty, and she has a scratch on her cheek and a bruise on her forehead. "Get me out of here."

Charlie helps her out of the trunk and her bare

feet are bloody. "Do you know where you are?"

She begins to cry, "No idea." She grabs her stomach and manages to utter, "Oh God, I feel sick..." before running to the corner and vomiting.

"You're okay. We're calling the police." I grab my phone and dial Gekas. Busy signal! Of all the times...

Charlie comes over to me. "Tony—"

"I was right."

"Yeah, whatever. Listen, we have to get her out of here and find Robbie."

I'm pissed and ready to express it when—

Bzzz.

"Gekas?" Charlie asks.

I look. "No. Jessie." I read the text: *Asked around. Robbies at Brent Chans.*

Charlie shakes his head. "Brent lives down the street from the school. He's a dropout and a dealer and all the kids go to his place to get stoned. God, Robbie, you're such an idiot."

I gesture to Chrissy. "Maybe a bigger idiot than we thought."

"I doubt that."

I dial Gekas again.

This time, she answers.

"Detective?"

"What, Anthony?"

"We found her. We found Chrissy." I look over and see she's propped herself against a saw horse, pale and exhausted.

Gekas sounds distracted. "Where are you?"

I look over at Charlie, knowing he still has his doubts, but Chrissy needs help. "3212 Crawley

Crescent."

Again, a long pause. "Thank you, Anthony. Can you stay with her until I get some officers over and the paramedics arrive?"

"You're not coming?"

"I'm sorry, no."

"Detective—"

"Make sure Charlie stays around to give his statement."

"Okay, but Detective—"

"Thank him for me, will you? Okay, I have to go. Good bye." She hangs up.

Charlie looks at me. "What?"

"Something's up."

100

We help Chrissy out of the house as discretely as possible and wait on the curb. A few cars come down the street, slowing down. We must make quite a sight for this neighbourhood—a black kid, a shaggy haired troublemaker, and a girl who must look like—well, I don't really want to know what they must think we've done to her.

Charlie gives her the iced tea he's stolen and wanders to the car to get his coffee and bag of doughnuts.

I look over at Chrissy and know I have to ask, "Can you tell me what happened?"

She's quiet for a bit. I think she wants to cry but there's nothing left inside of her. "I was working day shift at the movie theater. It was quiet and boring and no one was coming because all the crappy shows are out. I was thinking about the party I went to the night before. I met a really nice guy and gave him my number and was hoping he'd call."

I smile, knowing it's Mike.

"Anyway, I had to go to the bathroom and went to the one we had in the back for employees. No one was around. It was quiet"— her voice cracks — "And then…" She breaks into big drying heaves.

I put my arm on her shoulder and she grabs my

hand.

"You don't know who grabbed you, do you? Someone you might have recognized?"

She shakes her head. "He had a mask on. Some creepy thing. I just…I can't"

I nod and squeeze her hand. We see Charlie on his way back and she wipes her eyes, running her fingers through her hair. I let her have her space and go to Charlie, who's on his phone.

"What's up?"

"Checking social media."

"See if there's anything about where Gekas is going?"

He nods. "Damn news moves too slow here." He sits beside us and I watch as he switches though his apps.

I see Chrissy staring at us. She's calmed down now that we're in the sun and the adrenaline's crashed. She nods at Charlie. "You go to my school, don't you?"

"Uh-huh," he mumbles without looking up from his phone. It seems he's turned off all of his empathy again now that we're back in the sun.

"And you were Sheri's boyfriend, right?" I notice the question is in the past tense, but I let it go.

"Yes."

She takes a sip of the iced tea. "Are you two some kind of undercover cops?"

I can't help but laugh. I shake my head.

"Then, how'd you find me?"

Charlie looks up and smiles. "Cuz, that's our job." He goes back to his phone.

Until he said it out loud, I never thought of it

like that, but now I understand his vigilance.

A police car and the paramedics arrive shortly afterward. We stick around to give our statements, but I can tell Charlie is annoyed. One more report to add to Gekas's growing file. Yet, by the time we are free to go, Charlie rushes me to the car.

"What's up?"

"I found Gekas. I think the cops are raiding Brent Chan's."

"The dealer?" I ask as I put on my seatbelt.

Charlie nods. "Somehow Gekas is onto Robbie."

"He's our only suspect."

"Yeah, but he's not the right one. You saw. It doesn't make sense."

I agree but we have no other leads. I pull onto the street, trying not to drive too recklessly in front of the cops.

"How did Gekas get to him?" Charlie pulls a doughnut out of the bag and bites into it. He runs the scenario in his head first, then out loud to me, "She has the photo and sees the car. But there's no license plate visible, so there's not a lot to go on. Unless the car got picked up after he lost it and it went in the system. But still, that's slim. They run the records and have to get a few hits." He looks over at me, "When you gave her the address, you're certain she was dealing with something big?"

"She didn't say it but I assumed."

He glares at me. "For Robbie's sake, I hope you're wrong."

101

By the time I get close to the school, the police have the streets blocked off. We find a place to park and get out.

A bunch of students stand by two cop cars that are angle parked on the street. When we push to the front, an officer says, "Stay behind the line for your safety, please."

I can see Gekas further down the street, looking at a map on the hood of a car and talking to another officer. None of the police have their guns drawn, so despite whatever's going on, the tension isn't too high yet. When I look over at Charlie, I realize he's already disappeared.

I push back through all the students and catch sight of Charlie moving towards a side street. I run to catch up.

"Where are you going?"

"I've spent time at Chan's."

"Is he dangerous?"

"Only in his own mind. But if Gekas tries to negotiate with him, she'll just make it worse."

"So, what do we do?"

Charlie stops and looks back at me. "You don't need to do this Shepherd."

I shrug. "No? But then who will?"

He smiles. "You're alright, when you're not being such a whiny baby."

I take it as a compliment and follow his lead. We move along the street until we are near Chan's. A police car sits in the street and I can see another cruiser down the block. Charlie moves into a backyard but I hesitate. The officer steps out of his car.

"Excuse me? Where do you think you're going?"

Charlie turns, acting innocent. "Oh, sorry, officer. I was just heading to my house."

The officer glares at him. "You have any ID on you?"

Charlie shakes his head. "I don't like to take my wallet to school, chance losing it, and have someone steal Mom's credit card or something."

The officer looks at me. "What about you?"

"Sorry, no."

He studies the two of us. "Well, we have a situation and I can't have you going back there. You'll just have to wait down at the end of the block."

I expect Charlie to argue his way around this, but he surprises me. "Sure thing, officer." He closes the gate and the two of us head back onto the street. As we walk away, Charlie pulls out his phone and flips through his contacts. "The backyard is covered, and although we're not going to get past all the cops, maybe we can bring Robbie to us." He takes a photo of the officer across from us and sends it.

He and I walk back to the intersection. "Who was that to?"

"Chan's supplier."

"Should I even ask how you have his number?"

"I've been doing some work for him on the side.

He figured Chan had been charging more than he's been saying and then smoking the overages."

"Was he?"

Charlie nods. "Remember, on the second day you came, I had Robbie bringing me some proof."

"The pipe?"

"What? No, dude, that was a test tube full of product Chan was selling." He looks at me. "Man, you should seriously get your eyes checked."

I don't believe him and I guess it shows.

"I needed Robbie's help to get me proof that Chan was cutting his supplier's stuff down to a lower grade."

Bzzz—he looks down at his phone. "Yup, it's amazing what you can do with your phone these days."

The doors to Chan's house bust open and stoner kids pour out, scattering to every corner. It's pandemonium and Gekas and her officers reach for their firearms but don't unholster them. The general nature of the stoners is a hazy disorientation, and their legs aren't interested in keeping up with the rest of their bodies. I laugh as the police corral the herd into a tight box. I look over at Charlie, but he isn't laughing.

"I don't see Robbie."

I scan the group. "Neither do I. You think he went out the back?"

"He's stupid but not that stupid."

The police are moving toward the house, guns drawn. They go through the open door and Charlie and I walk up to the police line. No one's talking now, except for the hushed radio chatter as the officers proceed through Chan's house.

I hear two gunshots and students standing next to the line duck to the ground. I don't move and then I see Charlie's face. He looks scared.

The radios sound off—*clear clear clear*—and go silent.

Suddenly, a radio crackles, "We need EMTs in here now."

Immediately, two paramedics race across the street with their kits and through the front door as more cops follow. Gekas comes out of the front door and I know it's bad. The radio chatter comes in short bursts of police code, but there's enough to know that someone's bleeding out and someone's dead.

102

I see where Gekas is and I move towards her. She's not thrilled to see me.

"Detective, what happened?"

"This isn't the place for you."

"Is Robbie in there?"

When I see her face, I know it's bad, but she deflects, "Why are you here?"

"Robbie's not the one."

"All the evidence says he is."

It isn't until Gekas looks over that I realize Charlie is behind me. "Is Robbie…?"

"It's not good, Charles."

Charlie gets in her face. "But he's too stupid to have done all those things."

Gekas pauses. "I know, but all the signs point to him."

"So you shot him?"

"No. By the time we got in there, Brent Chan had a gun on him."

"But you weren't there for Chan."

"No, but he was going on about Robbie being a rat, saying it was his fault we were there. Before we could do anything, Chan shot him, then turned the gun on himself."

Charlie stares in disbelief. Gekas reaches towards his shoulder before pausing and pulling back. She sighs, shaking her head as she moves back towards the house

I stand beside Charlie, not sure what to do. In the few weeks I've known him, I've seen nothing faze him, and now this guy he barely would call his friend has been shot and he seems rattled to the core.

"Charlie?"

He looks at me, at the house, and back at me before walking away into the milling crowd.

103

I find Charlie sitting on the curb down by the school, his hands propped on his knees, his phone hanging down. I hand over his coffee and bag of doughnuts that I grabbed from my car on the way over. He sets them between his feet.

"You okay?" I ask, knowing that is the stupidest thing to lead with. Me, of all people, should understand how annoying that question is.

"Getting Robbie shot was not my intention."

"Gekas says that—"

"I know what Gekas says. But I sure as hell didn't plan any of this."

I nod, not sure what to say next.

Charlie grabs the bag of doughnuts, rummaging through them until he pulls out a maple dip. "It doesn't make sense."

I can't imagine how Charlie must feel. It must suck feeling responsible for another person's death. "You couldn't know how Chan was going to react—"

"No, not that. That Robbie is some serial killer."

So much for Charlie's empathy—I never can keep up with this guy. However, I have to agree with him, Robbie isn't the right guy.

Charlie stares at the asphalt. "What are we missing?"

The siren of the ambulance interrupts our train of thought and we see it pull through the crowd, zooming down the street towards us. It hits the main thoroughfare, cutting through the red light and speeds off.

"The fact they've got the siren on is a good sign. Means they have something to fight for."

Charlie stares down the street for a long time before picking up his coffee and looking at me.

"Robbie moved recently. Why?"

104

Charlie's on his phone. "He came from some city out west. I've searched his name but nothing comes up." He takes a sip of his coffee, thinking it over.

"Wait a sec." He taps into the search bar and waits for the page to download. He taps again. "Kingstown! That's where he's from." He scrolls some more. "Oh, look at this. One article, dated a year ago about a Kingstown senior, unnamed of course, who was attacked in the school bathroom. No one was caught."

"Similar MO."

"Yes, but because us teenagers never know to keep our traps shut…" He works away at his phone. I can't help but be impressed watching him harness the power of the web. "A lot of social networks have semantic search engines that query all their big data."

"What are you talking about?"

"I can search age, location, likes, dislikes, relationships…anything."

"So?"

"So…by searching what the teens of Kingstown talked about a year ago, I'm ninety percent certain that our senior is Jayce Morgan."

"Who?"

He shows me his phone and I look. There's a stock photo from graduation of Jayce—a pretty girl with long, blonde hair.

He takes it back and searches some more. "And that's likely her phone number." I see his look and realize what he's asking.

"No."

"Come on. She's our only lead right now."

"It doesn't matter. I can't call a girl out of the blue that I've never met and ask her about an attack in a bathroom from a year ago."

"Well, I sure as hell can't but...you're a smooth-talking criminal."

I shake my head at his weak attempt to cajole me.

"Seriously, we need this. I need this. To make it right."

"For who?"

He doesn't answer and wobbles his phone in my face.

I weigh it in my mind. I know Robbie isn't the killer and I'm certain we're getting close to finding out who took Sheri.

"Okay, what's the number?"

105

As I dial Jayce, I shake my head. In the last few weeks, I've felt exhilarating rushes and real fear for the first time in my life. I've felt my heart pound, my palms sweat, and I've placed myself in uncomfortable, awkward lies that have twisted my stomach into knots. But this moment is not one of them. Now is when I might finally close in on the answer that I'm seeking.

ring ring

Charlie takes a bite out of his doughnut and follows it with a slug of coffee. Strangely, everything that's happened today seems to have taken its toll on him and he looks like an old man sitting on the curb.

ring ring

I feel my nerves tighten.

ring ring

The phone picks up and a teen girl answers, "Heya—"

"Hi, is this Jayce—?"

"—my phone is way over there and I can't get it, so don't be lame. Leave a message or send a text. Later." *Beep.*

I hang up abruptly.

"What the hell, Shepherd?" Charlie spurts out his sentence as quickly as he can swallow the rest of his doughnut down. I'm annoyed at him for being on my case, and I'm annoyed with myself for hanging up.

"I got her voicemail," I answer curtly.

"And, what? You couldn't say something?"

"Like what?"

"You don't have to hang up like some...like some freshman kid trying to get a date with the senior cheerleader." Charlie has this magical way of disconnecting and pushing buttons to provoke me and I can never tell if he's actually mad.

"What am I supposed to say? Hey Jayce, it's Tony Shepherd. You've never met me, but I was wondering how you feel about plastic bags and bathrooms!"

Charlie gets that 'what the hell?' look on his face. "Geez, Shepherd. Gear down, man."

I glare at him but he breaks into a big grin and I smile.

"Take a minute or two...or ten. She'll pick up eventually."

We walk to my car and get inside. I try a second time. It goes straight to voicemail. Charlie scrolls through his phone looking at what was happening in Jayce's world a year ago. I try one more time, ready to give up, knowing I'm verging on acting like the psycho that we're hunting.

"Hello?" It's her. My heart leaps. "Hello?"

"Hi. Is this Jayce?"

"Yes. Who's this?"

"My name's Tony. I was just wondering if you could help me out?"

"Who?"

"Tony Shepherd."

"Sorry. Do I know you?"

"No, but—"

"Do you work for the newspaper?

"No."

"Are you a cop? How do you know me?

"I'm not from—"

"How did you get my number?"

"I'm from—"

"I don't know you, so goodbye."

Click

"Shit."

Charlie looks at me. "That went well."

I dial again.

Charlie raises his eyebrows. "What are you doing?"

"I'm calling back."

He may know how to do a B&E, he may know what gadgets he needs to spy on someone, but I know how to talk to people. This is what I do.

ring ring

"Look, psycho, I told you not to call me! I'm going to trace your number and the cops will be on your doorstep!"

"I'll give you my phone number, address. Heck, I can give you the name of a nice detective who'd be happy to help you out...Jayce, please...I promise, just give me a minute and when that minute's up, and you don't want to listen anymore, you can hang up. Just one minute. Deal?"

Silence.

"Please? Almost everyone's got at least one minute to spare."

It seems like the longest pause in the world right now.

"Okay. Go."

"I know something happened to you about a year ago—"

"Stop. We're done—"

"No, no, no. You promised me one minute."

I hear her exhale but she doesn't hang up.

"I'm calling because the same thing is happening again and I think they're connected." I hold on a moment waiting for what I say to sink in, but not giving her too long. "I want to stop what's going on, but I don't have enough information, and I need your help. I know what happened to you was scary—is scary—and you didn't deserve it either, but I don't think anyone else should go through what you did. I just need a little more information. Can you help me?"

Silence. I hear nothing and hope she hasn't hung up.

"What do you need to know?"

I breathe again and Charlie gives me the thumbs up.

"Thank you."

"Whatever. Just because I'm giving you more than a minute doesn't mean I won't hang up."

"Fair enough." I pause, wondering how I'm going to proceed. I decide to jump right in.

"Last year you were attacked?"

"Yes."

"In the bathroom?"

"Yes."

"Did you see the person?"

"No. Well, not completely. I saw parts of him."

"Him? So, there's things you noticed?"

"Why can't you get a copy of the police report and leave me alone?"

"Because you'll tell me some things the police may not have asked."

"You're really not a cop?"

"No." I'm not sure why she keeps considering this.

After a long silence, she asks, "What for?"

I take a deep breath. "My girlfriend went missing a few weeks ago. The cops have tried everything but it all comes up a dead-end and I'm trying to find out where she is and what happened to her. I love her and I miss her, and to be honest, I think you may be my only help."

She breathes out. "Okay, Tony. Keep asking."

Charlie leans in and listens.

106

"Do you know Robbie—?" I realize I don't know his last name. I look over at Charlie and he looks back at me, clueless to the question. I muffle the phone. "What's his last name?

Charlie shrugs.

"What do you mean? You don't know?"

"Why would I?"

"A few seconds ago, you were upset that he got shot."

"So? Doesn't mean I have to ask him all his personal details."

"You know my last name!"

"Yeah, but why do you think I only called you Shepherd?"

"You can't remember my first name?"

"Sometimes I can…on and off. Look, it's not my style."

"It's his name."

"Yeah, if I needed to know, I'd just steal your wallet and look."

I'm dumbfounded and I hear Jayce in the background ask, "Hello?"

I go back on the phone. "Hi."

"Who are you talking to?"

"Um, my… uh… colleague." I'm frustrated with

the lameness of my answer.

"Is he listening in? You didn't tell me—"

I'm going to lose all my hard work if I'm not careful. "I'm sorry, Jayce, I really am. My name is Tony Shepherd and the other guy is Charlie Wolfe." I exaggerate my first name and give Charlie a look. He rolls his eyes.

"We just want to catch the guy we think did this to you."

"And your girlfriend?"

"Yes, and my girlfriend."

Silence.

"What's her name?

"Sheri." Saying it does something to my insides.

Another long pause, but I can't keep waiting.

"There is a boy, Robbie, in Grade…" I look at Charlie and he shrugs again and I shake my head "…I'm not sure, maybe Grade 10 or 11. He went to your school."

"I was a senior last year, so I probably didn't know him."

"He's kind of a screwup. Hung with the drug crowd…" I run through my head what I know and it's really not a lot. I grasp at straws. "He's short—"

Charlie grabs the phone out of my hand. "Hi Jayce, this is Charlie here. I don't know Robbie's last name but he got shot today and he's having a really bad day, so I can't ask him his last name. What I can tell you is that he likes Skrillex, Henry Rollins, Howard Stern, the Grateful Dead, Pink Floyd, and Deep Purple. He's also probably and almost certainly got kicked out of school more than once. He was also the kid in bio or chem class that asked about hydroponics a lot, which got him sent to the office a lot because he's a druggie, right? But he actually liked growing strawberries and basil and mint and—"

"Oh my god, are you talking about Catnip?"

We look at each other confused.

"Who's Catnip?" Charlie asks.

"He was this kid who went to our school last year. Stoned all the time but turns out the old ladies loved him because he'd get all their gardens going great at the start of spring because he'd sell them the best plants. I guess he had a real green thumb.

"Anyway, the rumor was that he was growing small quantities of marijuana in his patch and selling it to other students. Teachers hear about this, they plan to come down hard on him—"

Charlie interrupts her, "And they bust him and find out that it's catnip?"

"Better. He found out beforehand and swapped it out. Still got expelled though because administration thought he scammed a bunch of students."

"I don't think Robbie would be that smart—"

"Nah, they said he had help."

"Who?"

"Robbie's brother, I think."

I look at Charlie and he shrugs.

Charlie asks, "The brother, he went to your school?"

"No, he went to some private school that's a feeder program to some of the bigger universities."

"I don't get it."

"They are places where Mommy and Daddy pay big money to give you a high-end education and you live in dorms and it's all fancy pants."

Her cynicism is strong.

"So, why do you think he helped Robbie?"

"He was in some big play and he was worried Robbie was going to mess it up all up for him."

This peaks Charlie's attention.

"He was in drama?"

"Yeah. They'd always force us to see the plays each year."

I guess Jayce is not a lover of the arts.

"What grade was he in?"

"Don't know. They didn't really use grades at his school. More about who you were than your grade."

"But if you had to guess his age."

"Maybe my age, maybe a year older."

Is this our guy? Charlie leans into the phone. "What ever happened to his brother? Did he get to do his play?"

"I'm—I don't know."

There's hesitation in his voice and before I can stop Charlie, he charges on like a bull. "Why not?'

"Because just after that, I got attacked."

I punch Charlie in the arm for being stupid. He seems not to realize how insensitive he was being. I take the phone away from him.

"Thank you, Jayce. I think you helped us."

She's quiet again. "You don't think—?"

"I'm not sure. But we're going to find out."

"Okay," she says. I can hear the worry in her voice, like everything is happening all over again.

"Jayce?"

"Yes?"

"Do you know the brother's name?"

"Yeah. His name was Connor."

107

I hang up with Jayce and look over at Charlie.

"So, what do you think?"

"I think we should go grab a sandwich."

"Really? You just finished a bag of doughnuts."

"No, I still have one left."

"You're not going to eat it?"

"Nope. It's special." He gets off the curb and starts heading to my car. When he realizes I'm not behind him, he turns. "You coming?"

"What about what Jayce? What about everything she said?"

"Come on, let's go. I'm hungry."

We're so close. This could be our guy. And he wants to eat?

"Why don't you weigh 400 pounds?"

"Cuz." He grins and heads to the car, acting like Ollie when he knows a squirrel is in the backyard.

"Can I drive?"

I laugh, imagining what he'd do in the driver's seat of Dad's car.

"Don't you trust me?"

"Do you even have a license?"

"Do you think it would matter?"

I pop open the lock with the remote and point to the passenger side. He obliges and takes his usual seat. I climb in and he's got the window down and is already going through Dad's CDs, looking for music. He chooses *Bones* by Bodhi Jones. He listens to it for a few seconds and slowly grows into the mood, tapping his hand against the roof of the car.

"Where to?"

"South."

There's lots of traffic and the drive is slow but it doesn't seem to faze Charlie. He's on his phone, but I can't see what he's scrolling through.

"I think he's our guy," Charlie announces.

"How can you be sure?" I don't want to be biased by hope.

"First, the car. When Robbie said he lost it, he called it the family car. As you pointed out, it's a piece of shit, not a family car—especially not for that family. Maybe it's the second vehicle for the kids. It also explains the difference between his first attacks and the next few. They were closer to the city, simpler. After Robbie lost the car, the bodies were dumped near the places where the girls were attacked. At some point, when he got the car back, he started moving them again."

I pull up to a light and look over at Charlie, watching his mind work through the puzzle.

"Second, the mirrors and the camera. Early on, we felt he was performing, first for himself, then for us. He's a theater student, and from what Jayce said, a serious one at that." He hands me his phone. "Look at the guy left of center."

Charlie's brought up a photo from the university newspaper of a recent production by the Theatre Department. I see three rows of the cast and crew

362

standing on the stage. They're smiling, goofy, having fun—except for one guy.

Charlie flips to another tab and shows me another image. This time, they are production promo photos. Same guy in two photos, again the people around him are engaged and laughing. He is stoic and separate.

I look close at him and I can see a slight resemblance to Robbie, more of a distant cousin than a close sibling.

He's tall with dark hair and looks utterly boring. Over these past few weeks, I've imagined the sort of person who attacked Sheri, and who's been killing all of these teenage girls. I imagined the Devil, a monster, a sex freak, some hillbilly with a chainsaw full of perversion and bloodlust. I want to hate him, to be scared of him, but I don't know if I can. He's nothing like what I thought he would be—only a screwed-up teen, who seems to float along just like everyone else. Well, almost everyone else.

A horn honks behind me and I realize the light is green. I hand Charlie the phone and quickly make my turn. I drive down the block and make my decision. "We're not calling Gekas on this," I say confidently.

"We're not?" He looks at me, a little speechless.

"No, we're not. Not until we're certain. Not until we are without a shadow of a doubt."

"Well, all right then." There is no debate from Charlie.

108

We sit at the sub place by the window. I finish off some potato chips and Charlie chows down on his 12-inch meatball sub sandwich. He eats it slowly and with what appears to be wicked pleasure. It's a sloppy one but he's careful and tidy—much tidier than when he eats doughnuts.

I think about the comment he made about how a person's fridge reflects on the household. I think about mine, stocked with fruits and veggies and carefully labelled leftovers. I wonder what his must be like. Is it empty or filled with food he hates and that's why he seems to eat out so much?

"Good sandwich?"

"Yeah. Thanks."

He continues to enjoy it and I let him eat in peace. He puts the last bite in his mouth and leans back in his chair.

"We should go to the university." He wipes each finger one at a time with his napkin.

"That's what I was thinking." We're on the same page. Perfect.

Charlie stands picking up his fountain drink and slurps the last of it out of the cup. He takes everything off the table and tosses it away into the trash bin. I walk with him.

"Any idea where we're going when we get there?"

"Nope. I don't." He says with his usual certainty. That's good enough for me.

We agree en route that to save time we should just go directly to the Theater Department. Asking registry if they have a student named Connor in all the thousands of students attending is a shot in the dark. Going to the Theatre Department where the faculty is small may be a much better strategy.

As I drive onto the campus, I realize I have no clue where I'm going.

"Been here before?" I ask casually.

"No, you?"

"I played a couple of basketball games, so I know where the courts are."

"But the Fine Arts Department?"

"Nope."

"Nice." Charlie smiles as he says this.

"Really?" I don't know how two clueless teenagers can navigate this scenario one bit.

"Yeah. It'll be an adventure." Charlie grins and I shake my head, equal parts amused and worried but I'm game. Besides, nothing in this place can beat what we saw and faced in that basement.

I find a parking meter near the Kinesiology building and park the car. I dig into my pockets looking for change while Charlie stands there. I don't expect him to contribute, because I have a feeling there's no use, whether he can afford it or not.

We walk through the main doors with no idea of how near or far we are from the Theater Department. I recognize the area, having come for tournaments and summer basketball camps, but I've not strayed far from this one building. While I'm confident around people, my sense of direction could use some work. I pause, trying to get my bearings.

Charlie pushes past me. "Keep walking," he says quietly.

I speed up to catch him. "But where are we going?"

"If you stop right in the doorway, you look like a deer in the headlights and everyone notices the lost guy. Look while you walk, and we'll figure it out as we go."

I wonder if this is the mantra that Charlie lives his life by. It also makes sense, like a play on the court. I don't know what's coming, but I can't stand there like an idiot trying to figure it out.

We get to the end of a hallway and I finally know where I'm going. The pools are to my right and to the left is a long corridor. We head down it.

Students and adults move past me. I always assumed they'd be self-assured and I'd look like a kid to them but most of them seem as confused or stressed or bored with life as I sometimes do. I think about mentioning this to Charlie, but I realize that university may not be his thing—or that he may not even have the grades or money to get in. I hold my tongue, feeling another difference between us that I'd never considered.

I see one map as we walk and casually look over at it to discover that it only tells us where to find things in the building we're in. I'm thinking we should stop and ask for directions, but I know Charlie will ignore the suggestion.

We get to the end of the long hall and it breaks in a T. On the right is a set of double doors that curve up and lead to another set of doors behind it. A sign above guides us to student residences and the library. Charlie goes left and I follow. It's another long hallway and a turn right. We turn at a sign that directs us towards the Film Department. We move down a narrow hallway full of closed doors and come out on the other side, feeling even more lost than we were before.

"Well, that was a bust," Charlie states.

He turns left and heads down the hallway, and we make our way back to the first hallway. We move back to the T and this time we turn right and head through the doors.

We go through a bright corridor with windows on the left and make our way between the buildings. It leads to an older section with dark brick and tile and another T intersection. I watch the flow of students and teachers moving around me and can't figure out how they know where they're going. "This place is a maze."

"Haven't you ever played a video game? When you're in a cave or dark tunnels, you always turn left, that way you'll eventually end up where you started."

"What if the Theatre Department is on a right?"

He doesn't want to even acknowledge the question and turns left again.

We move past the library and zigzag through the hallways. Surprisingly, we get to another T and Charlie asks, "Do you have two dollars?"

"Sure." I hand him some coins and he heads to a

pop machine.

"You need a drink?" I ask, incredulous.

As he waits for his bottle to drop down, I realize he's looking around at his surroundings. He sees me watching him.

"You're sneaky."

He smiles at me. "Like a fox."

A guy, not much older than me, walks over to us. He's got an accent that I can't quite place. He struggles to ask, "Do you know—how I get up-stairs?"

Charlie looks at me and smiles. He points down the hallway to where we came from. "Go halfway down, turn left. Go halfway down that hall, and there are a set of stairs that should get you up there."

The student smiles and nods and heads off. I stare at him.

"What? I pay attention."

We head left and walk past a cafeteria packed with students.

"I suppose you'll be here in a couple of years?" he asks.

I'm surprised he brought it up, but I try to downplay it. "Maybe."

"Oh, whatever. You'll be nerding out with the rest of these geeks."

"What about you?" I ask, hoping to sound sincere.

"I don't think this place could handle *this*." He gestures towards himself like a showgirl. It seems like a deflection but he says it with such confidence I wonder if a part of him believes it.

He veers right and stops beside a map.

"I thought you didn't believe in asking for directions?"

"That's before I realized how disorganized it was here." We look down the legend on the side and find the Theatre Department. We look at where it is and where we are on the map—somewhere on the bottom left, on the second floor.

"We've almost gone around the entire campus!"

"The whole place is a big square, to herd us sheep in circles and keep us from realizing we're being indoctrinated into their system," Charlie states casually.

We move on and head towards a bright building made of concrete before slipping back to the brown tile and brick. Now that we have a direction, we move with the flow, like we really do belong. We come around a corner and a set of metal stairs rises in front of us. We head up the stairs and are immediately lost again.

"What's with these people? Maybe when you sign up, they implant a chip in your skull to guide you around this zoo."

I catch sight of a sign for the Theatre Department on the far side of the building.

Charlie nods. "Good eyes."

I take the compliment from Charlie. Although Dad has glasses, I seem to have Mom's genes for good eyesight.

"We'll need to figure out his last name or at least where he may be, his courses, anything." I say out loud. While Charlie does most of his thinking in silence, I feel I have to narrate my thoughts.

"Yes. Follow me."
"Isn't that what I always do…"

109

Instead of heading towards the Theatre Department, Charlie doubles back down the stairs to an open food court packed with people.

"But you just ate, man."

"I know." Charlie smirks.

"You're not eating again are you?"

He considers it and then answers, "No. Not right now."

He grabs us an empty table in the centre of the crowd. He hands me the student newspaper and I know the drill. I open it and try to look inconspicuous while he pulls out his phone and flips through it.

I look over at him. "What are we doing?"

"Relax. You want to find him, right?"

"Yes."

"Then we need an access point to figure out more about him and who he is. Look to your three o'clock."

I turn slowly. Sitting a few tables over is a man in his late 30's or early 40's, multitasking between his laptop and phone. He nurses a coffee in a travel mug.

"What do you see?"

"A professor?"

"And?"

I notice his eyes darting around the space and barely looking at his computer.

"He's waiting for someone?"

"Uh-huh. And I'm guessing not for long."

We scan the area, trying to figure out who he's looking for.

Then I see her—a very beautiful, leggy redhead walking up the stairs to the second floor. I look over at the professor and she's caught his attention.

She moves along the walkway to a space upstairs, and although she's trying hard to look older, she's definitely a student. I point her out to Charlie. "I'm pretty sure she's not a colleague."

"Nice work, Shepherd. Just like that ancient Police song, huh?"

I don't get the reference, but he doesn't care. He stands up. "Two cream, two sugar?"

"Um, sure?"

"You stay here and keep watch."

I say, "Okay," but Charlie doesn't hear me and takes off. He walks over to the coffee shop and stands in line, looking around, waiting.

I watch the professor take one last look at the redhead before leaning over to a couple of guys sitting beside him. He gestures to his computer and they nod back. This dude can't be that stupid. I'm dumbfounded when he rises and heads towards the stairs, leaving his computer behind.

I watch the silent movie of Charlie shooting out of line and walking straight to the computer and taking a seat. The guys beside him glance over and he convinces them that everything he's up to is legit.

I look up and see the professor and the redhead. His hands are in his pockets, acting cool, and she has a pretty smile but an exaggerated laugh that she follows with touching his arm.

Charlie's now hacking away at the computer, taking a sip out of the professor's coffee, cringing at the taste, and going back to work.

The redhead has her phone out and the professor points at something on it. I look at Charlie and signal that he needs to hurry up. He nods and holds up a finger indicating he still needs a minute but I'm not sure if we have one.

The professor is done wheeling the redhead and she puts her phone away—I'm guessing with his number now. He's on his way down the stairs and I get up to intercept him but it's too late. He sees Charlie and yells but everyone in the cafeteria turns and looks to him and no one sees the kid at his computer. When I get to the bottom of the stairs, the professor rushes past me, pushing through the bottleneck of hopeful scholars, but it's too late. Charlie is out of his chair and on the move.

I can't help but linger.

The professor gets to his computer, asking the boys beside him who Charlie was and why they let him on it. They all shrug, indifferent to their temporary task of protecting the laptop while the professor was working it with the redhead. I'm also certain they'd heard a convincing enough story from Charlie to not give a crap. My phone buzzes and I look to find a text: *Upstairs*.

I head up and hear someone call my name. Charlie's down at the end of a hall and I move his way. We travel down a corridor, far away from the professor, and the noise of the crowd falls away. We are left only with the quiet hum of the building and the *tap tap tap* of our running shoes echoing off the bare walls. We carry on past the Music Department.

"I got it. All his details. Class schedule, marks, how much he's paid for his books. By the way, I'm definitely not going to university! "

"You're crazy."

"Maybe, but aren't we all."

"Does he have class right now?"

"Nope."

I'm disappointed, feeling like we're out of runway on this crazy trip, but something's up because Charlie's smiling.

"What?"

"He's not around, because he's practicing for *this*."

I look over and see a poster for the Theatre Department's production of *As You Like It* starring our own in-house serial killer.

110

We take a back stairwell and come out in the middle of the Theatre Department. Props and sets line the hallways and music echoes out of a room to our left. Around the corner, we come to a lounge where students sprawl out in bunches, working on homework or playing on their phones. I pull Charlie back around the corner before we're noticed.

"We barely know what he looks like."

"So? We know enough."

"He knows us better. Remember that he spent Saturday afternoon beating the crap out of us." I don't usually have the pleasure of making Charlie pause, but I did this time.

"Fair enough. What's your plan?"

I don't know if I have a plan. He's never deferred to me and I'm a little surprised. "Well, he's been so busy watching us and setting up his little performances that I think it's our turn to watch him."

"Nice."

I head back around, keeping my eyes open for anyone who might look like Connor. There's no sign of him. I note a girl, looking like something between a hipster and a punk, laying on a couch reading a graphic novel. I can't help but think that university doesn't seems that hard. I tap on her shoulder so I don't startle her.

She slowly slides off her headphones and looks at me, annoyed.

"I'm looking for rehearsals for *As You Like It*."

"We're way past rehearsals, dude."

"What do you mean?"

She looks at us a bit more carefully. "Are you even in the Theater Department?"

Charlie steps in. "Are you?"

She glares at him. "Hey—!"

"Hey, yourself." He nods at her book. "Superheroes? Seriously? Why not try something a little more above your reading level."

I interject before someone starts swinging, "Can you just tell me where they're practicing?"

She sighs and with the most laborious of efforts, raises her arm and points. "Down the hall, but be quiet. There's a matinee on." She pulls the book in front of her face, blocking herself from sight.

We head around the corner and find a staircase. We descend a flight and find a locked door. We move back up to another level and find another locked door.

Charlie shakes his head. "What is with this place? I'd hate to be stuck here in a fire."

We hear a door shut below. A young guy with spotlights in each hand runs up the stairs.

"Hey, can you grab the door for me."

"It's locked."

He looks at us like were idiots. "No, the one on the next floor."

"Uh, sure?" I race up all the way to the top of

the stairs and we find ourselves on a walkway, high above the stage, and open the door for him.

"Thanks." If he paid any attention, he'd notice Charlie and I have wandered in behind him.

Down below, the auditorium seats are packed with high school students, sitting silently and bored in the darkly lit theatre. I'm sure some are watching the stage, but from what I'm seeing, I'm positive many are asleep. A beautiful set of a forest with sculpted trees rises up to the archway, leaves and branches crisscrossing between them. Two men stand below, speaking to each other, and I'm not sure, but I think the one guy wants to lay down and die.

I look at the kid we followed up here. "How do we get down there?" I point to the seats below.

The guy looks at me. "Don't you work here? Shit, you shouldn't be up here."

Charlie steps in. "Relax. We just got turned around on the stairs."

The lighting guy ushers us out the way we came. "Out the door, down the stairs, through the hallway, cut across to the right and try the door."

Charlie can't let it be and nods and smiles. "Oh, so *easy*, then?"

The guy gives us a look as I push Charlie out the door.

"You can't just let your mouth stay quiet some times, can you?"

He looks at me confused. "What?"

We follow the instructions, but of course, the door is locked. We move further down and finally find one that's open. We head inside.

377

111

We come out on a second floor balcony. Light from the bright lobby outside floods in and I rush Charlie to get the door closed before we attract attention. My eyes take a moment to adjust to the dark. It's quiet up here and we wander down to the first row and pull down the seats.

Two new actors are on the stage talking and one I don't recognize says:

"How now, monsieur. What a life is this,
That your poor friends must woo your company?
What, you look merrily!"

I stare as the other actor walks out onto the stage and stands under a spotlight. My heart pounds loudly in my head. Is that him? All I have to go on is a couple of small, blurry photos, and from up here, it could be anyone. However, there's something about him that feels off, over-rehearsed, like he's planned every move, every word, to the point that his very presence is stiff, almost empty.

Connor, or at least who I think is him, speaks:

"A fool, a fool! I met a fool in the forest,

A motley fool. A miserable world!
As I do live by food, I met a fool…"

I stare at him, trying to imagine him as the guy behind the mask or the guy that killed Bonnie or Maggie. Or Sheri. It's all a blur of white noise and my head pounds with confusion. This is not the monster I imagined, the ugly evil that disembowels dogs and murders women. If this is him, he's a dumb kid, clueless to reality. He's not much different from his brother Robbie, except his way of dealing with being trapped in suburban hell with helicopter parents and the pressure to be perfect wasn't to numb himself, but to experience the world by destroying it.

"O worthy fool! One that hath been a courtier,
And says, if ladies be but young and fair,
They have the gift to know it: and in his brain,
Which is as dry as the remainder biscuit
After a voyage, he hath strange places cramm'd
With observation, the which he vents
In mangled forms. O that I were a fool!
I am ambitious for a motley coat."

Charlie watches intensely, his back flagpole straight. I'm not sure I've seen him so hyper-focused before.

"It is my only suit:
Provided that you weed your better judgments
Of all opinion that grows rank in them
That I am wise. I must have liberty

Withal, as large a charter as the wind,
To blow on whom I please; for so fools have—"

I can't help but think he speaks as himself and not as Jaques.

"What do you think?" I ask Charlie.

He nods. "It's him."

112

Connor moves off the stage, pleased with his performance of the last scene. He's frustrated, because the fool playing Orlando choked on his lines again. He's not jealous that Orlando has more lines—everyone knows that Jacques is the better role—but every other actor's mistakes trickle down to the delivery of his own.

He doesn't go too far, since there's only a brief scene and a half before he needs to return to the stage. He sits in a chair at the back where he can look out and see the audience. He likes the one way mirror the theatre offers: while on-stage, he can be seen but can't see the people watching him, and when he is backstage, he can peer out at them, without them knowing.

He tries to focus on the present moment, remaining in this world, in this character, but he struggles, his mind shifting to the girl in the trunk. He's kept her at home, safe from detection, keeping her alive before he decides what to do with her.

He grabbed her on Sunday while at a matinee. After the excitement of the past few days, the movie had been boring—some stupid show about a guy fighting his drug addiction—and he left to wander.

He found a doorway at the end of the hall that

led to some stairs and he followed them up to the projector room. The space was long and wide with ten machines spooling film onto big platters. It was dark and noisy, and although he saw someone sitting at a desk hand-cranking through a reel of film, they never heard him or looked up. He found another set of stairs that lead him down to a staff room somewhere deep in the belly of the theater. A young girl that seemed his type walked by and he knew he wanted to follow her. *Opportunity only knocks once*— and he had fortunately fallen into the habit of carrying his supplies with him in his bag, including the mask he slipped on.

He found her in the bathroom and by now had fallen into a routine. In fact, it had become too straightforward, and as he rushed her he immediately felt an emptiness inside as he realized that her fight with him had become more irksome than elated. However, he was in the middle of the act now and he could not simply bow out and apologize for the mistake. He had to follow through somehow.

He punched her in the temple, hoping it would knock her out. He was successful and she went limp beneath him. He went into his bag and pulled out a roll of duct tape and wrapped her arms and feet and taped over her mouth. After checking the hallway quickly, he carried her out of the closest exit and placed her behind a dumpster. He went around the building and grabbed his car and brought it to the rear, backing up so that the open trunk would cover him from any possible witnesses. He moved quickly, placing her inside, uncertain whether he was seen.

The physical exertion of moving the still breathing creature with the possibility of being caught helped his heart to race. A new challenge was emerging. He shut the trunk and drove back to his residence.

He no longer felt connected to the people that had raised him. At one time, he saw them as Mom and Dad, and that idiot, Robbie, as his brother, but ever since he focused his energy on his new work, he felt those relationships slip away. He could never share with them the skills he had acquired, the audacity with which he performed, the agility he was able to display. Besides, they likely wouldn't have cared. They only worried about keeping Robbie on the straight and narrow, longing for the day that he would correct his course and make it through school so he could get a career. He was never certain when it happened, but he knew his parents had become blasé about his existence, indifferent to his successes. He had proved to them his ability to achieve and they had become disinterested in his future prospects.

In the quiet times, between acts, he'd ask himself why he was doing what he had begun. He loved the rush and the challenge, but wondered if there was a deeper meaning to his deeds. Was this a cry for help or a desperate attempt for the attention that he felt he deserved? When he gave it thought, the answer was always no. There was never a corollary between his actions and his parent's approval. He was not seeking their attention—in fact, he was resistant to the ramifications that such attention might elicit.

He preferred the silence of the vacuum, so that he might carry on as he had, because what he sought was perfection. As he watches the players on the stage, marking their exits and entrances, he believes that murder is an ideal, a refinement of action and reaction. He was above everyone: the other actors, the director, the audience, and the people working in the wings around him; his role was to be the force that ruptures the heavens, and his performance would be the shining example for all to remember.

He was perfection.

113

Connor is off the stage and I watch intently until he returns. I've never been a big fan of Shakespeare but this wait is solidifying my opinion more so. It isn't until I feel Charlie tap on my arm that my attention is drawn away and I see two police officers standing in the dark shadows by an exit.

"Are they here for him?" I whisper.

Charlie doesn't answer and continues to watch.

"Charlie…?"

"I don't know, Shepherd."

Their presence feels like a confirmation that Charlie and I are on the same page as the law, and it thrills me as much as it terrifies me.

I sit on the edge of my seat, scanning the audience, wondering if there are more cops. I look for anyone out of place among the teenagers, presuming there might be others not in uniform. However, except for the officers at the door, nothing seems out of place. In fact, judging by their casual stance, it feels like we are the only ones holding our breath.

They make their way to an illuminated side exit and lean against the wall without urgency, but my eyes dart over to Connor as he returns to the stage. Two women who I've figured out are playing Rosalind and Celia follow him. I wonder if his character, Jaques, is hitting on Rosalind. Although I know it's only a performance, he's a messed up person and the thought of him touching another human being repulses me. He seems disinterested in everything, a dark shadow amongst the otherwise bright, funny characters, and again, I teeter in uncertainty over whether or not it is Jaques or Connor I am looking at. Is he the player or the man?

He moves across the stage stepping into a spotlight near the front:

"I have neither the scholar's melancholy, which is

emulation; nor the musician's, which is fantastical,;

nor the courtier's, which is proud; nor the
soldier's, which is ambitious; nor the lawyer's,
which is politic; nor the lady's, which is nice; nor
the lover's, which is all these—"

His focus shifts, his view moving to the police officers, his body becoming rigid and straight. He falls into silence.

Charlie and I sit straight up in our seats.

114

They are here.

He always felt that one day they would catch up to him, and all the work, all the training, all the practice will come down to this one live, unpredictable moment. He feels a steady wave of energy. He is neither nervous nor afraid. All of his practice has made him perfect, as the saying goes. On this stage, here and now, he will fulfill the role he has always been born to play.

It's time.

The final performance is about to begin.

115

We watch as Rosalind and Celia look at each other, confused and concerned.

An awkward cough rises from the audience.

A voice from the wings whispers, "But it is a melancholy…"

Someone giggles in the audience.

The hushed voice repeats the line, louder this time, "But it is a melancholy of mine own…'

Rosalind puts her hand on Connor's back. "Jaques, is it a melancholy of your own?"

He jerks, looking at her, swallowing, then a smile, a shift in his face, a change in his demeanor. Finally he speaks again:

"But it is a melancholy of mine own,
compounded of many simples, extracted
from many objects…"

The tension in the auditorium dissipates slightly.

"…and, indeed, the sundry contemplation
of my travels; in which my often rumination
wraps me in a most humorous sadness."

Rosalind smiles. "A traveller! By my faith, you have great reason to be sad."

She turns her back and Connor reaches into his costume. I feel what's about to happen before I witness it. He slowly pulls a plastic bag out of his costume, drawing it tight in his fist. He takes a step toward Rosalind. I look down at the cops. They don't make a move.

"Stop him!" I yell.

The officers turn to look at me and the entire auditorium joins them. It's then that I realize whatever reason they are here, it isn't to arrest Connor.

Charlie grabs me. "It's up to us, Shepherd," and I'm shaken out of being an innocent bystander. "It's time to move. Now!"

And I'm up, racing towards the exit.

116

Charlie hits the stairs first but I pass him on the way down. I break right as he heads for the auditorium doors.

"Keep going for the backstage. We'll cut him off!" Charlie yells as he races away.

I sprint down the hallway, balls to the wall, full throttle. Holy shit! I'm chasing after a serial killer. On purpose. I don't even have a plan. What the hell?

Whatever fear had seized me early today is now gone. Whatever monster mask I had feared that Connor wore in my imagination has disappeared. He was flesh and bone and not much older than me. I know that if I catch him, I could make him bleed.

I turn right, then left, and I shoot past the hipster/punk girl reading her comic as someone yells at me to slow down. I zip past doors and props and rooms filled with actors dressed in costumes. I turn left and race through a door into a blackened hallway and onto the dark wings on the sides of the stage. An actor dressed in period costume glares at me and tells me to be quiet.

I look on stage and it's soundless mayhem. The actors stare, lost in silence, and I realize Connor's nowhere to be found. I shift, looking for Charlie or the cops, and I can't see any of them anywhere.

A guy with a headset shouts, "What the hell else am I supposed to do? End the show?!" I want to feel sorry for him but I don't have time.

"Where's Connor?"

"I have no idea but when you find him, let me know because I'm pretty sure I'm going to kill him. I can't handle this crap!" He pulls his headset off, rubbing his already messy head of hipster hair.

I run off backstage, feeling the strategy of the court coming to me as I work to anticipate what will come next. I shoot back out into the hallway, checking every door. It's like a drill, with me using my legs to bolt, stop, start and my hands to shake every handle on every door I pass. I'll have to thank Coach Davies for all the hard work he's put me through to help me chase down criminals.

Someone yells, "Hey!" and I hear a crash and I follow the noise around a corner. I find a pile of hats and fabrics and feathers and a poor stagehand cleaning up the mess. I hurdle past her.

"Asshole!" she yells and I want to apologize but I don't have the time.

I return to the large hallway behind the stage and hear the *thuck* of a stairwell door close. I rush to it, swing it open, and hear the *ratatat* patter of footsteps descending. I look over the edge and see a hand disappear off the railing.

I race after the person, unsure if it's Connor.

I spill out into another open hallway, but it's quiet and deserted. I move left, travelling quietly around the corner, hoping to hide my position and hear if he might reveal his. At the end of this hall is a locked door with a keycode, so I head back the way I came. There's an office to the right of the stairs with a big window and the lights on. Unless he went through another locked door and is hiding under the desk, I'm pretty sure he's not there.

Where the hell is Charlie? I could really use his help.

I proceed around a corner and find yet another hallway with a big, solid bay door on one side and long metal beams with hanging lights above. At the end is a doorway, and I race towards it.

Inside is a small dark room with only a chair, a wall length mirror, and a door that says it leads to the stage. I'm about to head through it when Connor slams against me, sending me hurtling into the mirror, my head cracking the glass.

117

I collapse to the ground, my body crunching against the daggers of the broken mirror.

Connor plans to deal with me like he did before and swings to kick me in the side, but I'm ready for him this time and I hold my arm low to block the blow. As he connects, an intense pain shoots into my shoulder, but I know it would've hurt worse if he landed his boot on my rib cage.

I grab hold of his foot as he pulls back to kick again and I yank him down, hoping to knock the brain out of his skull. Unfortunately, he twists onto his side as he topples. I have to push him down, but he shoves against me and I can't get enough leverage to get my weight on him.

He kicks against me, catching me in the shin, and it's enough that he's able to get the upper hand. I make a fist and swing, connecting with his jaw. I'd barely been in a fight before I met Charlie—I was always able to talk my way out of them—and now I've been in three. I punch again but this time he's ready and blocks it. He pushes his hand into my face, rubbing my cheek against the broken glass. I feel pain as the shards cut through my skin, and I try to push him off me, but he's too heavy.

His hands slip around my throat and he squeezes hard. I try and break his grip but it's too tight. He sinks his finger into the windpipe below my Adam's apple. It burns in my throat. I feel a gagging and a sucking of air at the same time. I can't breathe. I grab at his face, claw at his cheeks and eyes, but he keeps himself far enough away that I can't get hold of anything.

Connor's face hovers above me, wild and bloody, and I finally see him as the monster I always imagined him to be.

My head throbs and dark spots pop in the corners of my eyes and I know he's playing for keeps and I'm sure as hell not getting out of this alive.

The spots become bigger, blacker, and the darkness closes in.

I can no longer fight. I have no air and I know I'm dying.

But then his weight is off me as his hands are ripped free of my throat, and I can breathe again even though I can barely move. I inhale hard.

118

Charlie has come out of nowhere, slamming his body into Connor's shoulder and face. I look over and see that he's lifted Connor right off the ground with the tackle and slammed him hard against the wall. They're in a tangled sprawl but Charlie pulls himself from the heap, pushing the knocked out Connor to the side. I get up onto my hands and knees, still trying to inhale. Comforting my throat by putting my hand on my neck.

"That's for the stairs, asshole!" He yells at the heap that was Connor.

He looks at me. I stand, sort of. Both us are doubled over and breathing hard.

"You okay?" he asks.

I'm only starting to think I can straighten up without barfing all over the place. "Think so. You?"

"Oh yeah. Piece of cake," he grunts.

119

The two uniformed officers arrive shortly after.

When Charlie rushed the stage, they must've responded and went after him. He never made it to the stage and went through a side exit. Connor had slipped away in the pandemonium. So when the cops showed up, they still had no idea what was going on. They saw the unconscious actor on the ground, the broken glass, the cuts on my face, and Charlie is the only one looking moderately okay. When they rush towards us, I'm pretty sure they're only going to arrest him.

"Wait!" I call out, my throat feeling like I'd gargled asphalt. I point at Connor. "He's the one you want. He's the guy who's been killing the girls."

They ignore me, knowing to lockdown the situation before sorting out the mess. They put us against a wall, with a warning that if we try anything, they'll handcuff all of us. I try and explain to them again what's going on but they tell me to quit speaking while they help bring Connor around. They're checking his pupils and asking for responses when the door behind us opens. It's the stage manager.

He sees Charlie and me against the wall and the cops dealing with a semi-coherent Connor before he explodes and lunges at the barely conscious killer.

"You! You piece of crap! You destroyed the play."

The officers react, quickly pushing him back against the wall.

"I worked so hard and you ruined it! I'm going to kill you!"

The absurdity of the situation makes me want to giggle but Charlie beats me to it.

"Jeezuz!"

120

Paramedics and more police arrive to deal with all of us. After they check Charlie and I out, they stick us in a small theatre classroom somewhere behind the stage and an officer waits by the door.

"Where's the other guy?" I ask. All I care about is what's going on with Connor. If they don't realize who he is, I'm worried they'll let him go—we're so close, I don't want to lose him.

The cop ignores my question.

I look over at Charlie and he shakes his head. He has no use for police and there's nothing he'll share with them, even if it means not helping me out. I'm on my own. I try again.

"Excuse me. What about the other guy?"

The officer looks at me. He's neither annoyed nor friendly.

"Your buddy?"

This riles Charlie. "He's not our buddy!"

"Easy, kid."

"Go screw yourself." Charlie's cornered and he's doing his best to be a punk. I, on the other hand, only care about making sure Connor goes to jail—well, maybe I'm a little worried about what I'm going to tell my parents and whether or not I need a lawyer—but right now Connor's still my focus.

"Whatever you do, don't let him go," I plead.

"Don't you worry." He looks at Charlie. "Your *friend* is in the next room being babysat by my partner."

I sigh relief. "Can you please call Detective Gekas and tell her what's going on?"

"Why do you want her?"

Charlie pipes in, "Why don't you go shove your head up—"

I step in before he makes it worse, "Can you tell her you're holding Tony Shepherd and Charlie Wolfe? Please?" I suspect he's being difficult on purpose and I have to work around the system.

He scrutinizes Charlie and me, until he decides to make the call.

"I'm right outside, so don't try anything."

We say nothing and he leaves the room.

"Charlie, you okay?"

"Yup."

"You nervous?"

"Nope."

"What are we going to tell Gekas, the truth?"

"Are you mental? I think we need to be very selective of what we tell her."

I have a sinking, nervous feeling. I know Connor is our guy and don't want a loophole or something we did to allow him to walk away.

The officer returns.

"Get up gentlemen. Let's go. Looks like Detective Gekas wants a visit with you down at the station.

"What about the other guy?"

"He's coming along with you."

121

They have me in an interrogation room that looks nothing like the movies. There's a table and two chairs but no big one-way mirror—just four walls and some fluorescent lighting. I wait for a long time, stuck in my own thoughts and all I can think about is Sheri.

One night, only a few months after we started dating, we hung out at my place watched a movie. I don't remember what movie it was, but I remember it was awful and we both fell asleep halfway through. I woke, a little disorientated but feeling so comfortable with my arm around her, cuddling. Then, she looked up at me, half awake-half asleep, and she smiled and I knew she felt the exact same way. I knew then I wanted to spend a long, long time with her—

Now, that's changed and nothing can be the same. I know I'm crying and I wipe my eyes with my sleeves. I finally allow myself to let some of this pain go piece by small piece.

I force myself to think about other things. I wonder where Charlie is, feeling nervous for him, knowing this place and how he feels about it. I think about my parents and how much trouble I'll be in depending on how all of this goes. I worry about my future, whether I've ended any hope of going to university or playing basketball in some place without barbed wire fences.

The door opens and Gekas enters, holding a bottle of water. She takes a seat across from me. She takes a moment to notice the cuts on my cheek but she doesn't address them.

"Thirsty? Water?"

"Yes, please."

"Sorry it took so long, Anthony. I needed to debrief the officers who brought you in."

I take a long drink before I feel I can speak. "Why were they there?"

"Connor was Robbie's number one contact at school."

"Not his parents?" I feel a sense of being judgmental that quickly turns to a matter-of-factness when I consider how screwed up both Connor and Robbie are.

"When they weren't able to get a hold of him on his cell phone, they tracked him down there."

"Is Robbie dead?" I feel a heaviness.

"No. He's stable."

I'm relieved. "So they didn't know about Connor?"

"None of us had even figured it out." I feel pride, or accomplishment, or something. Gekas makes eye contact as she acknowledges the significance of the moment.

I nod. "How's Charlie?"

She grins. "From what I've been told, he's taking a nap." Her smile looks good on her and I can't help but laugh as my worries about him are quickly allayed.

"And Connor?"

Her smile fades and I expect the worst.

"He confessed."

The moment sinks in. The longest minute in the last few weeks passes between Gekas and I.

"To all of it. All of the girls."

That feeling I had weeks ago in the office at school springs right up into my belly, that wicked, familiar, dark feeling in the pit of my stomach but this time it's not just nervousness. It's real. It's connected to the thing I feared.

I wait for her to say it, holding my breath.

"Including Sheri."

Everything drops away and the silent clamp around my insides releases. I gasp to handle the shock of it all. I know that the way Gekas phrased it means she's dead. That leaden feeling sinks in. It's consuming, but at least I now know what happened.

"We barely interviewed him before he volunteered the information. He wanted to take credit for it, for what he called his 'performance.'" She pauses, waiting for me, but I don't know how to respond. I want her to stop talking and I want her to tell me everything. She continues, "With his confession, I think all charges will stick. I don't think he's getting out of it."

I nod, my mouth open, realizing that it's done. Everything that has transpired in the last couple of weeks has come to an end. Gekas pushes away from the table and stands.

"Good job, Anthony. You and Charles, you helped us get him."

122

They release Charlie and I later that day. Mom and Dad are there to pick me up and I see no one is around to pick up Charlie.

I'm about to say something, when Mom interrupts, "Charles? Do you need a ride?"

Charlie objects, trying to wave away the offer, but he doesn't realize Mom's persistence. "Nonsense, come with us."

If he tries to say no again, she'll likely drag him and shove him into the car, and I'm pretty sure he realizes this too, so he comes along.

Charlie doesn't talk during the trip, staring out the window, watching the houses go by. Not even Dad's music seems to change his mood.

It isn't until we're heading to the southeast end of the city that I consider that I have no clue where Charlie lives. I'm curious to see what his home will look like, since all he talks about are trailer parks and his absent mother.

"Do you mind stopping up ahead? I'd like to get a coffee and a doughnut."

Mom and Dad look at him, at each other, at me. It's a strange request, but I nod, hoping to help him out and get him out of his funk.

They pull in. "I won't be long," Charlie says before heading inside.

We wait in the car and I suddenly become aware that my parents have me trapped where they want me. I need to beat them to the punch.

"Mom, Dad, I—"

Mom interrupts, "Not now."

"But—?"

"Nope. It'll be a conversation for later."

Dad looks in the rearview mirror at me. "Maybe over a cup of tea."

Crap—it's going to be one of those talks. I sigh, leaning back in my seat, knowing I need to wait.

We continue to wait and when ten minutes pass, we know something is up. I head inside to get Charlie. I look around the coffee shop and check the bathrooms but I can't find him anywhere. He must have slipped out a backdoor, out of sight, and back into the mystery that surrounds—and seems to protect—him.

123

After a long interrogation with Connor, Gekas found the resting spot of Sheri. He had taken her only a mile south of the trails and dumped her weighted body into the bottom of a dugout. An autopsy still needs to be performed as they continue to build the case against him. She tells me that she and her people will be at it for weeks afterwards to make sure Connor is dealt with properly.

Gekas tells me that officially we were never involved in the case. I appreciate that. It's a complication I don't want, although I never told her about half the stuff we did. Tampering with crime scenes and evidence is not what the lead detective needs to hear. We left a pretty big mess behind us that I'm guessing she'll be able to figure out. In the end, she cut our path of destruction out of her investigation, reducing us to the conversations I had with her and the final incident at the theater.

A week later, Sheri's parents have her funeral. They ask me to attend. Although the involvement of Charlie and I wasn't officially associated with finding her killer, I find out Gekas may have hinted to the Beckmans that forgiveness was in order.

The church is full of Sheri's friends, her parents, and family. I stand by her coffin, and when I close my eyes all I see is her big smile. Finally, that thick, heavy weight releases in my gut and I can't help but feel the pain rising up. I decide not to hide it away this time. I let it go and cry in front of everyone.

124

Mom, Dad, Heather, and I come home from Sheri's funeral and head inside the house.

Heather gives me a final hug before she runs upstairs to change out of her dress. I'm thankful for her love.

I sit at the kitchen island and, without realizing it at first, Mom and Dad are there, with a cup of tea brewed and set between us.

"Is it that time?" I ask.

They smile.

"You know you drove us crazy the past couple of weeks," Mom says. It's more of a statement than a question, but I nod anyway. I don't want to fight. My strategy is to let them say whatever they need to.

Dad carries on her thought, "You did a lot of stupid, stupid things."

"I know—"

"But you also made us proud."

"You fought for what you believed in. And you fought against something that neither your Dad or I could imagine."

I look at them, not sure what to say.

"But if you ever do something like this again, you'll be grounded for a very long time."

I laugh, even though I know it's true.

I sit in a chair in the backyard, wrapped in a thick fall jacket, eyes closed, feeling the last rays of warm sunlight on my face. I'm certain winter is right around the corner.

"You know if you sit on a cold surface, you get hemorrhoids, right?"

Just like that Charlie walks into my backyard.

I don't open my eyes right away. "That's only rocks or sidewalks."

He sits down beside me. "Really? Hmm...I guess you do know some things."

I look over at him and see he's brought me a coffee. "You sure took the long way to get that."

He shrugs. "Yeah, well, it's still hot."

I take a sip and have to agree. It feels good, warming my body.

"What happened back there?"

He doesn't look at me. "What? You wanted to see my place? Meet my Mom? You serious, Shepherd?"

Always the deflector, always the joker. Still, he makes me laugh.

"Charlie—?"

"Oh, don't say it—"

"Thank—"

"Here it comes—"

"You."

"Ugh, now it's out there. Next, you'll start with the crying and whining, and I won't get you to stop."

I let him be, letting him have his moment. I take a sip of coffee and finally sigh, "Good coffee."

"Yup, it is."

"You pay for it?"

"Of course not."

We both smile.

"Oh, that reminds me." He searches his jacket and grabs a small paper bag that he hands to me. "This is for you."

I look inside and find a doughnut—a Boston Cream. I pull it out and take a big bite.

It tastes fantastic.

ACKNOWLEDGMENTS

Angie and David would like to thank our first readers: Lana LaFontaine, Anna Gane, Kate Gane, Charlene Hilkewich, and Kevin Leflar. We'd like to extend our extreme gratitude to Dimitrios Kounios for all his artwork and Nathan Mader for his excellent editorial work. We'd also like to give a special thanks to those early readers who caught our mistakes: Kevin Leflar, Kevin Johnson, and especially Lucas Frison and his eagle eyes.

Angie would also like to thank her students and Blair Randall for fielding her many questions.

David would like to thank his family, Kate, Anna, and Peter, for all their love and patience.

ABOUT THE AUTHORS

David Gane is a writer, teacher and stay-at-home dad. He writes film scripts and fiction, but also has composed poetry, plays, and academic film reviews. Occasionally, he teaches screenwriting at the University of Regina.

Angie Counios teaches by day and writes by night. All other times, she's packing her bag to see the world, completing goal lists, painting, playing with a camera, or practicing yoga.

Find them at www.couniosandgane.com.

Made in the USA
Charleston, SC
20 November 2015